Broken Symmetry

Broken Symmetry

A NOVEL BY
Rosalie Osmond

Nevermore Press

Library and Archives Canada Cataloguing in Publication

Osmond, Rosalie, 1942–
    Broken symmetry / Rosalie Osmond

ISBN 978-1-7753717-0-0 (softcover)
Canadiana
LCC PS8629.S547 B76 2019 | DDC C813/.6—DC23
20190075880

This is a work of fiction. All names, characters, places, and events are
products of the author's imagination. Any resemblance to actual events
or persons living or dead are purely coincidental.

Cover and book design by Jayme Spinks
Author photo by Grant Dixon

Printed and bound in Canada

Nevermore Press, Ltd.
P.O. Box 369
Lunenburg, NS B0J 2C0
Canada

PART I
Stained Glass

CHAPTER I
August 1943

Emma stands holding her small daughter up to the light. Multicoloured, it slants through the stained glass transom above the oak front door in rays of purple, green and rose—grapes, leaves and flowers, supporting scrolls—dyeing the child's white, smocked dress. She strains in her mother's arms to touch the warm glass, to feel the streaming colours. "Pretty, pretty."

Emma's arms ache. Gently she puts Eleanor down into the pool of coloured light on the polished birch floor. Surrounded by toys—some nesting cups, a cloth book, a small stuffed bear—it is still the light that absorbs the child as she sits moving her hands to make shadow patterns in the brightness around her. Emma leaves her there and goes back to the kitchen to make the cake for her first birthday. It must be, like her daughter, perfect.

The stained glass window is the one touch of opulence in the wooden clapboard house, as if the sea captain who built it one hundred years ago allowed himself this alone to compensate for the Spartan life on shipboard. Everything else is as plain and functional as a mind centered on eternal rather than temporal reward could wish.

The hall runs straight from front to back through the symmetrical house—a kitchen and a living room on each side. A staircase, brown with varnish, narrows the hall where it ascends and curves around to lead to bedrooms that are mirror images of one another, like the rooms below. It's darker here. The large five-sided bay at the end of the landing has been enclosed, appropriating the view of sky, masts of fishing boats and gulls, for the common bathroom. The rooms behind the heavy bedroom doors are narrower than those below, confined by sloping eaves.

The house is almost silent now. In one kitchen Emma shakes a flour sifter and scrapes a spoon across a bowl; in the opposite kitchen her sister, Virtue, rubbing her rolling pin along the pastry board, lets out a muffled sigh.

Suddenly, there comes a high-pitched cry from Eleanor. Both run, but Virtue gets there first, scoops up the screaming child and sticks a finger in her mouth. "A tack. Just look! She might have swallowed it."

The wound is not severe. A pinprick to the tongue, a red drop staining the white dress. Still Eleanor howls and Virtue coos and rocks her in her arms.

Emma stands by, accused, alone. She reaches out for Eleanor, but Eleanor will have none of her. She hides her face in Virtue's shoulder, cries some more. "Poor lamb, it's all right now."

Then rage, pure rage. "Give her to me." In a surge of fury Emma wrests Eleanor from Virtue's grasp and bears her, screaming, to her own kitchen. She sinks into the wicker chair, tries to calm the frightened child, and tries to calm herself as well, as anger yields to guilt and shame. The rolling pin is active now across the hall, staccato on the wooden pastry board, and interspersed come imprecations that could be to the pastry or the gods but that Emma knows are for herself.

A nursery rhyme to blot it out! "The little pigs?" Eleanor, recovered now, nods and tugs at her socks and shoes so that her toes can be exposed. Virtue's voice fills the gaps, antiphonal.

"*This little pig...*"

"Poor baby."

"*Went to market...*"

"Too careless for words."

"*This little pig...*"

"Thinks only of herself."

"*Stayed at home...*"

"My very own sister."

The child is mine. How dare she! "My very own sister," indeed.

Hot tears run down Emma's face even while she continues whispering rhymes to Eleanor, who has seemingly forgotten that she was hurt and is fondling and examining her toes intently as if trying to unlock some profound secret they contain.

Are there profound secrets? Is there any plausible explanation for how she, Emma, has ended up here in this unpromising house on the lower street of Lunenburg, living with husband, sister, and brother-in-law? It had all seemed so simple, so natural, even. Obadiah and

Nathan Wentzell, two brothers, married Virtue and Emma Miller, two sisters. As children, each pair of siblings had slept together in their crowded country farmhouses in the tiny village of Waldenstein.

The brothers moved to town, started a barbering business together, and bought the next-door house as well as the barbershop. After they married, all that changed were the pairings of the sleeping arrangements. Then they had lived happily ever after—or at least for seven years.

Now this—the jealousy, the muttered accusations, the sidelong, accusing glances, all because of the child. Eleanor begins to squirm. She is no longer interested in her toes, the little pigs. It is getting late, eleven o'clock, and Emma has been so busy concentrating on the birthday cake that she has barely begun to make Nathan's dinner. He will not be pleased if he has to wait because it will delay his return to work. That will only give Obadiah and Virtue something more to complain about. Emma puts Eleanor down softly on the kitchen floor, and gives her some tin measuring cups to pile up or bang together.

❧

The trouble began as soon as Emma knew she was pregnant. After Nathan, Virtue had to be the first to know. So Emma went to the open door of her sister's kitchen, breathless with excitement. It was late afternoon; Virtue was peeling potatoes for dinner. The knife went precisely round and round the potato, the string of peel unbroken.

"You'll never guess what has happened. At last..." Emma said.

Virtue looked up, the potato peel curling down from her left hand. Already she seemed removed, as if she anticipated the news. "I'm going to have a baby! After all these years. Seven lean years. Dr. Willis told me this afternoon."

Virtue stared at her white, blank potato. "Oh," she said. "I see."

Emma stood in the doorway, waiting for something more. "Aren't you...aren't you happy for me, for us?"

"Yes, of course. How good that it's happened at last." Virtue's words fell like a dull knell. After a minute more, Emma went back to her kitchen, sat down on the old wicker chair and wept silently. Of course Virtue had always been "touchy," like when Emma got her

Grade Ten and her Grade C teachers' licence and Virtue had to make do with the D licence, which was all her Grade Nine qualified her for, or all the boys wanted to dance with Emma because she was prettier. Those times had been difficult, but that seemed normal, somehow. It was the way sisters were. This was different. Virtue might still have a baby herself, she still might, even though she was two years older. Emma too had despaired, and now look—the miracle had happened.

When Nathan came in for supper Emma cried again, telling him. He held her, as she knew he would, told her it didn't matter, that they were having a baby, a son, and that was all they should care about. Virtue was just jealous.

From across the hallway that evening floated whispers and muted exclamations. Nothing more, but as she was about to go up the stairs to bed, there was Virtue standing in the hallway. Emma felt afraid, thinking, "Don't say it. Whatever it is, just don't say it." Virtue's arms were crossed in front of her chest; she held herself firm and erect.

"It's not safe for older women to be having babies. You'll need to be careful."

"Mama had lots of babies after she was thirty-five."

"But they weren't her first baby. And…it may be…people say…" Virtue's voice trailed off.

Emma could not reply. How could her sister think like that? She went up the stairs without looking back. Later in bed, she whispered to Nathan, "I want to leave."

The bed covers heaved as he turned to face her. "Leave? Leave for where?"

"I don't care. Somewhere…anywhere. Just the two of us. Alone. Without anyone else. Where we can talk without being overheard, where we can have as many babies as we like without interference." She raised herself on one elbow; the beam of a streetlight outlined her determined jaw.

Nathan quailed. "Darling, you know we can't. The shop and house go together. I don't have the money to buy Obadiah out, and even if I did, he wouldn't sell. How could he?"

Across the hall a door opened. Footsteps padded on the smooth linoleum. The bathroom door opened and closed. They stopped whispering. Nathan drew Emma to him and held her as closely as he could, allowing for the baby, and kissed her again and again. After a while her body relaxed, her breathing slowed, and she fell asleep.

It was hot and sticky the summer Eleanor was born. Emma sat in a chair in the tiny garden reading books—Dickens and Trollope, mostly. Virtue stayed in her kitchen, cooking pies, gingerbreads, cakes with elaborate decorations. Who ate them all, Emma couldn't imagine. Must be Obadiah; he was getting a bit of a paunch.

It was strange, Emma thought, to be sitting so peacefully in a garden, even an inadequate one, when overseas men were being killed in droves. Luckily, Nathan hadn't had to go to fight. It had been close. The age of conscription kept getting older and older. Finally Nathan was called for the medical examination, which mercifully he failed. If he'd gone...well, there would be no baby; that was certain. Of course, he did his duty and went off in his hard hat in the evenings when the practice siren sounded to make sure everyone had their lights out and blinds down, but that was like playing soldiers, not quite real. Fishing boats were being blown up just off the coast by German submarines, but that too seemed unreal. She didn't believe in the war, she decided. It was a story, like *A Tale of Two Cities*. What was real was the garden, the sun, and the slowly turning baby inside her.

One particularly hot day in late July a man appeared in the garden. He walked purposefully up the alleyway between the barbershop and the house. Seeing Emma sitting in the garden, he halted his approach to the back door of the house and came towards her.

"Mrs. Wentzell?"

"Yes."

He removed his hat. "I'm Mr. Curtis. I knocked out front, but got no answer. The school board sent me..." He stopped in confusion, focusing on Emma's stomach. "I'm sorry...I didn't know...I guess they didn't know..." He blushed. "You see, there's a shortage of teachers, and Mrs. Kaulbach has just told us she's not coming back next year to teach in Garden Lots, so we thought...well, we thought you might be able to help us out, but of course..."

"Well, yes, of course..."

"I won't trouble you anymore." He started to leave, then turned and said, "You don't know of anyone else who might be interested, do you?"

To her amazement, Emma found she did. "Well...I don't know if she'd be interested, but my sister is a teacher as well. You could ask her."

He perked up at once. "Now where might I find her?"

"She's just inside the house. In the kitchen, on the left. We share the house, you see. We married brothers, so Virtue is Mrs. Wentzell, as well." Suddenly this seemed like a shameful secret, an admission of an incestuous liaison.

He knocked on the back door of the little house. Virtue appeared, wiping her floury hands on her apron.

"Mrs. Wentzell? May I come in and speak to you a moment?"

Emma could hear Virtue's fluster. "Well, I guess so. But...I don't know. I'm sorry I'm such a mess. My hair..." Meanwhile she was opening the door and letting the man inside. They disappeared from view and from hearing. Virtue must have taken him into the living room at the front of the house. Emma tried to continue reading, but the book no longer held her attention. The baby moved. It hung heavily inside her, cramped, weighing her down. Having a baby, especially after all these years of trying, was such a splendid thing, but Emma thought of how happy she had been in the classroom, standing in front of the children, telling them new things, wonderful things they would never forget. Now Virtue would have a chance to do that once more. Of course, she would make a mess of it. The children would adore her, but Virtue would tell them that there never had been an Ice Age, that evolution was just an idea a few nutters held, and that asking why math problems were solved in a particular way was a waste of time; you just got on and memorized the method. But none of that could be helped.

Half an hour passed. He's taking his good old time, thought Emma. Or maybe it's Virtue who's taking hers. The sun was too hot, but she couldn't go back into the house because that would look like snooping. She couldn't go into the barbershop. That would be improper for a woman in her "condition." So she sat with the book on her lap and steamed gently.

Eventually Mr. Curtis emerged. He was smiling and waved a cheery good-bye to her as he left the garden. So...success? She went back into the cool semi-darkness of the kitchen and started thinking what to cook Nathan for supper. Virtue was back in her kitchen again, mixing something. Emma could hear the sound of the wooden spoon against the pottery bowl.

Half an hour later Virtue appeared at her kitchen door, leaned against the doorframe, as was her custom, and said, "Guess what? They want me to teach school in Garden Lots."

Emma was tempted to say, "No they don't. They want me. But since I can't do it, they'll settle for you." She didn't. Instead, she inquired politely, "And will you?"

"Well, of course, I'll have to ask Obadiah."

"Of course."

"But if he doesn't mind, I just might."

☙

Four weeks later, at the end of August, Emma woke at midnight and knew that her time had come. Quietly, she alerted Nathan, and together they crept out of the house and made their way to the nursing home. Nathan kissed her and whispered, "I'll see you in the morning— with our son." And then he was gone, and she was left alone with the hustle and bustle of the nurse. She had known this was how it would be; still it was very lonely in her little room. After a while Dr. Willis arrived, all hearty cheerfulness. His attitude towards childbirth was that no one, not even the mother, should know too much about it, so when the time seemed right he gave Emma an anesthetic. The pain sank down into darkness.

The next thing she knew there was a pale light coming through the sheer curtains at the window. Someone was standing by her bed with a white bundle in her arms. The bundle was crying. Of course, the baby.

She roused herself and said, "He sounds like a healthy little fellow."

"Oh yes, she's healthy and beautiful as well," came the reply.

At first Emma did not comprehend. "She?" ·

"Yes, you have a lovely little girl, Mrs. Wentzell."

"A girl?" Why had she and Nathan been so sure they would have a son? Naturally, it was what Nathan wanted, and since God had finally answered their prayers for a child, it seemed unreasonable that he should withhold his bounty in the matter of the sex of the child. Sarah had given Abraham a son. Suppose God had just let him go on during the pregnancy believing that his name would be preserved for future generations and then, when the child was born, stood back and laughed, "Joke's on you! It's a girl!"

The nurse put the tiny screaming bundle down beside her. Emma opened up her nightgown as she knew she was supposed to do. The bundle stopped crying, nuzzled furiously, and latched onto her breast. She had never been so happy.

For two weeks Emma lay in the nursing home, cocooned from everything in the outside world. She slept, she woke; the baby slept and woke, screamed while her diaper was being changed, then sucked her way to bliss and oblivion. Time no longer existed—just the rhythm of sleeping and waking, eating and sleeping again. The two of them inhabited this finite space, alone with one another, needing only one another. Even Nathan's visits scarcely impinged on her happy solitude.

One evening, towards the end of her stay, Virtue arrived. Why had she not come before? Vaguely, Emma had wondered about this, but in her languorous and solipsistic state it scarcely mattered. Now here Virtue was, an envoy from the outside world, dressed in a smart new suit, her hair taken back in a tidy roll. Emma's hair had not been washed since the baby's birth. She looked up at this stylish apparition and perceived how she herself must appear—a shapeless lump in a floppy dressing gown holding an untidy child in a ball of blankets.

"I've brought you something—for the baby."

"Eleanor. Her name is Eleanor." So certain were Nathan and Emma that the child would be a boy that the baby remained nameless for several days. Suddenly it came to her with complete clarity. Eleanor of

Aquitaine. A feisty woman if ever there was one.

Virtue proffered a small white sweater in a lacy, complicated pattern. "I knit it myself."

"It's lovely. Thank you so very much." Virtue had always been better than her at knitting and crocheting. The sweater was truly lovely. But the formality! This was the person with whom she had shared a bed for sixteen years. Only when they went away to Normal College had they been separated. Virtue spoke to her politely, oh so politely, like a stranger.

After Eleanor had been admired, Emma allowed herself to say, "You look wonderful. That suit—I don't think I've seen it before."

"Well, yes, it's new. I decided to take the teaching job, so I needed to get some different clothes."

"When do you start?"

"I already have. It's the second week of September. School began a week ago."

The second week of September! How was that possible?

"And...and how's it going?"

"Oh, I absolutely love it. The children are sweet. I didn't realize how much I was missing teaching until I got back into the classroom."

Then she was gone. Emma sank back in her chair and wept.

⁊

When Emma returned to the small house on the lower street everything looked different. The kitchen suddenly seemed to have more stuff in it. The new baby carriage took up at least a third of the wall space on one side. There was the sink in the corner, the window with the wicker chair under it, a cabinet with china and a workspace below the hutch. Under another window stood the large kitchen table that also doubled as work surface, ironing board, and so on, and finally, a further wall of shelves with drawers, beside the large oil stove. Now all these objects that previously had lived agreeably together were shouting for more space, jostling with one another for light and air.

The living room pleased her no more than the kitchen. The brown plush sofa was beginning to wear at its corded seams showing the bare threads underneath the pile. The rocking chair with its buttoned leather cover was secondhand, the wooden arms worn. The fireplace wasn't real; it had been blocked up years before they bought the house, and on the mantel over it stood only a few glass ornaments and two candle holders. None of this was poor by Waldenstein standards, but this was not Waldenstein.

Outside though, there was the real problem. Situated on the street that ran just above the harbour, the house was crushed by the businesses that surrounded it. On Emma's side there was a shop that turned out oars, block tackle for boats, and galvanized metal buckets, particularly sinister because of the noxious fumes produced in making them that spewed straight into their bedroom window. Huge piles of lumber pressed upon the garden fence. On Virtue's side there was no need for a garden fence at all. The garden ran behind the barbershop up to the walls of a tall building that housed a plumbing business that clanked away eight hours a day and provided an impenetrable barrier. Workmen leaned cheerfully out of the upstairs windows, tapping their cigarette ash on the sill, whistling down to the tiny patch of green below. There was no lake, no field, no protective woodland as in her childhood. She tried to avoid telling people where she lived.

The first day Emma went to church in Lunenburg had been a revelation. She should have guessed how it would be, but she hadn't. Dressed in a respectable but very ordinary dark blue suit, she was surrounded by ladies in silk dresses and smart jackets. Everyone was very kind, of course. Perhaps they even envied her radiant good looks, her petite figure, but all Emma could see was that she was poor. These other women had all gone through school to the end of Grade Twelve, because that was natural in a town where Grade Twelve was taught. Emma had been lucky to get her Grade Ten in Waldenstein. Her husband was a barber. Their husbands owned fishing schooners.

Even their small car, purchased jointly by Nathan and Obadiah when they set up business in the town, and which had seemed so wonderful when she and Virtue first arrived, proved a cause of dissension. The trouble with joint ownership of a car was that you couldn't divide it in two as they had the house. The car, not understanding about dual ownership, would insist on going as a complete object in one direction only. So they decided that Nathan and Obadiah would takes turns driving it for a week at a time, and the non-driving couple could tag along in the back or not, as they wished. This seemed a reasonable arrangement, but how would it work now that there was a baby?

Then she heard Eleanor's cry, and went upstairs to the bedroom. She picked up the tiny child and unbuttoned her blouse. Eleanor snuggled in, and everything was transformed to quiet contentment once more.

⋅•⋅

When Virtue returned from school at four o'clock, sometimes she went across the hall to talk to Emma, but more often she simply busied herself getting Obadiah's supper. No one could accuse her of neglecting her wifely duties, even though she was now working all day and marking schoolwork all evening. Tonight, however, she took the time to appear at the kitchen door as Emma was settling Eleanor in her carriage while she cooked. Virtue cleared her throat to announce her presence. Emma looked up from the carriage. "How's your day been?"

The sight of Emma, fussing around her baby, raised up something at once sad and fierce within Virtue like a caged lioness, but she replied casually, "Oh just fine. I'm really getting into the swing of teaching again. The children are mostly just great. And the few big boys that seemed difficult at first—even they're beginning to come around, I think."

She could see Emma flinch. Was the baby alone not enough then? Perhaps Emma was remembering the excitement of those first mornings in autumn, the squeak of the chalk on the blackboard, the smell of the new books, the apples on the teacher's desk. Whose apple would you pick to eat at recess, and how would you convince the others their apples were quite as good, really, your hand just happened to light on Alice's apple first?

"Eleanor fine?"

"Yes, I've just fed her, and I think she may have a short nap now while I cook supper. I don't want to let her sleep too long, because we need her to sleep at night, not all day."

Still Virtue stood at the kitchen door, rubbing her back gently against the frame. Finally, she said, "Your minister's dead."

"Reverend Selig?"

Emma had acknowledged him as her minister, Virtue noted with wry satisfaction. "Yes. I heard today."

Virtue paused and watched Emma falter, then look down to hide what she was feeling.

"Not a natural death." Virtue said and went back to her own domain.

⁂

Emma forgot about cooking supper; she forgot about everything except that brief time when she had learned Latin with the priest, when he had, had he not, asked her to marry him. "I would wait for you," he said. Then she unwittingly betrayed him, helping drive him away, back to Germany. Emma found the page of the letter that he dropped, and instead of returning it or even throwing it away, she showed it to her mother. It alluded to the time he spent in a sanatorium before he came to Canada, and her parents decided everyone must be told. Those who didn't like him anyway, which was nearly everyone except Emma, decided that his new ideas of which they disapproved—two versions of creation, not all of Isaiah being written by one writer, Job being just a story—must be the result of insanity. Of course, he had to be stopped and sent away. That was what they did, and it was all her fault. Virtue never liked him. He hadn't chosen to teach her Latin. Now, he was dead, by his own hand no less, and doomed to eternal damnation.

Finally remembering supper, Emma dug out the eye of a potato with ferocity. If only she'd put the letter in her pocket, given it back to him, he would be alive and she would be living in the "old" country, be a minister's wife, and have beautiful inherited silver and china such as the women in Lunenburg had never seen or imagined. There would be wonderful music every Sunday, and her children would be brilliant and go to university!

She looked down at Eleanor, now drifting off to sleep. Well, that was one thing she could achieve. Eleanor would be brilliant! Eleanor, who thought only of milk and warmth and nuzzling, sucked her lips in seeming approbation.

At first, Virtue and Obadiah paid little attention to the new member of the household. They might yawn pointedly, or say something about a poor night's sleep. The shared car was an additional source of friction as Emma had anticipated. On Sunday afternoons when they were all about to go out together for a drive, Eleanor would need changing urgently, and Emma would dash off to make her clean while Virtue, already in her coat and hat, sniffed and shuffled in the hallway. There were other times when, having set out without any trouble, Eleanor would begin screaming in the middle of the journey. Feeding her with Obadiah in the car was out of the question. So, either they were all forced to turn around and go home or proceed with a shrieking baby.

"Can't you make her stop? There must be something wrong with the child. Mama's babies never cried like that!"

Now Emma was an ineffectual mother, compared with her own mother and found wanting. Indeed, that was how Emma felt. Years of teaching school hadn't prepared her for motherhood, and her mother was no longer around to give any advice. Sometimes Emma felt like joining Eleanor in wailing, though in the back of the car this was scarcely an option.

Autumn flashed a few brilliant colours, and then it was November. Soon it would be Christmas. They would have a big tree this year, a tree standing on the floor, taking up even more of the scarce space in the living room. But Eleanor must have a wonderful first Christmas.

Virtue also was aware of the approach of Christmas. The first week of December after a day's shopping trip to Halifax with Obadiah, Virtue came into Emma's kitchen and asked to borrow Eleanor for a short while. Emma could think of no reason to refuse, though this was a new and surprising development.

A few minutes later Virtue was holding Eleanor, wearing the whitest, softest, fuzziest knit leggings, jacket and cap ever devised for a baby. Obadiah chuckled. "She really looks sweet in that." Virtue turned the child around to face her and bounced her a bit on her knee. Eleanor smiled, then laughed outright. She brushed at the fuzzy edge of the cap and laughed some more.

Something moved within Virtue—a worm of an idea, a subterranean, crawling feeling. Eleanor would be hers. Born of her sister, fathered by her husband's brother, this child that she ignored for four months would be hers, bone of her bone, flesh of her flesh. She did not fully recognize the insidious seed of desire for what it was, but the worm was there, crawling ever deeper. She looked up at Obadiah's face, transformed with happiness. She hugged Eleanor, who stopped smiling and began to whimper.

Emma called out, "Everything okay over there?"

"Oh yes, she's just coming back." Eleanor, in her original clothes, was returned to the arms of her mother.

❧

On Christmas Day all was revealed. The green tissue paper parcel with the big red bow labeled "Eleanor" was opened, and there was the little white angora suit.

"How absolutely lovely," Emma exclaimed.

Virtue and Obadiah beamed with pleasure.

"Where on earth did you find it?" Emma asked. None of the stores in town had any such baby things.

"Remember that trip we took to Halifax a few weeks ago when I took the afternoon off? Well, we weren't just going to buy new clothes for me. We found this for Eleanor in Eatons. Not in the catalogue, you know—the real big store in the city."

That didn't prevent the angora from making Eleanor sneeze.

❧

On Christmas evening Emma rocked Eleanor in front of the multicoloured lights of their tree. Nathan had gone to the church Christmas concert with Virtue and Obadiah, so now the two of them, mother and child, sat transfixed by the lights. Outside the snow fell. Soon the ugly piles of lumber in the yard of the block shop next door no longer existed, but became terraced houses of snow on which the tree lights winked softly. The street itself was white and quiet. No one was about—only Emma and Eleanor and the tree lights, reflected in the snowy landscape. She wrapped the white blanket around Eleanor more tightly. The baby sucked her fist and stared fixedly at the tree until at last her eyelids drooped and she fell asleep. Time stopped. Emma felt nothing would ever change; she would always be here, insulated by the snow and Christmas lights, rocking her child, impervious to everything outside this moment, this timeless time of happiness.

☙

Virtue came home from school tired. Not that she could sit down and relax. Oh no, there was Obadiah's supper to get on the table. And what was that happening across the hall? Eleanor was fussing and banging something on the floor. Emma was saying, "Shush, shush, it's okay. Mummy needs to cook just now."

"Incompetent," Virtue thought. Emma did nothing the whole day but stay at home, and she still couldn't look after the child properly. *She* looked after thirty children for six hours. Why had Emma had a baby at all if she was so unable to look after it?

It was almost as if Emma got pregnant on purpose, just to get one up on her. Well, indeed she had done it on purpose, if not chiefly to that end. For seven years the two of them thought of little else except beginning a family. What else was a married woman for? They watched each other carefully every month. Were the disgusting red cloths going into the scrub bucket? Were they hanging out on the line? Each time this happened to both of them in turn there was a sense of despair but also of relief that at least they were together in their predicament. What to do? Was it their fault? It couldn't be; they were good submissive wives, and it couldn't be due to any lack of carefulness or hygiene on her part at least, Virtue reflected. Her douche hung on the back of the bedroom door and was always used after every "occasion." Cleanliness next to godliness.

Then one month, Emma's cloths did not appear. Well, she was getting old, Virtue thought. At thirty-five there could be some—some irregularity. Virtue said nothing and waited. Next month, the same thing. Could it be? God couldn't be so unfair. He gave Emma a prettier face, and she went further in school than Virtue, though heaven knew how. All that reading. Not that it meant Emma really knew more. Most of the stuff she read was pure fancy, Virtue was certain of it. Novels! What were they about? People whose lives it certainly didn't improve you to be acquainted with. And now this, the final thing they both desired. Emma was to be given that too. So, when Virtue was told, she was prepared—sort of, but the certainty still hit her like a blow in the stomach. She could hardly breathe and thought maybe she would make a fool of herself and faint. No, not before her self-assured sister, standing there already smoothing her stomach, as if there were anything visible to smooth. She muttered something. Emma wasn't satisfied. "Aren't you pleased for me, for us?"

How like her. Emma always wanted more, always expected people to be pleased for her, like when she got her Grade Ten and ran all the way home from the post office into Papa's arms, shouting, "I did it, I did it." After that her very own dear Papa had eyes for no one but Emma all that summer, smiling whenever he saw her, leaving her off chores because she was "reading." Now Emma would have a child, the only child between the two of them. Perhaps she would miscarry. Virtue killed this thought almost as soon as she was aware of it. It was wicked. Of course, she hadn't wished Emma would miscarry. The possibility merely popped into her mind, unbidden. Such things did happen. What was wrong with thinking of a perfectly possible event in a neutral, contingent sort of way?

When Virtue went to visit Emma at the nursing home, it had been a small death to see the tiny mite curled up in Emma's arms, but the next morning, there she was dressed up in her new skirt and jacket, standing in front of an expectant class. Emma, she knew, was almost certainly still lying enveloped in a nightdress that smelled of stale milk, doing nothing or at best reading rubbish. These boys and girls needed her; they respected her; they called her "Mrs. Wentzell." She was earning money. She knew Obadiah didn't like to be reminded of this, but she was. Soon they might be able to buy a car of their own and not have to share one with a screaming infant.

But Christmas had changed it all—seeing Eleanor in the fuzzy hat and sweater, reaching out to pull a button on her blouse. Eleanor smiled and made talking noises at Obadiah. She liked them! Maybe, in some convoluted way that she had not wholly calculated, she could make Eleanor her own. Now she was beginning to see the worm, but it did not look like a worm to her; it was scaled in green and gold, iridescent. Emma wasn't good at dealing with the child, anyone could see that. When Eleanor cried at night, Emma would sit and wail as well, or so Nathan told Obadiah. Then Nathan would carry Eleanor back and forth across the floor of the tiny bedroom until both she and Emma settled back to sleep.

Nathan, poor Nathan. What must Nathan feel, knowing Emma still carried a torch for someone else—even if it was someone who now was dead? The way Emma had looked, her face crumpling, when she told her Reverend Selig was dead. When had Emma last seen him? Not since the summer she was fourteen. Emma behaved very badly then, leading him on. Mama and Papa were very worried and even considered forbidding Emma to stay behind after confirmation instruction for her Latin lessons. It was odd, that, teaching Latin only to Emma. When Emma found the page of a letter in German that he dropped, she couldn't just wait to give it back to him the next week. No, Emma had to take it home to Mama, who could read German and did, and then showed it to the whole parish giving it "proof" of what it suspected all along: he was crazy. Of course he was crazy, and only someone who was half crazy herself, like Emma, could ever have liked him. So there! Better he was out of the way for good and all, but Emma still had a soft spot for him; that was as clear as her inability to care for Eleanor.

Eleanor was still fussing; indeed, at times the fuss rose to a wail. "I'm making Daddy's dinner, Eleanor. See, I'm putting the fish in the frying pan right now." But precocious as she might be, Virtue could tell from her continued protests that she didn't understand at all about Daddy's dinner. She marched across the hall and picked Eleanor up from the floor and gave her a hug. "You can come over to Aunt Virtue's kitchen until Mommy's not quite so busy."

Emma glared, but said nothing.

Returning from school one February afternoon, Virtue stopped in Emma's kitchen where Eleanor sat in her playpen banging some wooden blocks together.

"Can I take her over to my kitchen for a little? Maybe she'd like a change of scene?"

"Well, I suppose so, if you really want to, but she's perfectly happy here."

"I do, want to that is, and it'll give you a chance to get the dinner ready without any interference."

Eleanor was swept off to Virtue's kingdom. Virtue had no toys, but the measuring cups and spoons she offered to Eleanor were a delightful novelty and made even more noise floating out from one kitchen to the other than the wooden blocks. Laughter and baby talk emanated from the kitchen. "Is 'ooo a good 'ittle girlie, then?"

When Virtue returned Eleanor, Emma said, "Please talk properly to her. She'll be talking herself before you know it, and I want her to speak well. She's perfectly intelligent and should learn proper English."

Virtue sniffed, as of old. "She was having a lot of fun."

"I could hear."

Undeterred, Virtue continued to have an hour or so with Eleanor after school most days. Sometimes Eleanor was still there when Obadiah came in for supper; sometimes, Emma was certain, Virtue fed her—sweets, probably—and then Eleanor would not eat her supper and, when the sugar wore off, was cross all evening and slept badly.

As the visits continued, Emma was struck by an appalling thought: Suppose Eleanor turned out to like Virtue better? Suppose she turned out, in reality, to be Virtue's child? Eleanor clearly enjoyed her visits with her aunt. One day in June when she was ten months old, just about when Virtue would return from school, Eleanor said, "Voo, voo."

Voo? Her first word?

Virtue arrived, and there was another chorus of "Voo, voo." "Voo" scooped her up, and off they went to the magic kingdom across the hall.

Shortly after Eleanor's first word, as Emma was leaving church, Louise Wamboldt, one of the town's worthies, touched her on the arm and said, "Emma, you must be so tied to your house now with little Eleanor. Why don't you come and have tea with me tomorrow? You can bring the baby too, of course."

Emma said, "Yes," because any diversion would be welcome.

Mrs. Wamboldt lived on the highest hill in town, right on the isthmus of the peninsula. Her husband was captain of a fishing schooner and, Emma thought, rather uncouth, but he earned lots of money. Mrs. Wamboldt who, like Emma, had taught school, used the money to good advantage on clothes and her house. Emma laboured up the steep road, pushing Eleanor's carriage. At the top she turned around; the view was breathtaking. Up here, on the pinnacle of everything, or so it seemed, she looked out in both directions, first in front of her, down to the wharves and fishing boats, tiny from this distance as if sitting on a toy blue sea, then across the harbour to a clean green swathe of golf course that ended in a point of wooded peninsula. Down there somewhere, invisible, was her own house, mercifully cloaked by taller buildings from the sight of these gods who lived in the stratosphere above it. In the opposite direction, over the crest of the hill on the far side, was a smaller inlet and another peninsula with fields and little play cows.

This must be the house. Yes, 43, Mrs. Wamboldt had said. She walked up to the front door, lifted Eleanor out of the carriage, and rang the bell.

"Oh, do come in my dear. I've asked a few other ladies as well who would love to meet you."

Emma stepped inside a small entranceway that opened out into a living room that ran the whole expanse of the front of the house. On the left-hand side there was a grand piano and a few chairs covered in velvet upholstery. On the right at the far end was a fireplace with a large surround made of granite beach stones, above it a mantel covered with silver candlesticks and display plates with an elaborate gilt design. Grouped in front of the fireplace were two sofas and several other chairs where three women, who had been talking animatedly among themselves, paused and looked up towards the new arrivals. The largest woman got up, jangling silver bracelets, as she reached out to Eleanor. "I'm Isabel. Here, let me hold the baby while you take your coat off."

"This is Mrs. Zwicker. Her husband is one of our doctors, and Mrs. Langille, who's married to a lawyer," Mrs. Wamboldt said, pointing to a frail petite woman wearing a pretty tight-fitting shirt dress, "and last but not least, Miss Lohnes, chief fundraiser for all our endeavours." A tall and elegant woman, imposing in a pale grey suit nodded acknowledgement. All these impressions flooded in on Emma in the few seconds it took her to remove her coat, pat her hair, and sit down in the chair indicated. Eleanor was placed on the rug in the center of their little group and given some metal cups to play with.

"I don't have many children's toys anymore. I gave them all to my children for the grandchildren," Mrs. Wamboldt explained.

"It doesn't matter. She'll be happy with the cups." Eleanor wasn't really interested in the cups but the other people and the unaccustomed surroundings. She could crawl now and had never had such a large space to explore. So Emma was torn between keeping an eye on her and trying to maintain her end of the conversation.

"We're all members of the I.O.D.E.," said Louise Wamboldt with evident pride. "And we wondered if you might be interested in joining our little group."

"What...what is the I.O.D.E.?" Emma faltered. Perhaps it was a secret society, a lodge, she thought. She knew the church disapproved of these, but Louise was a good Lutheran. These other ladies, of course, might be anything.

"The Imperial Order, Daughters of the Empire," Miss Lohnes intoned in a low husky voice. "We raise money for books and supplies for schools both here and abroad—things they can't afford themselves. We give a scholarship every year to a student graduating from Lunenburg Academy, and at the national level we give very large scholarships to study abroad."

"And we thought that you...being a schoolteacher..." Mrs. Langille began and faded away, gesturing faintly with her hand.

"That sounds very good indeed," Emma replied. "But just now, with Eleanor..."

Soon the conversation turned to other things, chiefly Emma herself. "So how did you come to Lunenburg?" Miss Lohnes led the inquisition. "You came from the country, I believe?"

"Yes, a tiny place called Waldenstein, about twelve miles from New Germany. But I haven't really lived there since I left school."

"Oh yes, you went to Normal College, Louise told me that." Both Emma and Mrs. Wamboldt nodded. "So why did you choose to go there rather than to university? Most of the women who teach at the Academy seem to have degrees, like Louise here."

"But we don't know if that's really better or not." Louise diplomatically intervened.

"Well, I don't know which is better either," Emma replied. "But I had no choice, you see. My father didn't have the money to send me to university. In fact, he didn't even have the money to send me to town to go farther than Grade Ten."

"But I heard he had a lot of timber land up there around some lake. Hundreds of acres, so I was told." Mrs. Langille raised herself on one elbow to make this observation.

"Still, if it was all in timber, it wouldn't have helped to educate his children," Louise rejoined.

"But after he died..." Mrs. Zwicker said.

"My brother got everything," Emma said with finality, trying not to sound bitter.

"Oh...I see, but of course."

"You live with your sister and brother-in-law, I believe," Mrs. Zwicker continued.

"Yes. You see my husband and his brother bought the house and the business together. And then, when they got married, because we were sisters, they just..." Emma's voice trailed away as she imagined what her situation must look like through the eyes of these women, each mistress of an elegant domain all her own.

"Let's have some tea." Louise led the party to the dining room table in an adjoining room. There laid out was a silver teapot surrounded by small cups with trailing pink flowers and plates to match. The cups rattled nervously when you touched them—rather like Mrs. Langille, Emma thought. There were small sandwiches and little squares with pink icing on top. Emma lifted Eleanor up and offered her a plain cookie. But Eleanor wanted the pink-iced square, and a small tantrum ensued. "Oh give her the square. One won't hurt her," Mrs. Langille urged. So Eleanor dined on pink icing and licked her chubby fingers noisily. Then she went back to exploring.

From the kitchen behind the dining room a voice called out. "I'm going now, Mrs. Wamboldt. See you on Friday."

"Thank you so much Ida."

So she had a woman who cleaned and maybe even cooked?

A loud crash came from the living room followed by screams from Eleanor. A small potted plant lay on the floor, its dirt liberally sprinkled over the carpet. Mercifully, Emma saw, the pot was not broken nor was Eleanor really hurt, but at the sight of the mess in this perfectly ordered house, something within her gave way; she could not think rationally. All she knew was that she could not stay a moment longer. She had to go. Emma grabbed Eleanor up, and said breathlessly, "Oh I'm so sorry, but I really must get her home now."

She seized her coat and Eleanor's jacket and practically ran out the door. On the way home she knew this had been all wrong; she should have offered to clean up the mess, particularly since the cleaning lady had obviously just left, but she was propelled by an agony that drove her away from that house on the hill, down, down to the lower street where she obviously belonged. When she next met Louise in church Emma apologized profusely for the mess and thanked her for her kind hospitality.

"We did so enjoy having you dear, and hearing about your life. And Eleanor is a sweetie. All babies break things when they start to move around. Don't worry about it," she replied with a stiff smile.

There was never any further mention of the I.O.D.E.

Nathan knew something was wrong, but he had no idea how to fix it. The night when Emma pressed against him and said she wanted her own home had filled him with dread. He always tried to give Emma whatever she wanted, but this he could not give. It was impossible. From the beginning, that Christmas afternoon when he was thirteen and made the crazy journey through two miles of snowdrifts to see her, he had known he wasn't good enough. There she sat on an upholstered chair, dressed in dark blue velvet, holding a book. The candles on the tree in her family's living room had been burnt. His family would say that was wasteful, but the Millers apparently didn't care about waste. She had everything, at least as far as Waldenstein was concerned, and when he married her he vowed to give her that everything in abundance. But "everything" in Lunenburg was something more, something of which he had no comprehension, something quite beyond possibility.

Emma said the people here were "uppity." What did that mean? She was more beautiful than any of them. She talked about their silver, their china, their polished wooden floors. What difference did any of that make? The husbands of these women came to the barbershop and made amusing conversation, even laughed at his jokes. They lay back in his chair and trustingly exposed their throats to his straight razor. What was the problem? Was Emma going to be like some of those women in stories in his school books who never had enough of anything and eventually were turned into animals or fish and lost what little they had?

"But Emma," he would reason with her, "shouldn't we be happy with what we have? We have enough to eat, we have a good roof over our heads, you have some really nice dresses." Nathan believed this was true, however much Emma told him her wardrobe was lacking. "And now... just think, Emma, God has given us the very thing we most longed for." Then he would pick Eleanor up and give her a big hug and kiss.

"I know, I'm sorry. I should be so grateful, and indeed I am, it's just that... It's just that, when Virtue is away, I feel so alone. And then when she comes back she takes Eleanor away, and I'm even more alone." Nathan would sigh and wonder what he could do to make things better.

After the day when Eleanor said "Voo," she learned words with astonishing speed. "Mama" and "Dada" followed within days, and by her first birthday she was using individual words with great precision. "Cup," "take" when she wanted to be picked up and, as a special birthday present for Emma, "pretty," when she held her up to the stained glass window. What words were forming inside her for "hurt," "Mommy sad," "Virtue cross," "Mommy and Virtue both want me"? Even now, small as she was, these ideas were tiny hooks of unease, pricking within.

The evening of her birthday there was a big cake with a little fire on top of it. Everyone—Mommy, Daddy, Aunt Virtue and Uncle Obadiah—was there. They sang a short song with her name in it. Then they all said, "Blow, Eleanor, blow," and puffed out their cheeks to show her how, and in the end the little fire disappeared. She sat in her high chair and was allowed to eat as much cake as she wanted, which was a lot.

Eleanor felt happy, but she remembered when earlier something sharp had stung her, and Mommy had grabbed her from Aunt Virtue. Then Mommy had sat in the chair and played a game with her toes for a long time, but she could tell Mommy wasn't really thinking about the game or even about her, Eleanor.

That was this morning, a long time ago. Now Uncle Obadiah was making funny faces at her, and everyone was laughing. At last she was picked up out of her highchair, shaken gently to dislodge the crumbs, washed, and taken up to bed. Mommy and Daddy were there, and Mommy sang her a goodnight song like she always did, except tonight when Eleanor said "more," she sang it again. Then there were soft covers and tucking in and everything warm and quiet and...

CHAPTER 2
1944

Emma reached furtively into the post box. A letter. A letter addressed to her in her sister Joan's handwriting. Oh dear, what was the matter with Joan now? The postmark wasn't from Berwick, where she had last been known to be working in a bakery decorating cakes, but from somewhere in Massachusetts—Salem, it seemed. Crazily, Emma thought for a second that maybe Joan had been arrested as a witch. She laughed at herself, and opened the letter, not even waiting until she got home.

Dear Emma,

I do hate to bother you now that you have Eleanor and you must be so very busy, but I do need a bit of help. You see I left the bakery because I just couldn't stand it anymore. I came down here to find Hannah, but Hannah seems to have moved, and I don't know where she is. I'm staying in a boarding house here, and I'm afraid I've spent all my money—or will have by the time you read this letter. I wonder if you and Nathan would be kind enough to send me something just to allow me to get back home, and then I promise I'll find a job and repay you everything. I'm so sorry to be such a bother.

Joan

At the bottom was an address to which, presumably, the money could be sent. There was no "your loving sister," nothing—just plain "Joan." A graceless letter. Emma sighed. Of course they must help her, but Nathan would not be pleased. He worked hard. Having a child was so expensive, and there was the constant comparison with Virtue and Obadiah who now seemed to have everything in abundance. Only yesterday Virtue had told her that they were going to buy a new car, an Oldsmobile of their very own.

"So what will happen to the old Chev?" Emma asked.

"Well, I guess Nathan will just have to buy out Obadiah's share. Then you'll have a car of your own as well." As far as Virtue was concerned, that settled the matter, but Emma knew Nathan would find it hard to raise the money to do that. She also knew who would decide just how much half of a rusting old Chev was worth. Now, this additional demand on their resources! But, of course, Joan would not write to Virtue; she had more sense than to do that.

Emma said nothing about Joan until after Eleanor had been put to bed that evening. Then she spoke. "I've had a letter from Joan."

Nathan took a slurp of tea, looked up and waited.

"She's gone to the States."

"What on earth for?" Emma knew that as far as Nathan was concerned, the States was a den of iniquity filled with all manner of bad things—the Depression, guns, and an insatiable desire for liquor, which some of his fellow Lunenburgers had risked their lives trying to satisfy by rum-running.

"She went to find Hannah, but Hannah wasn't any longer where Joan thought she was, so now Joan's stuck there without any money. She wants to come home."

"She went to see Hannah? And then she wrote to you?" Emma sensed the unspoken outrage. Hannah was not Nathan's favourite person— brash, assertive, big-boned, she was just the kind of person who belonged in the States. Still, she knew that Nathan would do what had to be done.

"How much?"

"She didn't say. Twenty dollars, maybe? Do we have that much?"

"Maybe. I'll see. If not, I guess I could borrow it from Obadiah."

The injustice of borrowing the money from Virtue and Obadiah to rescue Joan who belonged, if she belonged at all, to the two sisters equally, sat between them unspoken. There were no parents, so to whom but her sister could Joan turn? And in the hierarchy of family, they both knew who took precedence and who paid.

Emma trustingly put the money in an envelope with a short note:

Dear Joan,
   I hope this is enough to buy a ticket to come home. Of course we shall be happy to see you.
   Your loving sister,
Emma

Two weeks later Joan arrived. Thin, emaciated even, she stood in the doorway with a cheap brown suitcase. Climbing the five steps up to the main floor of the small house seemed to have taken a great deal of effort. She kept her head down as if apologizing for the intrusion. Emma embraced her; it was the right thing to do. A year had passed since that first birthday, and Eleanor ran everywhere now, a rollicking bundle of flouncing skirt, chubby legs, and golden curls. She ran up to Joan, but stopped short. "This is your Aunt Joan, Eleanor," Emma said.

"Doan?" said Eleanor, eyeing her suspiciously. Joan reached out to her; Eleanor backed away. "Perhaps she's shy," Joan said.

"Well, not usually. Maybe it's the big suitcase." Turning to Eleanor who was about to retreat from the hallway into the kitchen, Emma said, "Come and give Aunt Joan a nice hug, Eleanor. She's going to stay with us for a little while"

Until that moment, neither Emma nor Joan had known that was what was going to happen, but once it had been said it was a fact. Joan was going to stay. Eleanor did not give Joan a hug. She stood in the hallway and watched her mother and Joan go up the stairs. Looking back, Emma saw Eleanor furtively crawling up behind as she took Joan's case to the empty bedroom on their side of the landing.

"My room," said Eleanor proudly, pointing to the door.

"Well, not your room quite yet," said Emma. "You're still sleeping in Mommy and Daddy's room. Aunt Joan can use the room for a little while before you're ready to move."

"My room!" Eleanor repeated with emphasis. Her face curled up and she began to cry.

Then Joan began to cry as well. Emma knew all too well why Joan might weep—for her lost home, for her parents in the graveyard, for her stupid and selfish brother back in Waldenstein, for her own messed up life. She had tried to be a schoolteacher and had failed. She had tried to decorate cakes so that they would be the pride of the bakery and had failed. She had gone to the States to find Hannah and hadn't even managed to do that. She could be crying about any or all of those things, but still Emma felt there was something more.

"What is it?" Emma asked.

Joan just shook her head and kept crying. Emma found herself murmuring things she didn't believe or quite mean. "You're safe with us, now. You can stay as long as you need. I'm sure you'll find a good job soon. It's quite a big town, and you've got lots of things going for you."

Joan stopped crying but sat on the edge of the bed silently for some time. Finally, she got up without saying anything, opened the unwieldy suitcase, and started unpacking her clothes. Emma left her alone and went downstairs to find that Virtue had returned from her day's teaching and was busy soothing Eleanor who was telling her in a pouty voice, "Doan in my room." Of course Virtue could well sympathize with Eleanor, Emma thought, but not to the extent of giving Joan her own spare room, which didn't belong to anyone else and most likely never would.

At supper there was macaroni and cheese, a favourite of Eleanor's. The kitchen table sat with one side against a wall, and Emma and Nathan were at either end, so Joan sat down on the remaining side next to Eleanor's high chair. Eleanor looked down on her encouragingly. "Doan, macaroni."

Joan gazed at her plate, which was piled high with a large orange squiggly mound of macaroni and cheese, with apparent horror. "But...but...I don't like cheese. We never had cheese at home."

"Oh." Emma was taken aback. "Never mind, I can make you some macaroni without cheese." Though what that might taste like, Emma couldn't quite imagine. Nevertheless, it had to be done, and the orange mound was eventually replaced by a white one, which resembled a colony of dead white larvae. Joan picked at these with a fork for the better part of fifteen minutes; when she gave up the pile had not diminished noticeably.

⸱⸱⸱

The next morning was sunny and warm. Joan watched Emma's white organza curtains, her summer curtains, flutter gently in the breeze that came in through the open kitchen window. Periodically there also came the sound of timber being piled up or shifted on the other side of the garden fence, which only partly hid the large red building and yard of the block shop. Joan sat silently eating cornflakes with milk; she would have liked a banana as well, but there were no bananas.

"The war, you know," Emma said. "Nathan and Obadiah have been lucky. Mrs. Wamboldt, her husband's fishing schooner was torpedoed by a German sub. He was grateful to escape with his life, but the six crew members..." She shook her head. Lack of bananas was a trifle, Emma gave Joan to understand. Eleanor sat at her small desk in the corner, "writing" with crayons and studiously ignoring Joan.

Without warning, the whining sound of a large fan filled the air, and with it came a cloud of white smoke, rising, falling, seeping through the white curtains into the small kitchen. The smell was sharp and acrid.

"We must close the windows." Emma ran from the sink where she was washing dishes and slammed down first one window, then the other.

"Won't it get awfully hot and stuffy? What are those fumes anyway, and why are they sending them out into your house?" Joan had thought of Nathan and Obadiah as rich (well, comparatively), and of her sisters as living a life of modest luxury.

"They do something they call galvanizing. I think it's meant to stop the metal they use to make boat parts and pails from rusting. Anyway, somehow it makes this steam or smoke, and it's horrid and burning, so they have a fan that moves it out of their building, but into our yard."

"That's awful. Can't you stop them?"

"How? That's what they make. I guess it's not their fault that there's a house right next to their business."

Joan was appalled. "But it's awful," she repeated. "I can feel my throat burning even with the window closed."

"I know. And I do worry about Eleanor. She has so many colds and coughs. Sometimes I think..."

"Why don't you move then?"

"Move! Wouldn't I like to! But how? First of all, the house and barbershop go together. They're part of the same lot. So, to move, Nathan and Obadiah would have to find another place for a shop. Then...I don't think Obadiah and Virtue want to move."

"Well, I suppose they don't get the fumes from the block shop in quite the same way since they're on the other side of the house," Joan conceded.

"No, of course not. But it's not just that…"

"What then?"

"I think Virtue at least wants to be here so…so she can share Eleanor."

Joan was starting to see that there were more forces at work here, burrowing under the uneven wooden floor, whispering through the ill-fitting doors, than she had imagined. She took her cereal dish to the white enamel sink, washed it out and dried it. "I should go and try to see if I can get a job."

"You might…you just might try the boat builders at the end of the harbour. They always seem to need office staff, and it's run by some good Liberals our father used to work for."

"Why should I do that? I'd like to get a job on my own, not because my father worked for the Liberals!"

"Okay. It was just an idea," Emma said, "but it's how things work here, whether we like it or not."

Joan stepped out into the balmy June morning. Her heels clicked reassuringly with a steady, metronomic sense of purpose on the concrete sidewalk as she walked quickly along. On the second floor of the block shop building she could see the fan whirring away, spewing out goodness knew what towards her sisters' little cape house. Across the road was another red building that seemed more benign. "Ship Outfitters" it said in big white letters against the red paint. Farther up the street was a little market shop with some fruit in the window. She wondered if that was where one might get bananas when there were bananas again. The war…it seemed so unreal here in this little town. Up on the corner was another store—or was it a store?—with bars on the window. A disheveled man came out with something shaped like a bottle in a brown paper bag. Of course, it must be the liquor store. How sad that Emma had to live in such an awful part of town.

She kept walking, catching glimpses of the harbour between the buildings. The water sparkled invitingly, but to get down there you had to cross a lot of railway tracks and a dirty, unpaved road. It smelled of fish—not fish cooked and steaming healthily on a plate but fish raw, salt-enveloped. She looked up at the wheeling gulls and decided that maybe the sky was the best direction to aim for, impossible though that was. What a mess she was in! Forced onto the charity of her sister, living in a room smaller than the one she had in Berwick. Maybe she should have stayed there. But no, that had become impossible. She walked faster as if escaping from something she wished to outrun.

Then there was the child. What a spoiled piece of work she was. "My room." As if she owned it by right. And "Doan." Not even "Aunt Doan." Virtue was no corrective to little Miss Saucy. Joan could see that she was even more indulgent to Eleanor than Emma was. Maybe that was something she could try to fix.

A short distance along, the road curved around the end of the harbour. Two boats sat on dry docks; men scrambled around with metal blow-torches and hammers making a great racket. "Knickle's Shipbuilding and Repair," the sign said. This must be the company Emma had been talking about. Oh well, why not? Pride was a useless luxury when you were in a situation like hers. It would be humiliating wherever she went.

The front store space was filled with cast iron stoves and fireplaces. So they must make things other than boats.

A young man came up to her. "Can I help you, Miss?"

"Well, yes, I wondered…I've just come here, and I'm looking for work."

"Ah. That's not my department, but I'll take you back to the office."

He led her to a modest rectangular room filled with four large desks where important-looking people sat scribbling with pens or, in the case of the one woman, typing. In one corner was a telephone with a small switchboard attached.

What on earth could she do here? "Wait just a minute." Her gentleman escort disappeared into a large dark-paneled room behind the busy clerks. When he reappeared it was to introduce her to a short, balding man with an air of impervious prosperity. "Mr. Knickle, sir, this is the young lady I told you about who is looking for work." Mr. Knickle gazed at Joan, his head set low in the middle of his large shoulders, his eyes scanning her as he might the hull of a ship for some cracks, some signs of weakness.

"Well, Miss…?

"I'm Joan Miller, sir."

"Ah." He thought a moment. "Not one of Aaron Miller's girls, are you?"

"Yes, sir, I am."

"Good man, Aaron. Carried Waldenstein for me every election but one. And the swing to Conservatives that year no one could resist. Sad he died so young. So...how can I help you? Can you type?"

"I'm afraid not, sir. I trained as a teacher, but I didn't like it at all." Joan stood trembling, sinking under her deficiencies.

"As it happens, the telephone operator we had has just left. Planning to marry a Norwegian soldier stationed here in town, I understand. Guess she needed to, quick." He smiled knowingly. "Strange things this war does to people." Mr. Knickle mused a moment, while Joan stood silently in front of him. "Would that sort of work interest you at all?"

"Of course, sir, I'm certainly willing to try." Then in a burst of what, for her, was positive enthusiasm, she said, "Perhaps I could learn to type."

"Indeed, that's the spirit." He turned to go.

"But...but when would you like me to start?"

"Oh come in tomorrow morning, and we'll set you up."

Joan left. She had not dared ask what she might be paid, nor had she dared to go into the connection between the war and marriage to Norwegians, though she could guess.

She stepped out into the sunshine of a late June morning. Why go back to the house and get in Emma's way? Or retreat to her small room, now enveloped in noxious fumes, and contemplate her sad life? Since she had settled the job issue with surprising expedition, she would explore a little. She kept on walking in the same direction, around the end of the harbour, then curving back again on the opposite side. On the left, the harbour side, was a large encampment of some sort—a two-storey rectangular building, wartime grey, with a one-storey spur coming out at a right angle that looked as if it had been put up in haste. Men in uniform strolled around the make-shift paths. A metal sign over the gate proclaimed "Camp Norway." So this must be where the impregnating Norwegians lived. Joan shivered slightly and walked quickly by.

After this the road was unpaved, but now trees framed the view of the water, and behind, on a gently rolling hill, a herd of cattle munched slowly. A few houses were scattered along the shore, but mostly it was a peaceful, rural road. Joan relaxed; this was more like home.

Home. That hadn't existed for nine long years. Her early years of teaching had been hard, so hard, always living among families who treated her like a servant. "Make sure that Johnny has his boots when he comes home from school"; "The last teacher always washed the dinner dishes for us before she went to her room"; "I don't know what you teachers get paid for at all—you only work a few hours a day for a bit more than half the year." Joan, always short of money for decent clothes—they still expected you to dress properly, "like a school-teacher,"—was constantly afraid the trustees would find some reason to complain of her performance. "Last year all our children passed with distinction." Yet in those early years she could think, "Only two more weeks till Christmas; only a month till summer vacation, and then I'll be home, I'll be taken care of." Then in the space of a month, all that had disappeared. Mother dead, father dead, and her sisters and herself gathered around the parlour, white and subdued, while their one brother, Harry, sat in a corner shouting "All or nothing; all or nothing!" At the memory hot tears stung her eyes anew. So, because he roared, because he was a man, because there was no will, because they had to stop the outrage that was occurring in their own house, they gave him all; they signed the piece of paper, and then it was no longer their house, their fields, their woodland. It was his. Their older sister Flora was his as well, though that was a gift he rued.

Flora! What awful things had been done to her. Whatever Joan felt about her own life, she was sure it could not be as terrible as Flora's. Joan could only remember her sister as she was now—with crossed eyes, pouting lower lip, and no hair. Many times her mother had told her how beautiful Flora had been before her "fits," how clever, how kind. Virtue and Emma claimed to remember some of this, but what they chiefly talked about was their walk through the winter snow, around the lake, to summon help. They were the heroines of the story; Flora was merely its victim. Now all of them had callously passed her on to Harry's care. In return for the "all" he claimed of the inheritance, they forced him to promise to look after Flora. Faced with that choice, he agreed. He would build her a house, he claimed; he would see she never wanted for anything. Emma and Virtue were made trustees to see that this happened. Of course it didn't happen, and Emma and Virtue were helpless or hopeless, Joan wasn't sure which, in holding Harry to his agreement. So Flora was farmed out to be the "companion," slave was more like it, to some demented old lady down in Vogler's Cove. Flora had been abandoned, as Joan had feared she might be. Emma and Virtue had refused to give Flora a home with them; that she knew. So why should either be delighted to take her in? Perhaps now that she had a job she could pay rent. Maybe...

The road rose steeply now, curving away from the sea. By the time she climbed to the top, it was already eleven o'clock. When would Emma and Nathan eat? Not later than noon, she imagined. She turned around and there, laid out before her like a perfect picture, was the dazzling blue of the harbour dotted with what seemed like a hundred fishing boats, the bright red fish processing buildings that ringed the water on the opposite shore, and behind them, rising grandly on a large ridge of hill, the town itself—innumerable little painted houses set in strict rows, rising up the slope, as if some giant child had amused himself, ripping them out of his toy box and planting them there. "See what I've built, Mommy!" Church steeples sprang out of the trees— five at least—and on top of the highest hill Lunenburg Academy stood like a fantastic wooden castle. The town itself really was beautiful, Joan realized with surprise. But down where Emma lived...

⁂

Nathan could smell the galvanizing as soon as he stepped out of the barbershop to go for dinner. Emma would be upset. He strode the few short steps up the concrete path from the shop to the house. As he opened the back door the acrid smell of the smoke gave way to the sweet smell of Emma's chicken stew—summer savory, carrots, parsnips all mingled together in one glorious medley of fragrance. He was a lucky man. He would hold Emma, tell her how much he loved her, how wonderful their child was, how there would be a house of their own someday, all this and more. And then Emma would forget the lower streetscape and the galvanizing and the pretty dresses and dishes all the other women in town had—or so she believed—because she would know she was the woman who was loved above all others.

He turned from the hall into the kitchen and there was Joan—short dark hair, small nose, tight lips, pale skin stretched like a garment shrunk too tightly over her scrawny frame. Everything changed in an instant. He pecked Emma on the cheek, went to the kitchen sink to wash his hands, and sat down.

"Joan has news," Emma said as she dished up the chicken.

"Oh? What's that?" Nathan tried to exert himself to show interest.

"She has got herself a job. She starts tomorrow."

"Where? Here in town?"

"At Knickle's Shipbuilding," Joan said. "I just walked in, and they hired me. I'm as surprised as anyone."

"So what will you do?" What Nathan really meant was, "What will you be paid," which translated into "Will you continue to be living here?"

"Well, it's only switchboard operator at first, but if I can improve my typing…"

Nathan's question was answered. He knew the wages at Knickle's were by no means the highest in town, and answering the telephone didn't sound like top dollars to him.

"Of course she can stay with us until she gets more settled," Emma put in.

So that was that. Nathan forked up a large lump of chicken and swallowed it whole. If he choked, who cared?

He watched Joan pick daintily with knife and fork through the detritus of a chicken wing. Eleanor also observed her critically.

"Doan, you should pick it up and chew, like this." She demonstrated most ably with her drumstick.

Joan winced. Well, Nathan wasn't going to reprimand Eleanor at the behest of Joan. Emma too kept silence.

So this was what it was going to be like now, he thought. No family conversation, no intimate sharing of looks or little jokes or asides. All would be observed by the silent and judgmental Joan. As he pushed his chair back and got up to leave, he reflected that at least he was better off than Obadiah, who had no company for his dinner at all, and would doubtless be eating molasses bread and pork pudding again. Still, maybe even that diet and solitude would be preferable to his own over-crowded kitchen.

⬥

"I wouldn't have Flora and I won't have Joan," Virtue fumed in her kitchen after a day of teaching with supper still ahead of her. If Emma and Nathan wanted to take Joan on, that was their business. They probably thought she should do it because she didn't have a child and had a spare room. Well, one misfortune was no reason to be taking on another. What about cooking the meals for Joan, what about the laundry? When did she have time to do that? It was all she could do to feed Obadiah. People thought teachers didn't work: just six hours a day in the classroom and then all those holidays: Christmas, Easter, the long summer. Well, they did work. All that marking, all that lesson preparation, the hours of talking to impossible parents, trying to get them to understand that children must be helped at home as well. It wasn't all up to the teacher! They couldn't send a child to school in jeans, or worse still, a party dress, and expect them to do well or to behave well. Clothes were important; homework was important, and she found herself saying it over and over.

After all that, now when she came home and tried to do her duties as a wife, there was all this kerfuffle going on across the hall; it was just getting to be too much. Of course she tried to look out for the child as well. Sometimes she thought Emma had no idea how to bring her up. Poor little thing. She wouldn't have a room of her own for ages now. "Doan in my room," she said yesterday when she came down the stairs to her kitchen. Maybe Emma thought children didn't feel these things, but they did. Eleanor was such a bright little thing, she'd feel it more than most.

⬥

After putting Eleanor to bed, Emma sat in the living room under the reading lamp and embroidered a blue bird on the collar of a small silk dress for her daughter. As she worked at the radiant bird, its head and beak tilted upwards, she carried on an urgent conversation with herself.

She knew Nathan thought they shouldn't have taken Joan in, the way he walked about silently, scarcely speaking. Dinner today had been just awful. He ate and left, hardly even noticing Eleanor. They hadn't taken Flora, but Joan was different. She wouldn't be there for long; she had a job already. A job. Pin money, at best. She couldn't support herself on that. It was going to be a long time! The bird blurred with the tears of her confusion.

"Mommy…Mommy." A small, high voice piped down the stairs. Emma put aside her embroidery and went up to Eleanor, who was standing, holding onto the bars of her crib. "Mommy, there's something scary over there." She pointed to the wall between her bedroom and Joan's.

"That's nothing. Just Aunt Joan moving about in her room."

"No. Not Doan. A creature. You stay here, Mommy."

Emma knew this was the last thing she should do. "No, really, there's nothing there. Now lie down and go to sleep."

Eleanor lay down on her stomach with her little rump up in the air, and her thumb stuck firmly in her mouth. Emma returned to the living room, but after a short while the voice called out, as she knew it would, "Mommy, Mommy."

Again the small being stood up, commanding her to stay with it. Again she resisted the urge to stay, but the third time she wearily hauled a chair out of the bedroom and agreed to do her embroidery in the hallway with a crack of the bedroom door open, a sliver of light falling on her daughter's blonde curls. Only after Eleanor had gone firmly back to sleep did she creep downstairs again.

The next night the same thing happened. This time Emma went up only once and decided that she would let Eleanor scream for a bit. Two minutes later, Virtue was standing in the doorway of the living room. "I hear Eleanor crying."

"Yes, I know. She just wants attention. She wants me to sit outside her door every evening, just like I did last night."

Virtue went away, but soon Emma heard the crying tail off into gasping snuffles, as Virtue's unmistakable tones floated down the stairs. "Is 'oo afraid of the dark, then?"

Reluctantly Emma went up the stairs. This time she did not grab Eleanor from Virtue's clutches as she had on that first birthday, nearly a year ago; she simply reached out, and Eleanor was transferred to her mother's arms. After that, Emma spent at least an hour every evening sitting on the landing outside Eleanor's room. Joan, at least, had enough sense to keep to her own room with the door shut.

When school vacation came Virtue was there every day from morning to night. Nothing passed uncensored.

"Don't you think it's a bit cool for that sundress this morning? The poor child must be freezing."

"She ought to be outside playing, not sitting looking at a picture book."

"Why have you made that skirt so long for her? Surely little girls' dresses should be short and perky."

After lunch Virtue would appear at the kitchen door and ask if Eleanor wouldn't, perhaps, like to share some of the apple pie and whipped cream she had made for Obadiah. Naturally, Eleanor would, even as Emma tried to explain she had eaten a perfectly good meal and really, was having a second dessert good for her?

"Well, if you're bent on starving the child…"

So Eleanor had apple pie and whipped cream and gingerbread and whipped cream and coconut cream pie and…

Eleanor spent long hours in Virtue's kitchen, disappearing into the pantry with dolls and stuffed animals, setting them up in a row against the cupboards, then sitting in the doorway, facing them, 'teaching' them lessons as Virtue did. "Don't be a bad child now, Billie, but read to me nicely." Emma heard Virtue laughing and carrying on the game.

Later Emma would claim Eleanor and take her out into the little back garden where in the spring they had planted asters, alyssum and peonies together. They would pull out the weeds and admire the growing plants. There was a small cherry tree and a swing, and Emma would push her daughter until her arms ached. Eventually, they would return to the house where, sooner rather than later, Eleanor would again be claimed by Virtue.

Joan had a box camera from her more affluent days as a teacher. One July afternoon, as soon as she returned from work, she took out the camera and suggested that Emma, Virtue and Eleanor come into the garden for a photograph. It was still warm and sunny, though the perfume of the mock orange was beginning to take on an evening intensity. So where should they stand, the two sisters and the little girl? "Eleanor's so short, why don't you kneel down and then you'll all be at the same level," Joan suggested.

Eleanor stood in the middle, and her aunt and mother knelt, one on her right hand and one on her left. Each of them clasped one of Eleanor's arms. There they knelt—antagonists, sisters, saints—tearing apart the child they both worshipped.

"Perfect," Joan said and snapped the shutter.

CHAPTER 3
December 1946

Emma wrapped the scarf around her neck and tried to stifle the cough. It came anyway, originating from somewhere deep inside with enough force to bend her over.

"Don't be silly," Nathan said. "You can't go out in this weather. No one else will be there."

Emma straightened up and caught her breath. "Well, we'll see. But at least I'm going to be there."

"You've got a cold already, and it's a blizzard outside."

"I've got to go. The children need the rehearsal."

"Maybe, but I'm telling you the children won't be there. Their parents won't let them out in a storm like this."

Nathan protested, but Emma grew more insistent. She had written the Christmas play for the older children herself, a modernization of the second shepherd's play, and nothing was going to stop her from trying to make it as perfect as possible.

"At least don't take Eleanor. Virtue can look after her."

"Virtue's busy. She's going to make the Christmas cake today, and she won't want Eleanor around when she's doing that."

Emma knew this was not really true. Virtue would welcome Eleanor to her kitchen at any time. Emma didn't want to give Eleanor up to Virtue's care. Besides, Eleanor needed to practise her song with the organist.

So she bundled Eleanor up in her boots, leggings, coat, hat, and scarf that stretched over her mouth and nose so that only her eyes peeked out accusingly at her: "What are you doing now, Mommy?" Out they went into the storm. Emma thought of her father making his way back across the huge frozen lake to their home, struggling from his logging camp at weekends to be with the family. But in her heart she knew that, for her, this wasn't bravery; it was vanity. Her play must be as good as possible. People would see that if Emma Wentzell didn't have china as fine as theirs or a house as grand, she could still write a play the like of which had never been seen at a Lunenburg Christmas concert.

Eleanor pushed her little legs through the drifts as fast as she could because Mommy was racing in front of her through the gusts of wind and snow, scarcely even looking back. Perhaps she would disappear altogether, and then she would be left alone in a vast and unfathomable whiteness. She knew the way to church, but nothing looked the same anymore, and even Mommy seemed different. She didn't care about her anymore—all she cared about was getting to some rehearsal, she called it, some practice for the Christmas play. "Wait," Eleanor panted.

Emma turned around for a moment. "Hurry up then. We're late," she said as the coughs came again, buckling her over.

It was scary being out with Mommy like this. Eleanor knew that only something as important as church could make Mommy do it and plow on without seeming to think about her at all. It seemed, in fact, that there was nothing more important than church, because while most things only had to do with living, the church had to do with dying as well, and even at four Eleanor knew that getting ready to die was the very most important thing one had to do in life.

Every week you went to church, the big bell donging and donging—louder and more insistently as you got nearer until it swallowed you up and hurled you through the black open door set in the tower of the white building. Inside everything was different—quiet, with only the faint reverberations of the bell and the softer tones of the organ playing as you found your seat. Then you had to sit very good and still while Reverend Schwarz talked on and on. Sometimes you could understand the things he said, but even if you couldn't, you could tell what he said was important from the way his voice rose and fell, rose and fell, declining to a whisper and then bellowing out in fervent affirmation. He dressed in a black robe that fell in folds all around his hands and body, so that you couldn't really tell what kind of body was under the robes, though you could tell it must be very big because of the way the folds of the black gown dropped in a curve down the front. But that was only right as well, because you weren't supposed to think about his body, just his words, and the things he did up at the altar. While all the church was holy, the altar was an especially holy place where the minister did some magic. Some Sundays Mommy and Daddy would go up to the altar to eat and drink some of the magic, and when they came back they smelled holy. Once when Eleanor was walking past the store on the corner just up from their house, a man came out of the store who had the same holy smell, but Mommy said it was different, that the store was not a nice place and little girls should not even walk past it on their own.

The church was full of interesting picture windows, and one in particular caught Eleanor's fancy because, she believed, it must be a picture of Reverend Schwarz himself. The man in the window was also big with a black robe and a mouth that was tightly shut as if no one could change his mind or what he was going to do. He had a big Bible in one hand, and the other hand was pointing to it, as if it were the most important thing in the world.

And then there was the music—firm chords sounding one after the other in absolute procession, as if nothing could ever be made different. This was the one thing she truly loved. Everyone sang together, almost drowning out the big organ. She could sing some of these songs now, hymns they were called, and doing that was the happiest thing of all. Mommy said she could sing one of them at the Christmas concert, standing alone on the big stage that they put up every year for the occasion. That was going to be splendid.

She was allowed to sing the song because she went every week to Sunday School, and this was going to be a Sunday School concert, but in fact she didn't like Sunday School very much. Every week there was a little leaflet with a picture on the front and a story inside. Sometimes this story was good and interesting, but other times the pictures were scary, and then the story was usually scary as well. One week there was a man all covered with blood on a dirty road, with another man and a donkey beside him. The man lying on the road looked so terrible and frightening that Eleanor began to cry. The teacher said it was only a picture, and didn't really mean anything, but if it didn't mean anything why was there a story about the man and why would anyone bother to paint it? So she had cried some more, and they had to go and get Mommy from the class of older children she was teaching, and some of the other children laughed when Mommy took her away.

Now, as she ran behind Emma, she suddenly thought that if the Church could make Mommy forget about her, it must be very important indeed, and she hated the idea of this thing driving them on through the snow on the week before Christmas when she could have been helping Joan make sugar cookies and decorating them with coloured icing at home.

꿍

Emma puffed up the steps to the black door and pulled on the latch. The wind howled against her like a desolate beast. Eleanor was crying. With all her strength, Emma gave a mighty pull, and the door swung open. Everything was dark and quiet, but in a corner at the front, she saw a small light shining down over the organ. Melissa, forty going on eighty, her dark hair shading a low forehead and penetrating brown eyes, sat there swinging her feet disconsolately over the shadowed pedal board.

"I thought maybe you'd come," were Melissa's first words.

"Of course. There's a rehearsal scheduled. Where's everyone else?"

"Home, where any sane person would be on a day like this. I tell you I wouldn't be here if I lived farther than one block away."

"So, no one is coming?" Emma was outraged. Why wouldn't other people make the effort? She had managed to get there, sick and with a small child in tow. What was wrong with these people?

Well, at least Eleanor could practise her solo with Melissa. She took off her coat, helped Eleanor with hers, and told Eleanor to walk up nicely onto the stage that had been built out over the front of the chancel. There Eleanor stood while Melissa began the organ introduction.

In the bleak midwinter
Frosty wind made moan.
Earth stood hard as iron,
Water like a stone.

As Eleanor's small voice echoed out in the empty church, Emma found herself struggling not to cry. The piece was more appropriate than she could have known when she chose it, but it was not just the melancholy of the words and Holst's melody that made her weep. It was the promise she now saw in Eleanor and the loss of that promise in herself.

"You will be brilliant!" she had promised over Eleanor's crib. Now that seemed indeed a possibility…but as for herself? The play she had written would be a disaster without the needed rehearsal. Perhaps it would have been a disaster anyway. People here didn't like the new; they liked the old, and they had mastered the old—the gabled houses, the wide-planked floors, the silver set out on a tray for all to see, the masts of fishing boats floating against the sky, bringing wealth to the town and most of its inhabitants. These were constant reminders that she didn't belong, that she couldn't belong, no matter how hard she tried.

Eleanor sang the song through twice, word perfect, note perfect. Then she sat with Emma and a rather disgruntled Melissa for half an hour, until they all had to concede that no one else was coming.

Eleanor tugged at her sleeve. "Let's go home, Mommy."

Once more they braved the blizzard. At least this time it was down-hill, and Emma, remorseful of her earlier neglect, took Eleanor's hand and led her all the way.

"How did it go?" Virtue's question seemed innocent enough, but Emma didn't reply. She took off Eleanor's coat and leggings and her own coat in the hallway, and went into her kitchen and shut the door.

That evening, after she put Eleanor to bed—first the story, then the warm milk, then the prayers, "If I should die before I wake…"— Emma went back to the kitchen to do some last-minute tidying. She had a cold, so she thought little of the slight tightness in her chest. Then it got worse. Her chest and throat constricted as if someone were choking her. She couldn't breathe. Terrified, all she could do was make strange, gasping noises. The more she struggled, the worse it got. She flopped into the worn kitchen chair and heaved about, trying to loosen whatever it was that was strangling her. She mustn't wake Eleanor; Eleanor must be protected, must not see her like this.

Suddenly, Virtue was standing over her. "Emma, Emma, what's the matter?" But Emma didn't know what the matter was. She was going to die, right here in her own kitchen, in this dilapidated chair, with Virtue watching her.

Virtue disappeared, and a few seconds later everyone was there—Nathan, Obadiah, Joan, Virtue. They stood around her saying useless things:

A glass of water, get her a glass of water.

Call the doctor.

He's coming.

Maybe if she stood up?

No, don't move her.

She was a spectacle of the fearsome struggle between life and death in the midst of them. The doctor came and put a needle in her arm. She was shaking all over, but she could breathe again.

"I told her not to go out in the storm," Nathan said.

"But she insisted," Virtue continued the litany of accusation. "She even dragged the poor child with her, and all for a Sunday School play." It was all her fault, Emma realized, of course it must be. Her whole life, somehow, was her fault. She had mismanaged it terribly.

Dr. Willis looked at her with sleepy eyes. "She'll be all right now for a while. But you should go to the drugstore and get this inhaler." He scratched some words on a piece of paper and handed it to Nathan. Finally, he addressed Emma, who had begun to feel she no longer existed. "Whenever you feel you can't breathe, just take a few puffs from the inhaler, and that will make things better."

"Whenever..." So it would happen again. The nightmare would recur. When? How? How often? But she couldn't ask these things just now. She simply nodded to show she understood.

"And you must stay indoors until the cough is completely gone. That's very important. Don't go outside in the cold. Things will only get worse if you do."

"But the concert?"

"Not even for the concert. It will go on without you. Don't worry."

"Eleanor's song?"

"Not even for Eleanor's song. She will do perfectly well without you."

If that was meant to be consoling, Emma did not find it so.

That night she lay awake in bed while Nathan and Eleanor slept. Thank goodness Eleanor had seen none of the drama. How would she manage to explain why she couldn't go to the Christmas concert? How could she bear not to hear Eleanor sing?

Eleanor stirred. Dawn had come with a sludge of grey wafting in through the window. The snow had turned to rain.

Nathan got up. Emma started to rise. "You just rest. I'll cope," he said. Gently, Nathan woke up Eleanor. "Come with me."

"Mommy, Mommy," Eleanor protested.

"Mommy's not well just now. She needs to sleep a little longer."

"No! Mommy, Mommy!"

Emma got up, lifted her out of bed, and smoothed her rumpled curls. "It's all right. Mommy's here. Mommy will always be here, shush, shush."

❦

Virtue, presiding over the evening meal, let outrage fly. "Whatever next. She wants attention, I guess. First she tries to kill herself by going out in a blizzard, and then when she nearly succeeds she makes it really dramatic, so that we all have to stand around and watch her struggling. What a mother! That poor child."

"Don't be too hard on her. She was really sick," Obadiah said through the roast beef he was chewing.

"Yes, and why? Because she cares more for the rubbish she writes and puts on in church than she does for her own child—or her husband, for that matter. And who's going to have to help out with the house-work now? Who's going to have to decorate the house for Christmas? You know all too well! And I only get two weeks off to do it all."

❦

On Saturday morning, Joan sat in her small bedroom, the bedroom that she knew should be Eleanor's, talking to herself. "It's all my fault. There's too much for Emma to do. She insists on cleaning my room along with the rest of the house. Probably doesn't think I'd do it well enough. I shouldn't be here."

She sat on a small wooden chair stuffed under the eaves of the room. If she stood upright quickly, she bumped her head. There was a tiny table as well that Nathan had salvaged from the basement. A single bed shared the sloping wall with the chair and table. Against the opposite wall, where the ceiling was higher, stood a chest of drawers with a mirror above it. This was supposed to be Eleanor's also, of course. At one end of the room, beside the door, sat a large metal trunk bound with wooden slats and covered with a fanciful and flounced shiny, pink-patterned fabric, a kind of pseudo brocade that lay quiescent on the trunk, apparently unaffected by how much Joan was busy hating it.

In front of her, on the table, lay a blank sheet of paper and a pen. But to whom could she write? Hannah no longer existed, apparently. At least she had no knowable address, which, as far as Joan was concerned, was much the same thing. Flora could barely read, and certainly was in no position to help or understand. Her sister, Rachel, had long since stopped teaching school and married someone most unsuitable. Her parents had died, one after the other, just a few weeks apart. Except for her two sisters in this house, she was abandoned.

Finally, she took up the pen and wrote, "I have done something awful. It wasn't my fault, but I did it." She crossed out "I did it" and wrote, "it happened to me." She could think of nothing more to say. She folded the paper up and stuck it in the top of the chest of drawers under a wooden box of clean, starched handkerchiefs, got up and went downstairs to see what she could do to help Emma.

Emma sat playing a drawing game with Eleanor. It entertained the child and didn't require her to exert herself. You drew a part of a person or animal and then folded the paper over. Then the next person drew something without looking at the previous drawing, and when all the paper was used up you opened it up and found a fantastic creature.

"Can you make a drawing, Joan?" Eleanor asked.

Joan ignored this and focused on Emma. "I wondered if there was something I could do to help get ready for Christmas?"

"That's very kind, Joan, but... Well, there's the tree, of course. I've got the lights and ornaments on, but it needs icicles."

Served her right for asking, Joan thought. Icicles! Most people didn't put tinsel icicles on their trees anymore, but Emma did, oh yes, Emma put icicles on with a vengeance. First each one had to be straightened between your fingers, then put on carefully with one end folded over the branch and spaced successively at absolutely regular intervals so that each branch, each subsidiary twig, was evenly covered by a tinsel curtain. Joan set to work.

It took hours. Eventually, at about five in the evening, she was finished. She turned on the tree lights and waited for inspection, which duly arrived in the person of Emma.

"That's lovely Joan. Thank you so much. But..."

Joan felt herself stiffen.

"But...that branch up there to the right...don't you think maybe you could take a few off where they're very thick and put them down here where there seems to be a gap."

Joan did as she was told. Emma surveyed the results. "That's better. But there's still a small hole here on the bottom branch. Maybe that could be fixed." Joan steeled herself again and moved silently to fix the offending limb.

She was only released when Emma collapsed into the armchair with a fit of coughing.

⁂

Everyone was in the living room opening presents. Emma looked around at all their faces. She should be happy. The turkey, stuffed with a summer savory dressing, was cooking in the oven; the vegetables, peeled by Joan, were sitting in pots, waiting to be boiled or roasted; the cranberry pie stood on the sideboard, and Eleanor danced with delight, running from one new toy to another. There was a doll and a little crib made especially for the doll to sleep in from Virtue and Obadiah; a little tricycle from her and Nathan; a tiny baking set; and everywhere books—books with pop-up pictures, books with fuzzy felt covers, books that smelled when you scratched them. Two of the books were all that Joan could afford, and Emma assured her that was fine; books were the most important thing one could give a child. But Joan seemed unconvinced as she shrank apologetically into a large armchair. For once Emma saw the spectacle through Joan's eyes. It was gross, overdone, like one of those round-bottomed rubber figures that smiled and invited you to punch it, and when you did it bounced back with the same infuriating smile. But if you pricked it, suddenly it deflated and nothing was left.

What was wrong with her? Why couldn't she be happy with Nathan and Eleanor and Virtue and Obadiah as they laughed and joked over the shiny crumpled paper and ribbon? Emma was feeling a bit better. She coughed less and had only used her puffer twice in the last three days. She was going to be fine. Of course, she couldn't go to see her play in the evening, or to hear Eleanor sing. Maybe that was what was troubling her.

Outside the sun sparkled on what was left of the snow, hardened to an icy sheen. The piles of lumber, towering over the wooden fence that separated the back garden from the block shop, were white and polished. The street was empty; everyone was inside enacting scenes similar to those in her own living room. Even the staggering drunks had disappeared to some winter wonderland of their own. Gradually her spirits began to lift. As they did so, Emma realized, without consciously thinking about it, that despite all the doctor's warnings, she was going to the church concert that evening. The play had long since passed out of her control, and almost out of her caring, but nothing was going to prevent her from hearing Eleanor sing. Of course, she couldn't go with the rest of the family; she knew they wouldn't let her. She must go alone and secretly.

At last supper was over. Joan and Virtue had washed up the dishes. Emma went upstairs to dress Eleanor. She put the white silk dress with the bluebirds embroidered on the collar over her small head. Little white stockings went on the chubby feet, followed by new white shoes with tiny gold straps and buckles. The light brown curls were all smoothed individually and tied back with a blue bow. Emma could not imagine anything more perfect.

"Are you getting dressed now?" Eleanor asked.

"No, sweetheart. Mommy can't go to church this evening."

"But don't you want to hear me sing?"

"I want to hear you sing ever so much, but you see the doctor says I can't go out in the cold yet."

"But I need you!" Eleanor looked as if she might cry and refuse to go herself.

"Now you must be Mommy's brave girl and go and sing for your Daddy and Aunt Joan and Aunt Virtue and Uncle Obadiah and all the other people who will be there. And I'll be thinking about you every minute you're up there. You'll do very well. I know you will."

"But I still want you."

"Well, you just go off now, and you never know what may happen."

She took Eleanor downstairs where Virtue was standing in the hall, waiting to take charge. "Here, Eleanor, put on your leggings and coat and hat. Make sure you don't crush that pretty dress," Virtue said.

Emma intervened. "Her father can do it." But Virtue already had Eleanor sitting on the hall floor, and was busy pulling on the white jodhpur leggings. Nathan hovered uneasily. Two minutes later the whole party had gone out the front door, leaving Emma alone.

She watched them go up the moonlit street and around the corner. Then she went upstairs, put on her warmest dress and cardigan, and covered this up with her heavy grey winter coat and scarf. There was a childish glee in being naughty, in deceiving everyone. Why should she not go? She had a bit of a cough, and there had been one or two nasty attacks of asthma, but now that she had the puffer she should be fine. Out the door she crept, taking care to close it softly behind her. Then she laughed to herself. Why was she being quiet? No one could detect her here. They had all gone. Of course she would not join them in the church; she'd just stand quietly at the back until Eleanor finished singing. Then she could walk home, no one the wiser.

Stars and moonlight on the snow! It was an enchanted landscape, and for a moment Emma remembered that other walk in the snow that she and Virtue had taken all those years ago when they were scarcely older than Eleanor. But goodness, it was cold! Everything down to the base of her lungs seemed to freeze as she took her first breath outside. She pulled her scarf up over her mouth and coughed experimentally, just to convince herself that at least the coughing mechanism was still working. Climbing up the hill, she began to labour, but turning back did not occur to her. Finally she reached the church. She grabbed the railing and pulled herself slowly up the ten steps to the door.

As she opened the outer door, she could hear them singing the first hymn: "Once in Royal David's City." This was good; the singing would cover her entry. She waited in the vestibule until the lights were dimmed for the stage performances. Quietly, she pushed open the inner swinging door. Eleanor, the very youngest, was first on the program. Emma entered the large, warm space. She saw a flicker of white and blue climbing up the steps to the stage that had been erected in the chancel. The organ began to play. Clearly, perfectly, Eleanor's voice rang out. "What can I give him?" sang the little girl in the silk dress, who nevertheless lived beside a pile of lumber and within range of a fan that spewed out poison. Softly, Emma began to cry.

The burst of applause astonished her, but at that moment she began to cough, great gasping coughs that shook her frame. She must get out before the applause died down and anyone heard. Bent double, she stumbled for the door and escaped. A few heads turned, but they were all strange people at the back who only ever appeared on occasions like this. She should be safe.

Sitting down on the icy steps, she took a breath of the mysterious thing in the puffer that was supposed to make everything fine. Except this time it didn't. Frightened, she could think of nothing other than to get home as quickly as possible. Coughing and gasping, she went down the diagonal of the Anglican Church parade, which was completely empty on this Christmas night, skirted one block of the main street with its dark windows, down past the post office, and finally back to the lower street and in her front door. There she collapsed until a great commotion surrounded her and someone (Nathan?) was lifting her up and carrying her upstairs to bed. He was both upset and (could it be?) angry. "Why did you try such a stupid trick? You knew what the doctor said!"

In the distance she could hear Eleanor crying and Virtue hushing her. "I wanted to hear Eleanor sing," Emma whispered.

"And did you?"

"Yes, I did!" she said with as much defiance as she could muster.

"Well, I hope you're happy! I'll phone the doctor."

Emma knew she would not venture outdoors again until the daffodils showed their heads in early April.

❧

On Sunday afternoons in January, Eleanor would sit in the front of Obadiah's maroon and cream Oldsmobile, squeezed between her aunt and uncle as they floated through the frigid winter landscape in a cocoon of warm luxury, listening to the radio. Her mother was ill, but here were Aunt Virtue and Uncle Obadiah, so very nice, so willing to do whatever she wanted.

"Where shall we drive today, Eleanor?" Obadiah would ask.

Eleanor would look at the map, with its little squiggles of lines and blue spots, and say "there," and if it was not too far away, Obadiah would set off in that direction with the car purring in lulling tones, "Everything's fine/Almost divine./You're safe as a bug/Wrapped in a rug." As long as the car whispered its song, Eleanor was content. But when it would stop again before the house jammed against the lumber piles, with its concrete step abutting the sidewalk, something would tighten in her stomach. Mommy would be cross now for the rest of the day; she wouldn't speak to Aunt Virtue, or if she did, it would be in short little bursts that showed the words were difficult for her to say, and it was only because she had to that she spoke at all. Even to her, Eleanor, she would be remote. "So did you have a nice time with Aunt Virtue," she would ask. And Eleanor would not know whether to say "yes" or "no."

CHAPTER 4
1947

Eleanor counted eight "bongs" of the living room clock. She was supposed to be asleep, but she wasn't. The late evening June light filtered through the blinds and left a thin sliver on her pillow. Mommy and Daddy were talking downstairs, talking quite loudly, but she still couldn't quite make out the words. She crept out of bed and went to the head of the stairwell.

"She's not ready to go to school in just two months. She's still a baby." Emma put her case forcefully. "And she doesn't need to go. The law says that you don't have to start school until you're six. She'll be just five in August."

"Well, maybe you're right. I don't know. I walked two miles to school when I was five and a half."

"Eleanor should have a better and easier life than we had. I've already taught her a lot at home. She can read some children's books, and she can do simple addition with numbers up to twenty. Why does she need to go to school?"

Eleanor listened, all attention. They were talking about her. They weren't going to let her go to school in the fall. It wasn't fair! Sometimes she had been allowed to go to Aunt Virtue's school, just for a half day or so, for fun, when Mommy wasn't feeling well and couldn't look after her, and it was all so exciting. There was lots of important stuff written on the blackboard, pictures pasted on the windows, and Aunt Virtue up at the front, telling everyone what to do. Why should she be shut out of this world?

Now there was a sound of footsteps in the hallway. Aunt Virtue was walking across to talk to Mommy and Daddy. She would tell them to let her go to school; she would say, in her official-sounding voice that "it would be in the child's best interest." She leaned forward, straining to hear every syllable. But what was Virtue saying?

"You know, I think you're right. Eleanor's so high-strung she just wouldn't cope with being with all those noisy children."

"Thank you, Virtue," Mommy said in her 'what-right-have-you-to-say-anything' voice. "It's good to know you agree with us." Mommy wasn't going to say anything more, and after a bit Eleanor heard Virtue retreat to her kitchen.

Eleanor knew she had to take matters into her own hands. She ran down the stairs. "But I want to go to school. Katie and Mary and all the kids in my Sunday school class are going to school. Their mommies have bought them bookbags and pencil cases and all kinds of things. Why can't I go?"

"Why aren't you asleep, Eleanor? Go right back to bed!"

Mommy could be very cross sometimes. Eleanor began to cry. "No, I can't go up alone."

"Well, you seem to have come down alone."

In the end it was Daddy who took her up, cuddled her, told her everything would be okay, and tucked the covers in around her. She snuggled down and was asleep before he left the room.

*

"I just don't know what's best for her." Nathan thought to himself. "I guess Virtue and Emma must be right. They're both teachers, so they ought to know."

Nathan found himself in a curious situation. Deep down, he believed his little daughter ought to be starting school with all the other children her age. Why be different? She needed some other children to play with. It was bad enough there were no brothers or sisters; with Emma forty and not very well, there were unlikely ever to be any. And Virtue and Obadiah looked like they'd never be having one of their own. But to be friendless as well…commonsense told him that this was no good.

"If Eleanor really isn't going to school in the fall…" he began tentatively one evening.

"Well, you know what I think." Emma was sewing a coat for Eleanor—a navy blue light wool material that she could wear with a white and red cotton dress, also sewn by Emma, for cooler days in the summer.

"Yes, I know, and I expect you're right, but don't you think…"

"Think what?" Since her illness Emma could be so sharp. Nathan flinched, but he went on.

"Think that maybe she should have some friends to play with."

"And who do you suggest? The little monsters that live up on the corner above the liquor store? I didn't tell you this, but the other day, when I was hanging out the wash, the middle girl, Opal I think she's called, was on the other side of the stacked wood by the fence and looking through the spaces in the wood pile and calling out in a tiny whiny voice, 'Mrs. Wentzell, Mrs. Wentzell.' When I looked over, she would duck down, then pop up and do it again. Mocking me, she was."

"I don't know what you can do about that. But the kid's only little, and I guess she just don't know any better," Nathan replied. He didn't feel these slights—"wrongs" Emma called them—the same way she did. He was well-liked by his customers in the barbershop; he didn't go around comparing himself with others.

Emma persisted. "She's ten. Old enough she ought to know better. And as for what we can do, you know what. Get ourselves out of here. Get us a house of our own in a decent part of town. Then there will be nice children for Eleanor to play with. That's all I want. Even my mother and your mother, if it comes to that, had houses of their own."

It all came back to this. A house of her own. "You know I'm doing my best. Business is pretty good, and we put haircuts up ten cents this year, but even so..." his voice trailed off.

"Even so, I'll be dead before it happens."

"Now Emma, don't be like that. I'm trying my best. And also, we've got Eleanor. It could be a lot worse. Look at Obadiah and Virtue."

"Virtue has a job, a career, even." Nathan was shocked. Did Emma mean this? Would she really trade Eleanor for a job teaching? He tried to get into Emma's head, but it was like staring into a murky lake where insubstantial shadows moved. You were trying to catch something, but the shape of that thing you were trying to catch kept changing. Sometimes it was all about Eleanor, then it was suddenly about a house, and then, just when you thought you were on the verge of seeing it all clearly, the waters were roiled again and it was about having a career. He sighed.

"And the way things are going, it looks as if she may have Eleanor as well," Emma said.

"Now you know that's not true."

"How do I know? Eleanor's over there as soon as Virtue comes home from school. She seems to eat half her meals over there as well—or at least her second meals. She's getting fat!"

"She looks all right to me. And, when all's said and done, of course she's ours."

"Ouch."

"What?"

"I just pricked my finger. Now I've got blood on the coat lining."

"Never mind. I'm sure the coat will be beautiful." Nathan rose to kiss her, but she brushed him away.

Joan came into the kitchen. Now, if there was one thing that Nathan would have liked to change about his life, it was Joan—not her person so much as her place of residence. If Emma found it intolerable to live with Virtue and Obadiah, Nathan found it as near to intolerable as he ever found anything to have Joan around all the time. She wasn't particularly unpleasant, though her eating habits were what he called "sneaky," which meant she was very difficult and particular about what she ate. But Joan was just there, all the time, breakfast, dinner and supper. Even in the night he felt her presence on the other side of the bedroom wall, breathing, listening, thinking—thinking what?

Joan sat herself down in the chair next to Emma, which meant she would stay there talking idly until he went to bed. He might as well do that right now.

❧

It was Wednesday, Daddy's afternoon off and they were going to pick berries, blackberries Eleanor knew they were called, that ripened in the late summer. They took some large empty red pails with "Dominion Shortening" written on the side, piled into the little green Austin that had replaced the old Chev, and drove outside town to a spot that Mommy said always had good blackberries. It was going to be a delightful expedition, Mommy explained, just like she used to go on when she was a girl. Already Eleanor knew that good things happened to you when you were a girl and lived with your Mommy and Daddy and lots of brothers and sisters in a house in the country by a lake. She sometimes thought that maybe her childhood was less than ideal because there was no lake, and no brothers or sisters either. But now they were going on a fun trip, even if it was just for the afternoon.

When they got to the berry place, Mommy gave her a special little pail, and she scrambled up the bank beside the road. There were the bushes, their slim branches bent down with large blackberries. Eleanor reached out to pick. But what her small hand encountered was not a berry but something else that scratched and made the back of her hand bleed. She began to whimper.

"Oh dear, I told you to be careful of the thorns. Come here, and I'll kiss it away." Mommy showed her how to reach in for the berries without getting hurt, and she began to fill her small pail, but already there was a shadow over the pure bliss that was promised. Had the thorns never hurt Mommy as a girl?

After a while she lost interest in the berries, and began to play with the stones on the bank. She would build something; she was unsure what, but she needed a good number of small rocks for a foundation. Mommy and Daddy were busy picking on the edge of the woods and not paying attention to her. She began to tug on one particularly large and important stone, when suddenly it gave way, toppling her backwards on the ground. There, under the stone, were lots and lots of ants, crawling everywhere in frantic haste. Some were even on her hands.

She screamed, and Emma and Nathan came running. Emma scooped her up, brushed her off, and soothed her. Holding Eleanor on her lap, Emma began to sing a quiet song to comfort her.

> *Down in the valley*
> *The valley so low*
> *Hear the wind blow, love,*
> *Hear the wind blow.*

The song was quiet and sad; it didn't make Eleanor any happier.

In the distance, came the sound of a train. The blowing wind in the song became the blowing train. It was not traveling very fast when it came into view on a track just across the road, and the afternoon light was already fading. Eleanor could see people sitting in the lighted carriages, going somewhere, where it soon would be night. The train's whistle was the saddest sound she had ever heard, and as it went by it got softer and lower, disappearing into some strange and empty place that was both out there and inside her. She began to cry in earnest now.

"Stop singing! Stop singing." Emma stopped and held her close while the train and its wailing song gradually disappeared into the distance, and Eleanor said, "I want to go home."

Emma had to admit Eleanor was a strange child. She found the oddest things sad—a lot of songs, stories about circuses. One evening when Emma had left her with Virtue and gone to a Ladies Aid meeting, she returned to find Eleanor in hysterics and Virtue at the end of her wits— all because Virtue read her a story about a poor little boy who ran away and joined the circus. He seemed perfectly happy at the circus, but that wasn't how Eleanor saw it. Where were his Mommy and Daddy she wanted to know? Why couldn't he sleep in his own bed anymore? And on and on. Perhaps Nathan did have a point. Perhaps Eleanor was too solitary. She talked wonderfully well with adults, but when she came into contact with other children she didn't seem to know what to do. Her inclination was simply to boss them around. This couldn't be entirely good. Maybe she should make some contact even with the unsatisfactory children on the corner. Opal had a younger sister, Heather, who was about Eleanor's age.

The next time Emma saw Heather outside playing, she went with Eleanor to greet her. "Would you like to come and play in our garden?" she said. There was no garden attached to the Murdochs' apartment, and Heather seemed delighted to have somewhere proper to play. Emma went into the garden with the girls and showed them how to make hats from leaves of the mock orange bush, and how to build a little house for Eleanor's tiny plastic dolls out of twigs and moss. Also,

Eleanor had a swing; she even had a wooden seesaw Nathan had made for her, so there was no shortage of things to occupy them. At four o'clock they came in for milk and cookies. Emma congratulated herself that everything was going well. Why had she not thought of this before?

After the cookies, Heather said, "Why don't you come up to my house and see my new baby?" Now this was a treat that Emma could not compete with. Eleanor was eager; how could Emma refuse?

Emma watched the two little girls walk up the street towards the Murdochs' apartment. What would Eleanor find there? Would it be messy, dirty? Would people be swearing and using bad language? Emma had a horror of poverty and everything she imagined went with it. Of course, most people would have seen her life in Waldenstein as poverty. They had no running water, just a pump in the kitchen; they had an outdoor toilet. But somehow that was not "poor." "Poor" was not cleaning your house, drinking too much liquor, not having your hair combed and tidy, not wearing fresh clothes every second day. And here in Lunenburg, where she knew two families living in one house must be considered "poor" by many people in the town, she was especially fearful of slipping over the edge, down that steep incline that led to something she visualized like a series of etchings in an old book she found at a used book sale. *The Rake's Progress*, the book was called.

To ward off this dreadful fate, she cleaned obsessively, ironed everything in sight including her underpants, took the deadheads off the garden plants the moment the flowers died. If she lowered her guard for a second, who knew what might happen. She had invited Heather into her home and now, instead of being rewarded for her Christian charity, her own beloved daughter was being swallowed up in a den of vice. But what else could she have done?

❦

Eleanor followed Heather up the sidewalk with both excitement and trepidation. When they reached the house, she looked fearfully at the door and window of the liquor store that took up most of the front. "Do we have to go through there?"

"No, don't be stupid. We use this side door and go up the stairs."

The door was ajar, and a narrow hallway leading to a flight of rough wooden stairs opened up before them. There were bottles standing along one side of the hallway and on some of the steps. "What are those for?"

"Oh, those are just Dad's empties—or other people's. He collects them to sell them back and make money."

"Oh."

They went up the stairs and through a door that led into a room with a table, sink, and stove. The wallpaper, pale grey with yellow and blue flowers, might have been pretty once, but was now grimy and loosening so that it hung down around the chimney. It smelled funny. Eleanor couldn't place the smell, but it seemed to be a vaguely foody smell mixed with something else. A large woman was sitting in a rocking chair cradling something.

"Mom, this is Eleanor," said Heather.

"Pleased to meet you. I can't get up because if I do he'll wake and cry again. He's not been well this two weeks."

Eleanor saw that the tiny bundle she was holding was a baby, wrapped so securely in a blanket as to be almost invisible in her arms. Heather led her towards the bundle. "This is John. Come and see. He's so sweet."

The baby was very white and tiny, and scarcely moved at all when she touched his cheek. It was so smooth and soft; she wanted to keep stroking it, but Heather's mother said, "Best not to wake him." Just then the baby made a little mew and stretched out a minute arm that trembled as he tried to move it. He seemed very breakable.

"Is this what all babies are like?" asked Eleanor in wonderment. Here was a toy her parents had not provided. It now seemed a significant omission.

"Well, pretty much, though he's the littlest I've ever had. Hope he makes it," Heather's mother said.

Eleanor moved slightly away and whispered to Heather, "What does she mean she hopes he makes it?" Before Heather could reply a door at the far end of the room was flung open and a chunky little boy burst in. "Mom, I need you to wipe me."

"Hush, get back there Darrel. Look, here's a little girl don't want to see you like that!"

Indeed, Eleanor was staring in wonder at the naked boy, a sight from which she had been carefully shielded. She particularly wondered about the funny little tube-like thing that was hanging down between his legs.

"What's that?"

"Oh that's his thing, his willie." Heather looked in surprise at Eleanor.

"What's it for?"

"Peeing, of course. Don't you know anything?"

"Oh." Up to this point, she and her mother had been the ones teaching Heather things—how to make leaf hats, how to swing, how to ride on the seesaw, how to read. But Eleanor saw that there were other kinds of knowledge. She didn't know everything after all.

When she went home, her mother wanted to know all about it. For the first time, Eleanor didn't tell her everything.

A week passed, and Heather was not to be seen. Even Opal was no longer cat-calling through the woodpile. Then it was late August, and they were going for a week's holiday by the seaside. The tiny Austin was stuffed with suitcases, and off they went to a white sand beach forty miles away. Of course they took Joan, which meant they had to rent a cabin with an extra bedroom.

Joan did her best to play games on the rainy days, and tried to frolic on the beach when it was fine. "Frolic" was a new word Eleanor had just learned. She wasn't sure it suited Joan. Eleanor had a big inflatable green whale called "Bulgy," on which she would ride the waves until, on the last day, an especially big one tipped her over. Daddy heard her screams and came and pulled her out.

When they returned, the lower street seemed hotter and more crowded with shops and people than ever. But there was one change; the door of Heather's house had a wreath on it, and when Eleanor looked up she could see the blinds on the second floor were pulled down. What had happened?

Their little baby must have died, Mommy said.

Died. Animals died, cats and sometimes dogs, Eleanor knew, and old people died. But could babies die as well? God had taken him, Mommy said. Why would God want a poor little baby? She remembered touching him, his little cheek soft and smooth and cool. His arm had shivered when he tried to move it. She wanted to cry, but didn't know whether she should if God had done it all. Then she wondered if the baby had a willie, like his older brother, and what use your willie was when you died.

❧

"This is Douglas." Joan's voice burst in upon Emma's reading one September evening. She looked up to see Joan standing, almost defiant, at the top of the five stairs that led up from the front door to the inner hallway. Beside her was a remarkably good-looking young man. He had blue eyes, regular features, and large hands that looked as if they were used to working. But, Emma observed, his most extraordinary feature was his hair, which stood straight up like a thick brown forest, now backlit by the setting sun. Only a mighty hurricane could flatten that copse of brush. She reached to grasp his outstretched hand.

"This is my sister, Emma," Joan informed him.

"Pleased to meet you," he said, and shook Emma by the hand. "I think I knew your father. My family lived in the next-door village to Waldenstein when I was little, and I used to go and watch the men driving the logs down the river sometimes. I thought it would be an exciting thing to do, but then we moved down here, just outside town. Now I'm starting up a business making boxes—wooden boxes for packing salt cod."

A long speech, Emma thought, and it established his credentials well. He was one of them, a country boy. She watched Joan squirm beside him, partly with pride, partly with embarrassment. Just as Emma was saying, "Do come in and sit down," Virtue stuck her head out of her kitchen door to see what was going on.

"This is my other sister, Virtue," said Joan.

"Pleased to meet you." Again, the automatic extension of the large hand, the broad and open smile.

Joan flushed and fidgeted, but Douglas seemed perfectly at ease. Emma guided them both into her living room, and the conversation continued.

"Joan tells me she comes from a large family," Douglas said. "I've got ten brothers and sisters myself, though only a few still live around here."

Douglas and Joan sat down, but much to Emma's annoyance Virtue still stood at the living room door, rubbing her back like a cat against the dark wooden frame. "Do come in and sit down, Virtue. We want to get to know Douglas, don't we?" Virtue came in at Emma's invitation, and perched on the arm of a chair.

Eleanor charged into the room, dangling a grey stuffed rabbit. "Oh, you must be the daughter of the family," Douglas greeted her. "I've heard so much about you. Come on over," he invited. "Sit up here," and he patted his knee. "What songs do you like?"

Eleanor immediately began to recite her repertoire. "Well, there's 'In the Bleak Midwinter.' I sang that at Christmas. But it's not Christmas now. I like some hymns."

"'Jesus loves me?'" Douglas suggested.

"No, not much. I prefer 'A Mighty Fortress.' But," and here she brightened, "I also like a song, 'Robin, robin on my lawn.' And the robins haven't gone south yet, so you could still sing that."

"Eleanor, you should be going to bed soon," said Emma.

"Don't have to go to bed yet. I'm not going to school. Don't have to get up in the morning."

Emma took in Joan's quick look at Douglas, a look that seemed to say, "You see, I told you she was a spoiled brat."

"Surely one song won't hurt," Douglas said.

Reluctantly, Emma agreed. "One song and then bed."

"I'm afraid I don't know 'Robin, robin on my lawn.' But I could sing you one about a frog. Would you like that?"

Eleanor nodded vigorously, and so he began:

> *A frog he would a-wooing go,*
> *A-ha, a-ha.*
> *A frog he would a-wooing go*
> *Whether his mother would let him or no*
> *A-ha, a-ha, a-ha, a-ha.*

On it went, through all the stages of courting and the asking of Uncle Rat's permission, until the happy frog went away with Miss Mouse to France. He sang with a true clear voice, and a total lack of self-consciousness, jogging Eleanor gently on his knee in time to the music. Emma could see that Eleanor was completely enchanted. Did Eleanor think she was Miss Mouse? Probably. And if so, who would Uncle Rat be? Nathan? Uncle Obadiah?

Emma knew that none of this pleased Joan. She tapped her foot impatiently, looking balefully at Miss Mouse, Eleanor sitting on Douglas' lap. "We're going out for a drive in Douglas' new car," she cut in. "We really just stopped in so that you could meet Douglas."

Eleanor was ejected from her seat, and Joan firmly took Douglas' arm as they moved towards the hall. "I'll be back before you lock up for the night," were her parting words.

"Well, I never," Nathan said later that night. "Never thought she'd get a boyfriend, as scrawny and shut-up as she is."

Emma said nothing. Deep down she agreed with Nathan, but to be complicit in this description of her sister seemed a step too far.

⁂

One afternoon in late October, Eleanor was playing by herself in the garden. Mommy was busy, and anyway she had a cold, and it wasn't good for her to come outdoors when she had a cold. So Eleanor was wandering around, going on the swing for a bit, piling up some of the fallen leaves and pretending the pile was a mouse house, when a little boy wandered into the yard.

"Hi. Who are you?" Eleanor always asked the question direct.

"I'm Oscar. We've just moved in one street up."

"Oh." And then remembering her manners, "I'm Eleanor. This is my garden, but you can play with me if you want to."

"I didn't see you in school this morning."

"No. I don't go to school." She wasn't sure whether this was a mark of distinction or of failure.

"That's funny. Don't you have to go?"

"No. My Mommy and Daddy say you don't have to go until you're six. I'm only five."

"But don't you want to go?"

"I guess not." Then, not liking the turn the conversation had taken, she asked, "What shall we play?"

"I don't care. But, look here...have you examined your lawn for holes?"

"Holes? What kind of holes?"

"Holes that the chickens come up through."

"I don't know what you mean."

"See. There's one!" Oscar pointed to a tiny hole with some worm castings beside it.

"They're nothing. I mean, they're just everywhere."

"Ah," said Oscar knowingly. "That's just it. They're everywhere. You've got to be careful of them, because there's lots of chickens down in the earth and when there's holes like that, they come up."

Eleanor thought having some chickens in the yard might be fun, but Oscar disabused her.

"No, they're not fun, these chickens, because there's so many of them. Once they start, they just keep comin' and comin'. There's no stoppin' them. After a while there'll be no place for you at all—or any of your family. Then they'll cover the whole world!"

"But the holes are so little. Chickens, even babies, are bigger than that." Eleanor was determined to stick to reason.

"The chickens are really tiny at first, but then when they get out in the air they just go 'poof' and blow up real big, sort of like a balloon."

Eleanor considered. Not for a moment did it occur to her that what Oscar was saying might not be true. No one had ever lied to her in her life. To lie, or to make up stories, was a sin, and would land you in hell. She stared at Oscar. "Really?"

"Cross my heart and hope to die."

"Well then...I guess maybe we better start covering them up." She and Oscar began scurrying around the garden, stamping on all the bare spots with holes, examining the ground between the blades of grass to find and cover holes that were hiding in the lawn.

Emma looked out the window. "What on earth are you doing?"

"We're filling up all the holes so the chickens can't come out." Eleanor stated this matter-of-factly. Presumably her mother would have known about the chickens, but just hadn't taken it seriously enough.

"What?"

"The chickens that come out of the ground and might fill up the whole world so that we couldn't breathe."

"Who told you this?"

"Oscar here." Oscar nodded solemnly.

"Eleanor, I think you should come in. And Oscar, it was nice of you to come and play with Eleanor, but you'd better go home now. I'm sure your mother will be wanting to know where you are."

"No she won't. She works in the grocery store and won't be home until six."

"Well, I think you'd better go home and wait for her anyway." Oscar disappeared up the back alleyway.

"That's a lot of silliness," Mommy said when Eleanor was inside. "Where did that boy come from?"

"He just came. He said he goes to school."

"Well, he hasn't learned much there yet," Emma said. "Where did he get such a foolish idea?"

Eleanor was not convinced. She was beginning to see that the world was a scary place—a place where mommies got ill, where some people had strange appendages to their bodies, where little babies died, and where, lurking under the ground, there was some secret disaster waiting to overwhelm everyone.

CHAPTER 5
1948

One evening in April, when the snow had finally gone and the first warm rain was making the lawn green again, Virtue reluctantly made her way to Emma's kitchen.

"Harry's coming to see us," she said. "Tomorrow night if it's convenient. Well, I guess from what we know of him, he'll be here whether it is or not."

It was after supper, but Emma was still busy ironing away with determination. She looked up. "I guess that must mean he's selling more land. How do you know he's coming?"

"Phoned Obadiah in the barber shop this afternoon. Didn't want to speak to either of us, of course."

Virtue knew that their only brother was the one subject on which her sister could be certain to agree with her. The enemy without that united the enemies within. This would make the fourth lot he'd sold since Papa died. He hadn't even told them about the mill until after it was taken apart and sold down the river to some guy from Bridgewater.

After their parents died without a will, he insisted that the inheritance was his, must be his, because he was male, and therefore the only one of them capable of carrying on the lumbering and sawmill business. He sat glowering in the corner of the old sitting room, throwing down the gauntlet to the six sisters: "All or nothing, all or nothing!" he roared. So all the sisters, signed off and gave him the "all" he demanded.

In a matter of years, though, everything had changed completely. Somehow, and Virtue didn't understand this, after he was in charge, it became impossible to make a profit from the mill, impossible to find good men to work, just impossible. In order to support himself and his wife, he started to sell the trees, the beautiful trees their father had loved and tended and treated as partners in his business, bit by bit. A hundred acres here, fifty there. The home itself was falling down. Harry and his wife didn't want to live all the way back there in the woods "cut off from civilization." Flora wouldn't live there, with or without Harry. Weeds now surrounded the house their father built, the pasture grew bushes, and trees sprang up obscuring the view of the lake. What could they do?

Now Virtue was sure Harry was coming to torture her and Emma with the accounts, because they were legally responsible for seeing that poor Flora got her share, one seventh, of the total price.

"We've got to make him do something about Flora," Emma said.

"What? And how?" Virtue felt a mild annoyance. Emma was always making these grand pronouncements, "We've got to do this...or that...," but the reality was, there was little they could do. Harry was supposed to provide for Flora "in the manner to which she was accustomed." He argued that the house of the old lady where Flora now worked as a general maid was better than the one she grew up in; there was running water and an indoor bathroom for a start. Besides, Flora was happier living with other people than on her own.

Virtue sighed. How could you put into the legalities such subtlety as the difference between living freely in a house and existing as a servant? Did Flora feel the difference? Who could know, really? Flora had never recovered either physically or mentally from whatever happened that winter night thirty-five years ago. Her life had been broken and, yes, to some extent the family had been broken as well. Never again had they felt that life was ordered for their greater good.

Virtue moved into the kitchen and sat down on a chair by the table. "Well, I don't know how, but we've got to try. It's our duty. That's what we said when we all signed off our claim to the house and land," Emma said.

"Sure, and we could have done our bit by taking her in, but we didn't did we? And we're not going to now."

And so it went on, the tidy ironing stacking up on the table and the messy lives desiccating all around them.

❧

The next evening, promptly at seven, Emma heard Harry's knock at the back door.

"Thought I'd better not come to the front, not being the kind of highfaluting company you're used to." Harry's laugh rang hollowly down the hallway; his sharp blue eyes pierced the dim surroundings.

He took one step off the mat onto the wood hall floor, then backtracked to the mat. "Boots. Almost forgot. City folk don't wear boots in the house." With elaborate care he removed them and set them neatly by the door. Emma was tired of the same false ceremony that was the preamble to every visit, but still gave the usual response that, of course, it was fine for him to come in just as he was.

Once all three were seated at Virtue's kitchen table and the preliminary enquiries about health and families were out of the way, he produced a sheaf of papers. "Just need you girls to sign a few things, as usual."

"So what are you selling this time, Harry?" Emma asked. He was silent. Emma and Virtue waited. Then, seeing there would be no reply, Virtue took the papers from his hand and began to read. "You're selling the home place! The house, the fifty acres around it, everything!"

Emma cried out, "You can't do that!" But Emma knew he could, and lapsed into silence. What was there to stop him? Then she added, in a more subdued tone, "Why?"

"Need the money," said Harry laconically. "You girls down here with your rich husbands, you've forgotten how poor country folk live."

"That's priceless. You, who got everything..."

"Now don't upset yourself, Emma, you know it's not good for you."

Of course he was right. But the condescension of it! Emma felt as if she were being bereaved again. To be sure, she and Nathan hardly ever drove up to Waldenstein anymore—at least not since Nathan's parents died three winters ago. Not even a small part of it belonged to her anymore, but she could still slip back across the fields if she wanted, stand on the old porch, look down at the lake.

One afternoon last summer she went there with Nathan and Eleanor. It was a brilliantly sunny day; the lake shone blue and placid like an all-forgiving eye. She felt at peace with the past. Eleanor, at her suggestion, planted a few hollyhock seeds in the ground where the old garden had been, in front of the house. "Will they grow?" Eleanor wanted to know.

"I expect some of them will," Emma replied.

Now Harry was talking again, breaking into her reverie. "Old Silas Herman wants the boards from the house to build a new barn he's planning, so it's a good chance for me to get value not just from the land, but from the house also."

"The house is going to be torn down?" Virtue burst out.

"Well, let's just say it's going to be taken away. You know I'd never be able to sell it to anyone to live in—way back there."

"We lived way back there." Emma felt she was about to cry. In front of Harry, that would be just too awful.

"Sure we did, but no one would now. Times have changed. And really, that's why I need to sell. Times have changed. Here I am, still trying to farm with an old horse. It just don't make sense."

Virtue cut in. "I didn't think you were doing much farming anymore."

"Well, not a lot, but some. I need something to haul the plow and the manure and stuff like that. Old Bess, the horse I bought off Jack Ramey, ain't too spry anymore. But she's spry enough to knock down the barn door if I don't keep her exercised enough. So I'm thinking of getting a tractor, and selling the house and the land will give me just enough and a little left over." Harry tipped his chair back in satisfaction and folded his hands across his chest like a judge saying, "case proved."

"Hang on a minute," Emma retorted. "Have I got this right? You don't have enough work to keep a horse exercised so you're buying a tractor to take on the work. If you don't have enough work for a horse, how will you have enough work for a tractor? I thought it was a more efficient machine, or have I missed something?"

"The point is, it won't have to be fed or exercised when I'm not using it. So, yes, it's more efficient."

"You're trading in our home for a pile of rusting metal, that's what you're doing!" Emma wanted to scream. She was beginning to breathe heavily, and she wondered where she had left her puffer.

"It's not your home anymore, remember? It's nobody's home. It's just boards and nails set on some rocks in the middle of nowhere. And if it belongs to anyone, that person is me, remember? All you girls have to do, and the only reason I'm telling you about it is because you have to sign off Flora's share. Now I've got all the papers here, so if you'd just sign them."

Emma knew they were beaten. The last of the spring evening light faded, and the three siblings sat in the shadows of one another cast by the central kitchen light. She took a deep breath, gave a disconcerting wheeze, and said, "We can't sign anything until we've had a talk about Flora. The agreement said that Flora must be kept in a manner to which she was accustomed. That wasn't supposed to mean working out for someone else."

"I tell you, she's fine. Mrs. Marriott values her a lot, treats her really well. She has her own room, and a lot more conveniences than I have in my own house." Emma knew Harry prided himself on still having an outdoor toilet and a pump in a corner of the kitchen.

"But she's a servant."

"No she's not, well, not really. She helps Mrs. Marriott out. At eighty-nine, she needs some help."

"And who looks after Flora to see that she has clothes and everything she needs?"

"My wife. She's as good with Flora as if she was her own sister. Took her to get a new wig in Bridgewater only a month ago. And that cost a pretty penny, I can tell you."

"Ah yes, I can see," replied Virtue. "But you made her pay for it out of her own savings. Here it is, in the accounts, in your own handwriting."

"Well, she has the money, why not? The wig was for her, not me."

"You know that wasn't the agreement," Virtue said. "You were supposed to provide all the necessities of life for her—her share of anything you sold was to be for her personal use, for luxuries."

"Luxuries. Well, yes, I can see that would be important to you, living here in town with washing machines, and refrigerators, and oil stoves. That would occur to you, I suppose. And if you're so concerned about her, why don't you let her live with you? There's a spare bedroom upstairs I believe."

This, Emma knew, was what it always came down to. If you want to complain, why don't you look after her yourselves? If you can't sleep at night for thinking about her deprived life, why don't you do something about it?

It was completely dark now. Emma could see their reflection in the window, two sisters and a brother repelled by one another like the opposite poles of the little magnetic dogs Eleanor played with.

In the end, Emma and Virtue signed the release. What choice did they have? There was no law saying once he had possession of all the property he had to take his sisters' sentimental views into account.

He left through the back door as he had come, putting on the muddy boots without a word. Emma and Virtue each went to get a cloth to wipe up the puddle where the boots had stood. Meeting one another by the door, cloths in hand, Emma suddenly burst out laughing and Virtue joined her. For a moment it was like the old days.

❧

Eleanor made her way out of the back garden, up the alleyway, and turned left on the next street to reach Mrs. Veinot's door. She walked purposefully and steadily, not looking back at her mother, whom she knew would be watching until she turned the corner. As she reached up to turn the door bell—it made such an interesting "brrring"—she could see Mrs. Veinot, having been forewarned by a telephone call, coming down the stairs to welcome her.

"Do come in Eleanor. My, what a big girl you're getting to be. And your Mommy says you're going to school in the fall."

"Yes, that's going to be a lot of fun, I think." She was allowed to visit Mrs. Veinot, a widow whose own children had long left home, quite often, provided it was "convenient," and usually it was. The house was markedly different from her own. First of all, it was spread out entirely on one floor; the downstairs flat was rented by another family. The large kitchen looked down on the back garden of her house. At the front of the house was a great big living room, shadowed by large ferns in pots, and with a soft squishy carpet on the floor and a huge piano against one wall.

Secondly, it smelled different. It smelled of all the exciting things Mrs. Veinot got down from the attic for her to play with. There were ancient dolls, and a wicker buggy to push them in. There was an old tin car that wound up and ran across the carpet. There was even a little house that opened up on both the front and back to disclose a tiny family with miniature furniture and beds. Eleanor loved the house because she could make up endless stories about the people living in it. There were only five of them, a mommy and daddy, a little boy and a girl, and a baby who was, as far as she could tell, sexless. It didn't have that thing hanging down in front—she had taken its clothes off once to check—so she guessed it was probably a girl.

She pretended they all went off to the beach every summer; and had vacations even longer than the one she had with Joan; she gave them a wonderful Christmas with all kinds of exotic food and a big Christmas tree that no one got cross decorating. The boy and girl went off to school and came back with the highest grades in their classes, and the mommy was really pleased. Whatever they did, they were always happy, because they lived in a big house all by themselves. That was what her life would be like when Daddy managed to save enough money to buy them a new house. Then everything would be perfect. Mommy wouldn't even have the thing called asthma any more, which meant she could go out and play with her all winter as well as summer. She would probably have a sister as well. She prayed for one every night, and God surely couldn't hold out much longer. Though, in the midst of all this, she did feel that she might miss Aunt Virtue quite a lot. Her gingerbread with whipped cream was amazing.

This particular afternoon, just as she was settling in to send her family off on a shopping trip to buy groceries for the fancy dinner they would have in the dining room, the doorbell rang. Up the stairs came another woman, younger than Mrs. Veinot, but similar to her in appearance—the same slightly ruddy complexion, the same small brown eyes, the same full lips and wide smile. "This is Eleanor, Emma's little girl from the house on the street below."

"Hello, Eleanor. I'm Miss Bailly, Esther's sister."

"Miss Bailly teaches Grade Primary," put in Mrs. Veinot. "I guess she'll be your teacher when you go to school in the autumn."

Eleanor stared attentively at Miss Bailly. This was an important person. Maybe she should concentrate on her rather than on buying groceries for the dollhouse family. She stood up and thrust out her hand. "I'm pleased to meet you. I'm only going to school this fall because Mommy didn't want me to start last year."

"I see. And do you know why she didn't want you to go to school?"

"Not really. I think she thought I might get sick or something. And she said she could teach me at home. She's a school teacher too, you know."

"Hmm. So what kinds of things has she been teaching you?" Miss Bailly seemed genuinely curious.

"Oh, mostly just math and reading."

"And can you read?"

"Oh yes, I can read lots of children's stories. I can't read newspapers yet, but Mommy says I'm not old enough to know about the stuff they write in newspapers anyway."

"So would you like to read for me?"

"Sure. If you've got anything."

Miss Bailly reached into a large case and pulled out a paper book with a colourful rabbit eating a carrot on the front. "The Adventures of Beatrice Bunny," said Eleanor. She proceeded to read the story, together with her own critique of it. "Not much happens, really," she concluded at the end. "And it doesn't make sense for Beatrice to be more afraid of the farmer than of the fox. The farmer would just chase her away, but the fox would eat her."

"Why do you think she's supposed to be more afraid of the farmer than of the fox? Does it say so?"

"No, it doesn't exactly say so, but that's the way stories work. Each new thing that happens is supposed to be scarier than the one before, until you get to the end and then everything works out all right."

Miss Bailly sat back in her chair and stared at Eleanor. "I see. Did your mommy tell you that?"

"Not really. But you can just know from reading stories that's how they work. The tests for the animals just get harder and harder, and then in the end they're okay."

Eleanor never got a chance to show Miss Bailly what she knew about math.

Early the following evening Emma received a phone call. Phone calls were always somewhat problematic, since the sole phone was located not in the house, but in the back office of the barbershop. There was an extension bell in the house, however, and when Nathan or Obadiah answered the phone they signaled through to the house by a kind of Morse code on the water pipes to let Emma or Virtue know who was wanted. Emma was one long and one short tap, so when this signal came through she flung on a sweater and ran the short distance to the shop.

"This is Miss Bailly, the Grade Primary teacher, Mrs. Wentzell. I'm sorry to disturb you this evening, but I met Eleanor yesterday at my sister's house, and I thought perhaps it would be good to have a little chat."

Emma gripped the receiver tightly. What was coming now? What could Eleanor have done?

"She seems to be quite a precocious little girl," Miss Bailly continued. She paused, apparently waiting for some response.

"Well, I've taught her a few things—nothing very extraordinary," Emma said. "She wanted to learn to read, and did so very quickly."

"Exactly. But that may put her at a disadvantage when she comes to school in the autumn."

Emma tensed. "How so?"

"She will be in a class with children, some of whom won't even know their letters. What will she do? She'll be bored, because with forty children in the class, I can't teach her individually. I just don't have time."

Emma was afraid. What had she done that was so wrong? How could knowledge ever be wrong? "I'm sorry if I've made her school life more difficult."

"Not in the long run, not at all. What I propose is that she skip Primary and go straight into Grade One. That way, she'll be in her proper age group, and she certainly won't have any trouble with the work. She'll get on beautifully." The voice on the other end of the line was placatory, wanting to be oh so helpful, wanting to cause no offense.

"But...is this possible?"

"I certainly think so. I'll speak to the principal, and if you agree, Eleanor can come in to school for the final week of this year and take a few simple tests. I'm sure she'll pass with flying colours."

"I'll think about it. I'll have to speak to my husband," Emma replied.

"Of course. I understand. But I do think that my suggestion would work out better for Eleanor in the long run."

That night, when Nathan had finished work, Emma broached the subject, telling him all about the call.

Nathan hesitated. "I don't know," he said at last. This, while not particularly helpful, was in fact just what Emma wanted to hear. It was decided. Eleanor would move straight into Grade One. She was already beginning to fulfill her mother's expectations. Eleanor was exceptional; Emma had always known she would be.

※

Pushing the child, Virtue fumed. That's what she's always doing. It'll make her nervous, high-strung. Fundamentally, she didn't believe in teaching children too much too young—it scared them. Or at least it scared her.

She remembered what Emma had been like as a child. Always finding out things other people didn't know, like those marks on the rocks that she claimed showed God hadn't made the world in six days after all. It took him millions of years, and it wasn't finished yet. The scratches were made by sheets of ice that covered everything ages ago, Emma said. Fantastic! And now she had to teach some of this rubbish to her students. Of course she told them she didn't really believe a word of it, nor should they.

But Emma believed all the stuff she read—and she read a lot. Then she had that crush on the minister who taught her Latin, a totally useless language. Virtue knew she still held a torch for him, even though he was dead now. But in the end she married Nathan, who was no better than her Obadiah—not as good, because he was the younger son. So what if people thought Nathan was more handsome. Obadiah kept all the account books in the barbershop, and Nathan let him, because he was the older and that was right and proper. She was older than Emma as well, but Emma didn't seem to think that counted for much.

Now here she was pushing Eleanor into an educational flurry that could only turn out badly. She tried to tell Emma this, but she just said, "Eleanor is my child, and I'll make the decisions about her education." When she spoke like that, Virtue just went back to her own kitchen and shut the door. Still, and here the little worm that had been growing quietly within her for six years gave a small, exquisite shudder. She could continue to invite Eleanor into that kitchen for gingerbread and whipped cream.

The early September day sparkled. Even the lower street looked attractive, the sky a pristine blue, the shadows deep and crisp, the air, for once, fresh and free of fish or smoke. Eleanor walked out the front door with Emma because this was an important occasion, the first day of school. She wore a pleated navy blue skirt, a white pullover sweater that Emma had knitted for her, and a navy blue jacket that matched the skirt. Her light brown ringlets were combed out to perfection; her new brown leather bookbag swung on her back.

Up the block they walked, turning right at the corner, past the red brick post office with its imposing tower, and then left behind the main shopping street. Here on the right stood the courthouse, another large brick building, that, with the post office, seemed to intimidate the little wooden houses with their funny five-sided dormer windows. Next they came to the Anglican church parade, cutting diagonally through a swathe of grass and trees, and beyond it, at the highest point of the hill, stood the Lutheran church, their church, its immense steeple disappearing into the empty blue above it. All these large buildings suddenly seemed frightening to Eleanor. They were shut tight now in the early morning, biding their time.

Finally, round another corner, came the building that scared Eleanor most of all—the school, isolated in a square of grass and gravel, surrounded by the cemetery. To Eleanor, it didn't look like a school; it looked like a castle. Three stories high, with small turrets on each corner and a bell tower in the middle of the front, its red, black and white grandeur dominated the landscape. The bell was ringing as they approached: Dong, Dong. It didn't sound like the church bell, which rang with the grandeur of God; at the end of this ring the sound just sort of went down a bit in pitch, as if it wasn't quite certain of itself. Then a new "bong" would come again, and fade in the same way. She didn't know just what to make of it.

Up the exterior wooden steps they went to the huge front door. Emma pushed it open, and said, "Now you know where the Grade One room is. It's just to your left. I'll be here waiting for you at lunchtime."

Eleanor gripped her mother's hand more firmly. Lunchtime! That was three hours away. It was an eternity. But she had wanted to go to school, and now she was doing it, and she was trying hard not to cry. Her mother kissed her and, immediately it seemed, she was in a long dark cloakroom with lots of other children laughing with one another and hanging up their coats. Eleanor took off her jacket.

"This is your hook, Eleanor. You can hang your coat up here," her teacher, Mrs. Black greeted her.

Eleanor looked. There indeed was her name, but where was the clothes hanger? Her mother always said that if you just put your jacket over a hook the shoulders would get punched out and it would ruin the look.

"Where are the coat hangers Mrs. Black?" she asked tentatively.

"We don't have hangers here; just put it over the hook."

Then she was in the classroom, being told to sit at a shared desk with Katie. This was all right, because Katie had gone to Sunday School with her, and was one of the few children she actually knew. So school began.

"The first thing we do every morning, class, is to sing 'O Canada,'" Mrs. Black said. "Then we say the Lord's Prayer, and after that we sit down and sing a hymn before we begin our work for the day."

Eleanor stood up and sang, looking steadfastly at the flag that hung above the blackboard at the front of the class. The Lord's Prayer she also knew; the hymn she didn't. She stared at the words and single line of music in the hymnbook before her. It was something about

God coming and jewels. Before they sang, Mrs. Black explained that they, the children, were God's jewels, and that they must never do anything wrong to displease God and rub the shine off His jewels. Eleanor imagined the jewels lying in a velvet box. There was something creepy about being in a box, Eleanor thought, even if you were a jewel. Fearful and sick, she began to sing.

When He cometh, when He cometh
To make up His jewels,
All His jewels, precious jewels,
His loved and His own.
Like the stars in the morning
His bright crown adorning,
They will shine in their beauty,
Bright gems for His crown.

God's jewel box. The words fell like cold pebbles around the small children sitting with their hands folded on the desks in front of them in the brightly lit classroom. Imagine being shut up in a jewel box with Mrs. Black for eternity! But Katie was singing away, untroubled. Eleanor looked at her complacent face with wonder.

The lessons began, and things seemed a bit better. She was called upon to read, which, since the story was much simpler than many she had read to her mother, she did with aplomb and composure. But why were some of the boys behind her sniggering as she sat down?

"Jeremy and Paul that will do." Mrs. Black's voice rang out with a strangely metallic reverberation. It had the tremolo of a bell, but with a hard, grating undertone. Everyone sat up straight after that and looked innocent.

Then there was math. They chanted the two times table in a sing-song that all the other children obviously knew. Mrs. Black passed out sheets of sums copied on a hectograph, and all was silence. Suddenly the silence was broken by the sound of a wooden pencil case landing on the floor. Eleanor looked down. It was her pencil case. Everything had spilled out. Now Katie was tittering, and Eleanor realized that gradually, imperceptibly, Katie had been pushing it slowly across the desk until it toppled over the edge. Mrs. Black glared at her.

"But…but…" Eleanor stammered.

"Pick it up. That will do Eleanor."

Tears stinging her eyes, Eleanor picked up the pencil case.

Emma knew something was wrong. Eleanor didn't want to talk about school. Was her teacher nice? Was she making any friends? After a few days she burst out sobbing and said, no, no. Mrs. Black wasn't nice; she was horrid. And no, she didn't have any friends. "They all hate me."

"What makes you think that?"

"They laugh at me. They play tricks on me." She told her mother about the pencil case.

"Well, that wasn't very nice, but I'm sure she won't do it again. Why don't you keep your pencil case in the desk? Then she can't push it off again."

"But she takes my things out from inside the desk and piles them up on top. She says they're taking up her space, and she's measured where half is, except that it isn't half, she's got a lot more room than me, and then she takes out any things of mine that are even partly on the other side of the line."

"Why don't you tell Mrs. Black?"

"Because she wouldn't believe me. And because she's always cross. Well, not quite always, but most days. I can tell when she's going to be cross by the way she does her hair. You know how mostly it sticks out all over her ears and on top of her head? Well, when it's like that, you know she's really cross. Some days it's more smoothed down, and she puts a clip in the side to keep it back behind her ears, and then she's happier."

If she hadn't been so worried about Eleanor, Emma would have laughed. The idea of a six-year-old working out a teacher's mood from her hairstyle, the very idea that a teacher's hairstyle dictated her behavior, was at least mildly funny. Who was this Mrs. Black, anyway? Emma decided she must find out.

Some days later, Eleanor came home from school in tears. "Oh dear, what's happened?"

"Jamie got the strap."

"From Mrs. Black?"

"No. From Mr. MacDonald, the principal."

"But then you couldn't have seen it, if he got it in the principal's office."

"No, it wasn't like that at all. Mr. MacDonald came into the room and gave Jamie the strap. First he started talking about birds. He seemed nice. He said the birds are our friends. They sing for us, and some of them are brightly coloured and look pretty. And he said they help us to know the seasons, because some birds, like the robins, went south in winter, and when we see them again on our lawns, we know it's getting to be spring. So he went on talking, and he started soft, but then his voice got louder and louder, and he said that still, in spite of all this, there were some bad boys who climbed up into the trees and destroyed birds' nests. One of those boys was here in our class! And he would have to take his punishment for destroying the birds' nests. Someone had seen him doing it. And then he called Jamie up to the front and strapped him."

Eleanor stopped, her eyes wide with the horror of it.

"Did Jamie cry?" Emma asked.

"Yes. He didn't at first, but then he started, and he cried even a long time after he went back to his seat, and rubbed his hands."

The next morning Eleanor didn't want to go to school. Emma knew that she had to go. If she stayed home one morning, why not another? Why should she ever go back to school again?

So she coaxed her with a lovely breakfast—scrambled eggs, and bacon, and toast and orange juice. Eleanor looked at the breakfast and decided she didn't want any of it. Emma insisted. "Just this nice bit of toast, and this crispy corner of bacon." Eleanor tried to swallow it. Two minutes later she threw up. Emma felt she had no choice but to allow her to stay home.

The next morning, Eleanor woke at six o'clock. Emma took her into bed and tried to persuade her that going to school would be all right today. At seven-thirty she got up, made Eleanor breakfast, and brought it to her in bed. Joan saw the tray going in and sniffed. But Eleanor could not eat this meal either, not even propped up with her furry animals, who were all eager to sample the pancakes and syrup that Emma made. This time, however, Emma decided Eleanor had to go to school.

It was a gloomy mid-October morning, with fog swirling down the street, hiding the ships' masts, hiding the few autumnal leaves still clinging to the trees, hiding some of the ugly buildings. The smell of fish clung to the fog, making even the act of breathing an effort. Emma clasped Eleanor's hand firmly as she steered her way up the main street where the shops were just beginning to put up their blinds, past the Lutheran church, that seemed to have lost most of its steeple to the fog, up and up to the imposing castle-school, where she left a tearful Eleanor on her own.

"Crybaby," Emma heard someone say, as Eleanor went in through the front door. "Where were you yesterday?"

Emma knew she had to go and see Mrs. Black. She arranged for Nathan to look after Eleanor when she came back from school, and walked towards the Grade One classroom with almost as much trepidation as Eleanor. Her coat was grey and shabby; the buttonholes and edges of the sleeves were worn. She had been a teacher herself once, but not in a school like this, and anyway all that had been in another life. She knocked at the door.

"Come in." Emma recognized the vibrato in the voice, exactly as Eleanor had described it. She opened the door; Mrs. Black was sitting at her desk, apparently marking some work.

"I'm Emma Wentzell, Eleanor's mother," she said, almost timidly.

"Oh do sit down. I'm so pleased to see you. Eleanor is a most delightful child, a pleasure to have in the classroom." Mrs. Black beamed; her wiry hair, earrings and bracelets bobbed and jangled her approval, like a fancy percussion instrument.

Emma sank into the too-small desk in front of her, which made her feel even more diminutive and suppliant. "I'm glad you think well of her." Deciding she might as well plunge straight in, she said, "The problem is that she doesn't seem very happy at school."

"Oh dear. How so?"

"Well, there seem to be two problems. She isn't settling in very well with the other children. She says they make fun of her and play tricks on her, like pushing her pencil case off her desk so that it clatters on the floor, or hiding some items of outdoor clothing so that she can't find them. I know these things sound trivial, but..."

"I shall have to look into that. I didn't know. That will not do at all." She added, as if in explanation, "Of course Eleanor takes things very seriously, too seriously."

Emma didn't know how to respond to this. Was life to be taken as some huge joke that didn't matter? She plunged on. "But the second problem is perhaps more difficult. You see, she has not been used to seeing children punished, that is, punished physically, strapped. When she sees this happening she gets very upset. In fact, she's so upset that she doesn't want to come to school. She's afraid."

Mrs. Black bristled slightly. Did the hair inch up a fraction?

"Discipline is always difficult, as you must know. I believe you were a school teacher once?"

Emma nodded assent, although now it seemed she could scarcely remember that time.

"I'm sure you would agree that order in the classroom is of the utmost importance. No one can learn anything otherwise. I certainly try to be fair, but I guess you could say I am strict." Mrs. Black paused. "But Eleanor herself has nothing to fear. She's been a model pupil so far."

"It's kind of you to say that. But I don't think she's just afraid she herself might get the strap. She's afraid of a place where...where these things happen with some frequency. It just seems unsafe to her, scary."

"You will understand that I can't change the school rules for one child. I'll have a chat with her, but school is school. She must understand that."

Unsatisfied, Emma went out into a glorious autumn afternoon. The morning fog had dissipated, and the brilliant leaves cast flickering shadows over the tombstones that surrounded the school and glimmered white in the sunshine.

Two days after Emma's visit to the school, Mr. MacDonald came into the classroom. All the children stood up and chanted in a sing-song, "Good Morning, Mr. MacDonald." Eleanor expected the worst.

After a few words to the class as a whole, he told them to get on with their work and sat down in an empty desk beside Eleanor. She froze. Nothing in her math book seemed to add up right; the very numbers took on a strange, foreign character. She kept her head lowered and pretended she was thinking. Suddenly, he reached over, picked her up and sat her on his knee. He began to talk to her in a voice that was no doubt meant to be kindly. But in what language would God address you if He were trying to be kind? The people of Israel had been terrified of seeing Him, Eleanor knew, and had sent poor Moses alone up into the mountain to have all their dealings with Him. Was she the appointed Moses, lifted up out of her place, to communicate with this superior being? What was he saying?

"Mrs. Black tells me that you're frightened of coming to school. Now a nice, pretty little girl like you doesn't have anything to be afraid of, does she? What bad could happen to you here? We all want you to be happy and able to do your best work. And your work is very good indeed, Mrs. Black tells me. You can read better than anyone else in the class! So, you see, there's nothing to be frightened of, nothing at all. And if the other boys and girls tease you, just let us know, and we'll put a stop to that as quickly as we can. We all want to help you. And, someday, I hope, you'll come to love learning."

Dumb with terror, she said nothing. He gave her a quick squeeze, set her back in her place and left the room.

Much later, when she saw him teaching high school mathematics with true passion, she would remember his last words and wonder what he had meant by "come to love learning." Did he simply mean that she would get used to coming to school? Or did he mean that elusive thing, real knowledge, would capture her imagination as it had his and sustain her through the trials of formal education.

At the time, she was so scared and somehow embarrassed that she told no one about what had happened—not even her mother.

CHAPTER 6
1949

The new year dawned cold and misty, and for Emma it seemed to promise little. There was no snow to hide the dirt on Water Street. It wasn't actually freezing, so in the afternoon the town drunks wandered to and fro, shambling along between doorways, always keeping the comforting sight of the liquor store within their view. Virtue went back to her teaching in Garden Lots; Joan went off to her typing—as good as her word, she had learned to type—at Knickle's Shipbuilding; Nathan and Obadiah shaved the sunken winter cheeks of the town elders and cut their hair; the fishermen struggled through their winter trip on the Grand Banks.

After Nathan left with Eleanor for school, Emma was alone. She cut out and sewed dresses for Eleanor; she kept the house clean; she worried about making something for dinner that Joan would eat. Sometimes she sat and read a book, but this always made her feel guilty. Reading wasn't useful. Nathan didn't approve of it; neither, if it came to that, did Virtue.

Occasionally she allowed herself to think about what her life had become, and it seemed to her very strange indeed. No one else would have judged it that way, of course. Even she could see that. She had married a good man, and settled down where he worked. She had been lucky enough, later on in life than most, to have a child. She had enough to eat and a roof over her head. There was the little matter of the two families living under the same roof, and Joan was an additional burden, but all families had their difficulties, and compared to some, these were mild. Hers was a perfectly respectable, ordinary life. So what was the problem?

It lay in that very word, "ordinary." She had never imagined an ordinary life for herself—at least after Reverend Selig came into it. Even after he left Waldenstein, disgraced, presumed mad, she had hoped somehow that he would come back for her. Or that, even if he didn't, the miracle of the unexpected having happened once, it would occur again. Someone would come for her.

As for Nathan, well, she might have been his sweetheart, but he had scarcely been hers. No, she was going away with Reverend Selig to Europe, where everyone dressed in silk gowns and spoke in Latin and went to concerts every evening. Of course she had never quite believed in her fairy-tale vision of the "old country," but it would, at worst, have been different, exotic. She had just let things happen, and now the time for initiative was long past. She was married, and she had a child. These were facts as incontrovertible as the square kitchen table at which she sat. Reverend Selig was dead, or so Virtue had told her years ago. No one believed in life more fervently than Virtue—on, on, on—just living, not necessarily having a plan, just taking life as it came. What did that mean, anyway? Virtue would have said it was God's plan, but then was her childlessness part of God's plan? Don't ask that question—at least not of Virtue.

She glanced out the window. Something was actually happening! Old Willy Franks who owned the little fish and fruit shop opposite was outside with a ladder and a long piece of rope or—no—it was electric cable. Normally he should be in a state of alcoholic torpor by this time in the afternoon, but there he was, climbing the ladder and fastening the cable to the wall of the shop. Emma was riveted. Next, he came out with two things that looked like wooden brackets and fastened them to the wall just below the eaves. Finally, he appeared with something that appeared to be a large gramophone speaker. Up he went again, carefully fixing the speaker to the brackets. Then he fiddled around behind the contraption for some time—probably fixing the wiring to the speaker, Emma reasoned. What was he doing?

She began to cough and put the dress she was sewing aside, lest she soil it. Naturally she had a cough; it was winter. She had never been quite so ill again since the occasion two years ago, but every winter she was confined to the house more than she was out. Nathan had to walk Eleanor to school, and Obadiah grumbled because it meant he was out of the shop and they lost business when people looked in the door and saw a roomful of men waiting and only one barber working. When men came off the ships they wanted a shave and cut immediately, not in an hour's time.

As soon as the coughing ceased, she took up her work again and forgot about whatever it might be that old Willy was up to. She dreamed of a house of her own. This was the one tangible thing she could still realistically hope for. A house! Yet compared to what she had once imagined, even that was a diminished dream.

The next morning at a quarter to nine, just after she had seen Eleanor off to school, she heard music—well, singing to be precise. It sounded like a hymn. It was a hymn: "Rock of ages, cleft for me" came blaring into her kitchen. She went to the front and looked out. Sure enough, the sound was emanating from Willy's loudspeaker. He was broadcasting the daily fifteen-minute religious service on the local radio to the entire community. Emma wanted to laugh; Emma wanted to scream. She imagined the sacred water and blood flowing in all its ridiculous and redemptive glory down Water Street. And here she was, trapped in its path.

❧

One Thursday, towards the end of January, Eleanor came home from school with a sore throat. The next morning, she had a low fever and was allowed to stay home from school. The following day she began to cough. Eleanor herself quite enjoyed this early stage of illness. The fever made her not care as much about things; she stopped worrying about school and whether she was really the best in the class. She could enjoy just lying on the sofa-bed Mommy made up on the living room couch and eating the nice soft buttery baked potato and tomato soup she made for her because her throat was so sore she couldn't swallow anything else, and reading lots of books. There was a radio as well that she could listen to, and in the evening when Aunt Joan and Aunt Virtue came home, they would come and read more stories to her, because by that time she was tired of holding up the books herself. One evening Douglas came and sang the frog song over and over to her until Joan said, "Come on. We've got to go. We want to look at the china on sale at Himmelman's before they close."

Douglas squeezed her hand before he got up and said, "The boss says I've got to go."

On the following Tuesday, it all changed. The day began in much the same way, but by mid-afternoon things got scary. The light in the living room ceiling began to do strange things. It didn't seem solid any more, but slid around as if it were made of jelly. Perhaps it would come down and eat her—though Mommy pointed out that, if it were jelly, it should be more afraid that she would eat it. Her teeth no longer seemed to fit her mouth. Nothing was real.

The doctor came and said she had a bad fever—scarlet fever, he called it. Her body got pink all over with tiny little spots, and she no longer wanted any of the food Mommy kept bringing her. It all tasted funny, and it was too much effort to sit up and eat it. This seemed to go on for a long time, and it was impossible to keep track of the days or the nights. Once she thought she heard Mommy say, "What if…" and Daddy put his hand on her mouth and said, "Don't say it…bad luck."

She was in her bed upstairs all the time now. Mommy brought in a chair and was always sitting there it seemed. When the noise of the fan that brought the fumes out of the galvanizing plant started up, it shook Eleanor's head and made it hurt.

Finally, things started coming back to normal. Mommy and Daddy told her that she was getting better, and they were so happy. She herself was neither happy nor sad—just tired and in a place that was very calm and remote. Nothing mattered much anymore. School and all its problems were in another world that she was not yet ready to enter.

Weeks seemed to pass, but eventually she was up and able to cut out the paper dolls in a book Aunt Virtue bought her. Later she was able to walk up the street and go to the ice cream parlour. The shop had little square tables with rattan chairs around them in the centre of the room and dark secretive wooden booths along the walls. At the back, a window looked out over the frozen harbour. She sat with Mommy in one of the booths and had a big chocolate sundae with marshmallow sauce. It was cool and delicious, but even the ice cream didn't make her feel really happy, and she didn't know why.

A few days later, Daddy took her back to school. It was strange to see that the class and Mrs. Black were still there, apparently unchanged. The class had been making paper pelicans, their moving parts held together with clasps. Mrs. Black said how very glad she was to see her back, and gave her a pelican she had made just for Eleanor while she was sick. Eleanor took the pelican and checked that its beak and legs were in perfect working order, but she knew that she was no longer interested in a world where paper pelicans mattered. She had left all that behind. What this new world was, she wasn't quite certain.

***

What a lot of fuss, Joan thought. The child had been very ill, of course, but she was always likely to get better. Children did, didn't they? Unless they died like the little boy baby that her mother had before Flora, but Eleanor just didn't seem the dying sort. The child was spoiled rotten, a little minx. In the evening when Joan stood over the hot air grate of the furnace, her skirts billowing out with the rising air—it was so cold in the kitchen—Eleanor would come and push her. "I'm cold, Joan. Move over for me." Joan knew what she was expected to do; this was how the household worked.

Now she had a hope chest. This meant that the small bedroom was more crowded than ever, because the big ugly trunk that was full of bedding couldn't go anywhere else; there simply was no room. Crammed up against the wall in the corner, the dark polished mahogany of the chest shone dimly, and when opened, it exuded a wonderful aroma of cedar. There her few treasured possessions lay—two pillow cases that she had embroidered with pale blue flowers, two more embroidered by Emma (a Christmas gift), a cushion cover that Virtue had tatted, and now, packed carefully in tissue paper, a small set of china dishes that she had purchased from Himmelman's out of her meagre savings. In the evening, when she was sure no one would interrupt her, she would take the pieces out one by one and lay them on the bedcover, as if it were a table. There they sat, the small pink flowers and green vines contained by a rim of gold around the edges. Much prettier than Emma's, she thought. Even Eleanor had been impressed. ("Those are beautiful, Joan. Can I have them when you're dead?")

Joan was not expecting to be dead for a long time. At last, she had a future. Douglas hadn't actually asked her yet, but he had encouraged her to get the dishes, hadn't he? He kept telling her how much better off he would be once the new mill he was building was up and running. Then he could hire twice the men. Of course, she was thirty-five, but people could have futures even at that age. Look at Emma. She didn't have a child until she was thirty-five—so anything was possible.

Still, as she put the dishes carefully back in the trunk, she sighed. There was a slight problem, and she didn't know whom to consult. Emma and Virtue were out of the question; they knew nothing and would be scandalized if she told them. It hadn't been her fault; she had been forced.

❦

It was June, and Joan was getting married. This came as a disappointment to Eleanor, because she thought that she might like to marry Douglas herself. Indeed, she once told him so on an evening when he was holding her on his knee and singing to her while waiting for Joan to finish dressing to go out with him. "I would marry you, you know...when I'm bigger...if you don't marry Joan first."

"Well, Miss Mouse, that's a very kind and generous offer. But I'm a pretty old codger to be waiting for the likes of you."

Now it was clear that he had decided on Joan, and Eleanor didn't quite see why. She was older and ready to get married right away, of course, and that, Douglas had intimated, was a major point in her favour. But she was too skinny, Eleanor thought, and not as nice looking as Mommy or as she herself would be when she grew up. Joan had straight dark hair—though Douglas mightn't know that because she always curled it—and eyes of an indeterminate brown-green, not nearly as pretty as Mommy's, which were blue.

Now Joan had a sparkling diamond ring, and that meant it was certain she was going to get married. The hope chest was filling up fast, and one Saturday afternoon Joan let her explore its wonders. There was so much more in it than before—all kinds of dishes wrapped in tissue paper, and little spoons Joan said were silver—or silver plate, she corrected herself—and embroidered tablecloths and napkins. Then, one day, Joan came back with her wedding dress. Eleanor knew wedding dresses had to be white, so she was surprised when Joan pulled a pale blue taffeta and chiffon gown out of the large bag.

"Why isn't it white, Joan?"

Emma interrupted, "It's Joan's special day, and she can have any colour dress she wants, Eleanor. I think the blue is quite pretty."

Joan's own explanation? "Oh, I thought maybe I was a bit old for white. And blue is Douglas' favourite colour."

❧

It was all a bit funny, Joan's wedding arrangements, Emma thought. First there was the blue dress. Well, it was a very pretty dress, and Joan looked nice in blue—or at least better than she looked in anything else. (That was a mean thought, and Emma stifled it.) At least, Douglas seemed a good man and, from a practical point of view, if she could just live through the wedding and reception, then Eleanor could have a room of her own.

The reception. Ah yes, Joan had decided that since there was no money for a large event, she would like to have a small party in the house, if Emma didn't mind. Well, Emma did mind, but she would do it anyway. So now she was baking and cleaning furiously, pressing Joan to know exactly how many people there would be, and trying to imagine how they could fit even twenty people into the small house. Virtue, of course, insisted that she could not be expected to bake for the event, since she would finish the school year only two days before the wedding.

Eleanor was not to have any official part in the ceremony. Joan said children at weddings were only for show, and this wasn't going to be a showy wedding. An older cousin of Douglas' would be ideal as a bridesmaid. And, really, she would just invite the family plus one girlfriend from work.

"You must invite Flora," said Emma. She could see Joan flinch.

"Why?"

"Because she's your sister."

"I don't know her."

"Well, that's a pity. Maybe we should all make more of an effort to know Flora."

"And I don't know where Hannah lives now, so we can't invite her, and do we have to have Harry?"

"I think we must invite all your sisters and your brother. There's no point in making enemies over what should be a happy occasion."

"What about Rachel? Do we have to invite Martin?"

Emma thought for a moment. Rachel, the youngest and most fragile of them all, had made a most unfortunate marriage. Cast out into the world by her parents' death at sixteen, she had become a fully qualified teacher like her sisters and, unlike Joan, enjoyed teaching, but she was always looking for something, someone to take her in—to love her, Emma supposed. She chose Martin. Like Douglas, he was from the next-door village, but very different in temperament. Fourteen years older than Rachel, there were rumours he had already fathered a child. But this was not what people held against him. He was cruel and a drunk. Nathan had watched him drive his father's cattle home one evening when he was still in Waldenstein, pointlessly whipping the beasts. "Stop that! They're going as fast as they can." Martin just flicked his whip at Nathan.

Still, he was handsome and seemed to have a mysterious magnetism for the opposite sex. He had toyed with Rachel while she was still in school until their father had put a stop to it. Then, for a time, he disappeared. The first anyone knew of his return was when he turned up at four o'clock on a sunny afternoon at the schoolhouse door in Waldenstein, as Rachel told it. All the pupils had left. He knocked on the door, and Rachel appeared in a white blouse with a lace collar, and a tight-waisted dark skirt. That was the last anyone saw of either of them until they were married. Later, Rachel told her sister, it was as if she had no choice. She opened the door, and there he was, waiting for her, and she simply fell into his arms. She would be loved, cared for, cherished.

Of course, it hadn't quite worked out that way. After a few weeks he discovered she was not as compliant in all matters as he would have liked, and he decided to beat her into submission. Rachel retreated into dumb acquiescence at first, then, roused by the need to protect her first child, to futile fury. Two more children followed; she was trapped. How could she complain to those very siblings who knew she had been warned against him? In episodes of drunken paranoia he accused her of harbouring men in the house, and actually searched the cupboards to find them, clattering the lids of the pots and pans in frenzy. If she had not been so desperate, Rachel would have found this funny. A man in her stew pot? He was mad, he must be mad! But she couldn't convince the doctors, because when he was with them he was a perfectly reasonable, charming man who had married a hysterical wife. Once a week, on Friday evenings, she came into the town to shop, brought by a neighbour who pitied her. Then she would seek solace with Emma for a few brief hours, and they would remember the hard life in Waldenstein as if it had been an idyll.

"Yes, you must invite Rachel and Martin too," Emma snapped.

"He'll be drunk."

"Well, he won't get drunk here, because all we're serving is grape juice and apple juice."

"That won't stop him. He'll arrive drunk or have his own supply to hand."

"Well, there are enough men to handle him."

❧

The day of Joan's wedding, Nathan and Obadiah closed the shop early, and by five in the afternoon Nathan was trussed up in his best suit and tie. It was all a pile of nonsense as far as he was concerned, this having a "big" wedding. He and Emma and Virtue and Obadiah hadn't made a great song and dance about it. Admittedly, that was in part because their wives' parents had just died, but even so. Trust Joan to make everyone work as hard as possible for her own pleasure. At least, after this she would be gone. His little household would be his own once again. Then he could start saving in earnest for the new house, because he was convinced the small amount of rent Joan paid didn't even cover her expenses.

He sat with Emma in the large church with about thirty guests. Where was Reverend Schwarz? At ten past six, his bald head and rotund figure appeared at a side church door. "When's the wedding?"

Typical, thought Nathan. Someone shouted, "Now." The head and body disappeared and five minutes later reappeared clothed in a Geneva gown at the chancel steps. Joan and Douglas came in hand-in-hand, and the service began. Nathan glanced over at Virtue, dressed in a pale green frock made out of some kind of floppy material with a neck cut too low for his taste. Trying to look young again, he supposed. He looked approvingly at Emma, who had a new dress that she had made for herself in a somewhat darker shade of blue than Joan's. It was snugly fitted in the bodice, showing her tidy figure, with a flared skirt and a bit of lace at the high stand-up collar and the sleeves. His wife knew what was appropriate.

⁊

Flora was not happy. Standing in the living room doorway in an ill-fitting dress with a large floral print, she held her glass of juice firmly in both hands. It was all too noisy. Fancy making such a fuss over getting married! Both Emma's and Virtue's living rooms were overrun with people spilling drinks and dropping bits of sandwich everywhere, even on the upholstered furniture. Someone would have to clean all that up—Emma, she supposed. Eleanor, silly child, was running around passing sandwiches and cakes, and talking to anyone who would listen. No one would make that kind of fuss if she were to get married. But then that wasn't going to happen, was it?

She moved to a large chair near the window and sat down, surveying the scene, her wrongs mounting. What had she done to be so singled out, stupid, ugly, never to get a husband, a servant in someone else's house? Her sisters didn't want her. Now that Joan was leaving she had thought maybe...but no, that stuck-up Eleanor would get Joan's room. That child didn't know her place.

There was Harry, her brute of a brother—brash, confident, laughing, tossing back the unruly lock of dark hair that fell down over his fore-head, making large gestures and more noise than all the rest of the room put together. What a show-off! Flora found herself getting up, shoving through the other people talking in little clumps, pushing her way towards Harry.

"Why, hello, Flora. How good that you could get here."

"No help from you!" Then, everything she had suffered since her parents died, burst out. "You, Harry, horrible! Taken everything, given us nothing. Where's my house? You were supposed to build me a house?" Other voices died down, overwhelmed by Flora's strident tone. She saw she had an audience. "Look here, this man, this brother, what...what..." She stumbled momentarily, but then hit her stride again. "Look what he has done to me! I have no home. I have no one to look after me. Look at my sisters," she said, sweeping her arms around the room, "look at all the nice clothes they got, and the houses, and the husbands. And I ain't got nothing. Here is the man who has made certain I got nothing—my brother, Harry! He's taken it all, and left me nothing, nothing, nothing." She began to beat Harry on the chest with her fists in time to the repeated refrain.

Nathan and Obadiah tried to pull her away. At first she struggled, but slowly she acquiesced and let them draw her back. She looked at Harry, who was standing transfixed as if an earthquake were engulfing him and he were powerless to escape, and shook her head. Emma and Virtue took her out to the garden and tried to calm and console her.

"Flora, you mustn't. Not at Joan's wedding party." Virtue was all sweet reason.

"Joan will be so upset," Emma continued. "Some other time we'll talk about it. Some other time."

Flora was not to be appeased. "Why some other time? For me, it's always some other time. You got married. I'll get married some other time. You have a house, but it's 'oh Flora, just wait a bit, I bet Harry will get you a house some day.' You know some other time is never or when I'm dead!"

❧

September. Another school year. Eleanor was allowed to walk to school by herself now, and she went up the little path that led from her own garden to the street above. She knew her mother was watching her until she turned the corner and found, to her surprise, that now there was a sense of relief and freedom when she was out of sight.

She trotted along in a business-like way, her bookbag bumping along behind her, up to the post office corner, where she met another girl who looked to be about her age. She had seen her on the playground before, but had never spoken to her. She was really pretty, Eleanor thought, with dark curly hair and huge brown eyes, and she too was walking with a bookbag bouncing on her back.

"Hi, I'm Eleanor."

"I'm Donna."

"Going to school?"

"Of course."

"What grade are you in?"

"Grade Two, Miss Parkinson's grade."

"So am I. How come I never saw you in Grade One?"

"I," Donna hesitated. "I'm having to take Grade Two over."

"Oh dear." Eleanor could not imagine tragedy on a greater scale. She could not even imagine getting less than ninety percent. And to fail...

"You see...my mom and dad don't get along real well. Last year it was awful bad. After he was out fishing, my dad would come home and beat my mom, and there was terrible fights, so I couldn't do my homework and I couldn't sleep at night, so sometimes my mom would let me stay home from school because I was so tired. But now," Donna continued, "it's okay because my dad's not coming home anymore."

"How's that?" Eleanor couldn't imagine things being better if her father never came home.

"I'm not sure, exactly. There was something called a court order that said he couldn't come home."

"So where is he?"

"Well, most of the time he's on a boat out at sea. But when he's home he mostly just wanders around the streets. Sometimes I see him, and he gives me a big hug. I'm scared of him when he's drunk, but when he's not, he's really nice. I feel kind of sorry for him, but Mom couldn't stand it anymore."

Maybe Donna's father was one of those mysterious "drunks" wandering about outside their house in the evening. How awful! Up to this point, Eleanor hadn't really seen them as people at all—people who might have wives and children, who might have been kicked out of their homes. Donna seemed to accept this as a perfectly natural thing, and probably wouldn't even have mentioned it except that it explained why she was repeating a grade. They walked together, and by the time they reached the school they were holding hands and making plans to play together.

So Eleanor entered her second year of school with a friend.

***

Virtue sat in church clenching her fists and pressing them down on the wooden pew. Joan was going to have a baby. It was unbearable. Skinny little thing, lucky to get any man at all, and she was so old! Much older than she was when she got married, but she was barren, and Joan was fertile. There was something positively Old Testament about it all. What did God want? She was a good wife, sober and faithful, even though she now went out to work. She was forty-four. Was there still a chance? What did God want of her?

Perhaps Joan's baby would die. No, she hadn't thought that! What was the minister saying? "We poor sinners confess unto Thee that we are by nature sinful and unclean..." She pressed her fists more fiercely against the wood. Fingernails bit into the palms of her curled hands.

Joan would be a terrible mother. She had no idea how to treat children. Certainly, she didn't seem to like Eleanor very much, you could tell that. Mothers were the very worst people to bring up children! Look at all the useless parents of the children she taught. They sent them to school either dressed for a party or in dungarees or without the warm clothes they needed to play outside at recess. They let them stay up late at night so that they couldn't concentrate the next day, and when she mentioned this to them casually, almost as an afterthought to the scholastic appraisal, they took offence and told her, more or less, to mind her own business. They were the parents, they reminded her. She was only the school teacher.

She looked up at Obadiah. He was sitting placidly as always, staring straight ahead, apparently concentrating on what the minister was saying. Perhaps it wasn't her fault at all; perhaps it was he who prevented her from having children. That disease he had when he was little—she couldn't remember its name—but she heard that it could make men—well, not able to father children.

For a moment she looked at his rounded face and his rounding stomach with positive hatred. Maybe she should have married someone else. But whom? It wasn't that she never had other suitors, it was just that her life had become so entwined with his that she couldn't imagine anything different. It had all seemed so convenient, so settled, she and Emma marrying brothers and setting up house together. Now she knew that Emma, at least, hated the arrangement. Of course she and Nathan would never have enough money to move, not with only one salary coming in and them spending ever so much on Eleanor. She didn't really want them to move. She would lose Eleanor, and the poor child needed her. Emma could be so irrational.

As she left the church she noticed that it had become late autumn. Sometime while she was busy marking schoolwork, making lunches for herself and Obadiah, cooking and cleaning after she got home from school, the weather had changed. Green had turned to red and now to rust and brown. The wind sent great swirls of leaves over her feet as she walked towards their new car. In the distance, she saw Douglas solicitously helping Joan into their less grand vehicle. He would be careful of her now, of course; she was bearing his child. She opened her car door herself as Obadiah got into the driver's seat with never a glance at her.

❧

"Why don't you come and sing with us on Saturday mornings?" Katie asked. Eleanor had been trying to avoid her now that they no longer shared a desk.

"Where? What are you talking about?"

"There's a singing class that meets every Saturday morning at Mrs. Schmeisser's house, back of town. Lots of us go there—Emily and Rose and Janet. It's at ten o'clock, and lasts for an hour, and then as you go out you put ten cents in a little pot to pay Mrs. Schmeisser."

"I don't know. I'll have to ask Mommy."

"Well, you sing really good, you know. Almost as good as I do."

Coming from Katie, this was high praise indeed. It won Eleanor over. "I'll see."

She went dancing home that day to Emma. "Mommy, Mommy, there's a singing class on Saturdays, and Katie wants me to go."

"I didn't think you and Katie were such good friends..."

"Well, we're not, really, but she asked me if I could go to this singing class, and it sounds really good. Maybe," and here a new thought struck her, "maybe Donna will go as well."

Donna's mother didn't want her to go—was the ten cents a problem?—and Katie lived in a different part of town, so the next Saturday it was Eleanor alone who walked to the dark brown house with its low eaves and two huge chestnut trees in front that were dropping chestnuts in a most inviting way. Eleanor stooped and picked up a few. Behind the house, down the hill, lay the town's back harbour, blue and still in the morning sun.

Lots of other girls were arriving, so she followed them down to a basement door cut into the side of the hill. Inside there was a large room with a grand piano in the centre and three tiers of benches along one wall. Eleanor climbed up to the top bench and sat beside Katie, who said, "I was saving this seat for you. I knew you'd come."

Mrs. Schmeisser entered, a loose dress flapping around her expansive form. She gave them all little orange songbooks, and before long they were singing a song about a gondola in a far-away place called Venice where "the streets [were] flowing rivers." Eleanor forgot that she lived in a house her mother hated, that her school classmates didn't like her, that stories could make her cry—she forgot everything except the fact that she was completely happy singing.

Going home, scuffling her shoes through the piles of fallen leaves, she was sure that this ecstasy would last forever.

🙙

One day in late November, Eleanor came home in triumph. Emma watched from the kitchen window as her plump legs came running down the slope of the back garden. "Mommy, Mommy," she cried breathlessly, as she threw her bookbag down on the floor. "I came top of the class, I came top of the class!"

Emma was surprised that this information was now given to the children. It certainly hadn't been in Grade One, but here was Eleanor, unstrapping her bookbag and drawing out of its depths, along with a flurry of other paper, a report card. On the bottom of the card it said, in large letters, "FIRST."

Emma's reaction was one of caution. "That's wonderful, Eleanor. But you mustn't let it go to your head. And, of course, this is just one set of exams."

In her heart, though, she was as pleased as Eleanor. It was even in the local paper. Under the names of boys and girls who had passed in each grade with "Honours," "High Pass," or a mere "Pass" was a list of those who had come first, second, and third in each grade. Emma felt vindicated. She had known Eleanor would be brilliant. Had she not told the child in her carriage that she would be? Top of the class in this small school in an obscure town was not the doctor's son or the priest's son, but the barber's daughter.

That evening, when Nathan came in for supper, the three of them danced to the music of Don Messer and his Islanders, around and around the kitchen until they were all breathless and Emma was coughing and laughing at the same time.

CHAPTER 7
1950

Eleanor was going to have a part in the school play. The senior school put on an elaborate operetta, directed by Mrs. Schmeisser, every Christmas, but Easter belonged to the junior school, and this year they were putting on a children's version of *Hansel and Gretel*. Naturally, she had wanted to be Gretel, but with her long curls she was destined to be an angel. This was not all bad, however, because she got to sing Humperdinck's beautiful lullaby. As the two lost children fell asleep in the woods, a small group of angels in long white gowns and tinsel halos came on stage and sang to them. "When at night I go to sleep/Fourteen angels watch do keep..." Katie was an angel as well, and with her rich voice sang the alto line, while Eleanor soared up to the high notes with ease.

Rehearsals took place after school. Sometimes they went on until well beyond four o'clock, and all the instructors wanted to do after the rehearsals was to get home as fast as possible.

One day shortly before the play was to be put on, all the children from Miss Paterson's class with parts in the play returned to an empty room to get their coats and boots and go home. Eleanor walked to the cloakroom, but before she could get her coat off the hook, it was grabbed by Mark, a large boy who had aspirations to unseat Eleanor at the head of the class.

Eleanor knew this with certainty because of what he had done at the last set of school exams in February. In the middle of their English paper, Mark had raised his hand.

"Yes, Mark," said Miss Patterson, assuming that he had a question about the exam, but Mark had no such question. Instead he launched into an astonishing speech.

"My mom and dad say that if I beat Eleanor in these exams, they'll give me a big train set, bigger than anyone else's in town. It's going to have robbers standing on the side of the track, waiting to rob the train, and police in the station ready to catch them, and electric lights on the signals and..."

"That will do, Mark."

"And a mountain with a tunnel for the train to run through..."

"That will do! Sit down and get on with your work."

Mark sat down. Eleanor's face burned. She pressed her pencil hard into the paper and wrote as fast as she could. Mark was not going to get that train set if she could help it.

Now Mark tossed Eleanor's blue coat in the air, caught it neatly, and then ran with it towards the stairs and threw it down the gap in the middle of the alternating flights of stairs. Eleanor ran after him, screaming, "My coat, my coat, you'll get it dirty!"

"Will I now? And what will your crazy mother say to you then?"

"Bring it back, and my mother isn't crazy."

"Yes she is. She hardly ever comes out of the house, my mom says."

"That's because in winter she's sick."

"I bet she's not. She's just scared of normal people. She and your pop don't even come to the club dances."

"I don't know what you're talking about. Why should they go to dances?"

"Because everybody who's anybody in town goes to the dances. Well...the people my folks know, anyway. They're great fun, my dad says. And at the end, all the men throw their car keys into the centre of a circle, and the women run to pick up a pair of keys and then go home with the person whose keys they've picked up."

"But why would they do that?" Eleanor was so intrigued she was almost forgetting about her coat.

"Because it's fun, that's why. My mom and dad say your parents are stuck-up country folk that don't know how to live in a town."

"That's not true." Another boy threw her boots down the stairs. Then came Jimmy, prancing around with her hat on his head, pretending he was a dancer. They were all ganging up on her; they all hated her! She began to cry, which only made them laugh at her harder.

"Crybaby, crybaby."

"Go home to your mommy!"

"Poor little girl. Nearly five o'clock. Past your bedtime."

Then Donna and, unbelievably, Katie came to her rescue. "Stop it guys, or I'll tell Miss Patterson tomorrow," Donna said.

"And so will I," said Katie, "and you'll lose your parts in the play for sure."

Gradually, the boys went back to the cloakroom, put on their own clothes, and disappeared. They weren't going to bring Eleanor's clothes back, of course. That was left to Eleanor and her two girlfriends.

At last everything was quiet. Even Donna and Katie had left, and Eleanor was sitting alone in the classroom slowly pulling on her boots. The late afternoon sun slanted through the classroom window, illuminating the honey-coloured desks, the books in shelves along the wall, the white pieces of chalk under the blackboards. Eleanor was tired after the rehearsal and the chase and sat humming "When at night I go asleep" to herself as she gradually fastened her boots. She felt strangely happy and at peace. The events of fifteen minutes before had happened in another world, and now she was safe, surrounded by the smell of old books and chalk and the music that she was making for herself. How long she dawdled she wasn't sure. Suddenly the classroom door opened and a teacher's head stuck into the room.

"What are you doing here? I'm about to lock up. I would have locked up if I hadn't heard you singing. It's late. You should have been home half an hour ago."

The spell was broken. She had done something wrong, some terrible transgression for which she would be punished. She stood up, hauled her coat on, grabbed her bookbag, and ran all the way home in tears so that Emma, seeing her arrive in this state, was convinced something awful had happened. "Is that all?" she asked when Eleanor had explained about the teacher who wanted to lock up. She didn't tell her mother about the bullying that preceded it. In fact, Eleanor couldn't explain even to herself why she was so devastated. She simply knew that she had been very happy sitting alone in a room singing, and then someone had opened a door and shattered it all.

❧

It was the middle of May, and Joan felt that if she grew any bigger she would explode. When she looked in the mirror she saw something a small child might draw—a big round circle for a body, a little round circle for a head, and little stick arms and legs protruding out from the body. She had never been this big before.

Before? She killed the memory, but it kept raising its subversive head. A baby. Her baby. It never had a chance. She had bound herself so tightly, because no one must know, and then it was "born"—or it came out of her—much too early. Of course the people in the bakery where she was working knew or guessed, so as soon as she came out of the hospital she fled to Hannah. At least that was her intention, but Hannah was nowhere to be found. So with her paltry savings she lived, almost destitute, in a small boarding house outside Boston until she received the reply from Emma. Then she had a place to go to, and there was never any need to explain.

Now she could never explain because Douglas would be appalled. The question still burned within her. Had he been able to tell? Eventually she decided that perhaps some men could tell the hidden secrets of women, but she didn't think Douglas was one of them. She could tell he was less experienced than she. Still, every time he spoke of her innocence, her purity, which he worshipped in her, she wanted to die. He must never know. Now he brought her flowers and insisted on doing much of the cleaning of their little flat, lest she get tired. The baby never seemed to get tired, however, and pushed and poked inside her day and night.

Then one night everything was still. Nothing. She turned and prodded herself a bit, hoping to arouse some action. Still nothing. Eventually she fell asleep. The next morning she waited, attentive for the slightest movement. Still nothing. At lunchtime she told Douglas when he came back from the mill. "I think...the baby...it's gone still."

"Are you sure? Maybe he just wants a rest."

"It's never been this long before. I'm afraid..."

"Do you think we should go to the hospital?"

"Well, maybe. What do you think?"

"Perhaps that would be best. They'll know what to do."

At the hospital in Bridgewater Joan submitted to everything—the examinations, the grave faces of the doctor, the solicitousness of the nurses. She was on a drip in a small room; then she was in an agony so intense that she ceased to care about the baby. Finally, out came a small, perfect, waxen figure that did not move or cry. Her baby. God had paid her back. Joan was beyond tears.

"Next time..." Douglas said.

Joan knew there would not be a next time. Divine punishment did not allow for next times. She had sinned; she had a child out of wedlock; there would be no children within wedlock. Douglas thought that her extreme grief was simply the result of losing their child, and some of it was, but beyond that, there was sin and grief she could not possibly share. What happened was buried far in the past and covered in such deep shame that she refused even to remember.

$\sim$

When Virtue heard that Joan's baby had been stillborn, her first reaction was panic. She had done it. She had thought, "Maybe the baby will die." And it had! Of course she could tell no one. How to go to Joan and say, "I killed your baby. I wished it would die." Joan would not forgive her. How could one forgive something like that? So she said nothing.

She turned to Eleanor. As soon as she got home from school, she called out to her and invited her to "come and see what Aunt Virtue has for you." Sometimes it was simply a delicious cupcake that she saved for her; sometimes it was a brand-new book of paper dolls; sometimes it was a shiny new pencil case. In some strange way, this seemed to expiate the guilt. It made Eleanor happy. It made Emma angry.

$\sim$

Obadiah sat alone in his kitchen eating his lunch of Lunenburg pudding and molasses bread. What on earth was the matter with Virtue? Why was she taking on so about the death of Joan's baby? You would think it had been her own. He knew she blamed him for their childless state, but what could he do about that? He was loving and good to her—though the 'loving' part had been rebuffed on several occasions since Joan's misfortune. She just turned over and pretended to sleep.

What was the point of her teaching if she was going to spend all the money she earned buying rubbish to give to Eleanor? He worked hard, and didn't complain when he had to lunch, as he did today, on cold meat and store-bought bread, or when there was no apple pie for dessert like Nathan, across the hall, was enjoying. It seemed only right that, in exchange for this, he should have the newest Oldsmobile and be able to buy his wife a fur coat if she wanted one. He chewed petulantly on the pudding. Maybe this was just a phase. Things might get better.

⁊

Another baby had died, Joan's baby. Eleanor had imagined how she would be able to play with it, take it out for rides in the carriage, teach it to talk. It would be almost as good as having a baby sister or brother of her own—and her hopes of that were fading. Aunt Virtue quashed the idea whenever she brought it up. "Your mother's not getting any younger, you know," she would say. What exactly did that mean? Even she was not getting any younger, and she was extremely glad of it. Now she was almost eight, and after that she would be nine and ten, and soon she would be grown up and able to do all the wonderful things she imagined. Still, under it all, she sensed that Aunt Virtue did not want her mother to have another baby. Why?

Against one wall of the house's common hallway stood a small table with the jointly-owned radio and some magazines including pamphlets that Mommy got when she went to the missionary society at church. Eleanor looked at the black and white pictures of sad women and babies in India. Perhaps she would become a doctor and go to India to help them. For several weeks she thought and talked of little else. She would learn to play the organ for them as well, like someone called Doctor Schweitzer, though he had been in a different place, Africa. She would work in a hospital all day, helping the poor women to have babies that didn't die, and play the organ all night—a thoroughly satisfying life, and one that must be pleasing to God. She would be famous as well. Whether this would or would not be pleasing to God she didn't know, but it would certainly be pleasing to her.

If she was constantly thinking about this wonderful future, it was perhaps because things in the present weren't going too well. She knew Mommy didn't like the fact that she spent more time in Aunt Virtue's kitchen than in her own. Mommy never told her not to go, but when she came back Mommy was cold and distant for a time. Mommy would look at whatever she had brought back from Aunt Virtue and say, "Now where on earth are we going to store that?" It was true that Eleanor's tiny desk in a corner of the kitchen was overflowing with paper cutouts, drawings, crayons, coloured pencils, cardboard houses, and so on. Then her mother would sigh and look down at her ironing or the vegetable she was peeling or the dress she was sewing and say nothing more until Eleanor felt bad for her but didn't know what to do about it.

Now something new was wrong with Mommy. There were things called "polyps" in her nose, and the doctor had to cut them out. This sounded rather drastic, but Mommy said not to worry; the doctor would make it so it wouldn't hurt when he cut, and then she would be able to breathe better. But Eleanor did worry, and on the day Mommy went to the doctor's office to have it done she couldn't concentrate at all in school and got less than ninety-five percent on a test for the first time. Then she temporarily forgot all about Mommy in the shame she suffered.

❦

Emma grieved for Joan; how could she not? Having a child was the most amazing thing that had ever happened to her, and she had thought her sister would know that joy for herself. Still, she could not understand Virtue's obsession. She talked about it incessantly. What could they do to help poor Joan? Emma thought she had done quite enough in the past for "poor Joan," and if Virtue felt she had not come up to the mark well, that was unfortunate, but it couldn't be rectified now.

What Emma grieved more for, however, was the loss of her own daughter to this strange sister across the hall. Virtue had always wanted Eleanor; she knew that, but her efforts now seemed to take on a new intensity. All this stuff that she was forever buying! Much of it was worthless junk that she got from the five and ten-cent store. Eleanor loved it, of course, but Eleanor was merely a child. Still, how could she stop it? She couldn't prevent Eleanor from crossing the hall in a house where the doors always had to be open, particularly in winter, because the single furnace grate stood in the centre. She would just have to wait and let whatever was motivating Virtue run its course.

Now she had other things to worry about. She dismissed the polyps when talking to Nathan or Eleanor, but, in fact, she worried. She thought of her own mother dying in her fifties, worn out by life in the backwoods. Worn out also by the despair that it seemed had over-taken her. Emma now felt a despair of her own. They would never have enough money to build a house; they would live forever down here surrounded by the smell of fish and commerce, and the sound of Willy Frank's radio. Eleanor was the only thing she lived for. She, at least, might eventually escape.

Her own escape came through reading. She had always read, but now she turned to something new—not the classics that nourished her in her youth, but the tawdry romances printed on the inserts of the weekend paper. They were rubbish, she knew that, but they were absorbing rubbish. At night she sat in a chair that she hauled over the grate of the front hall furnace, a place warm and comforting. Nathan and Eleanor were in bed; the house was quiet, and she was alone. On and on she read, regardless of time, until a small voice would call out over the banister, "Mommy, are you coming to bed?" Eleanor, the little tyrant, would not give her even this respite from reality. She refused to give in immediately, but eventually she would move her chair back into the kitchen, fold up the paper, and ascend the stairs.

"Kiss me, Mommy, I'm still awake."

"I can see that." Emma would kiss the recalcitrant child and then crawl into bed beside a sleeping Nathan.

❦

A fair little girl sat under a tree,
Sewing as long as her eyes could see.
Then smoothed her work, and folded it right,
And said, 'Dear work, good night, good night.'

Eleanor was the fair little girl, sitting with her work under the big tree in the garden, as the birds and the animals crept back silently to their homes for the night. She was the perfect little girl, making her Mommy happy by doing her homework, writing little poems for her, reading the books she suggested, going to bed on time. It was a life of perfect obedience to Mommy and, by extension, a life of obedience to God, because obeying your parents was what God wanted you to do. He also wanted you to do your work to the best of your ability because you were put on earth for a purpose, and that purpose had something to do with working, not just having fun. In fact, having fun didn't seem to fit into God's plan at all. She would work, then, and be good.

The evening light of late August slanted, coloured and dappled, through the fluttering leaves. A few robins called out to their mates. She thought she was happy.

PART II
White Light

CHAPTER 8
1954

A Sunday afternoon in early June. Outside the bathroom window Eleanor could see ships' masts perched like crenellations over the roofs of the red shipping supply stores. Inside white sunlight reflected off the pale blue bathroom walls, attempting to nourish the three straggly geranium plants on the bay window seat.

She stood combing her hair and looking at her almost twelve-year-old self in the mirror over the basin. She liked what she saw—wavy light-brown hair, serious blue eyes with eyebrows that turned slightly upwards at the outer edge like question marks, a finely chiseled nose. The last school exams of the year were over so there was no weekend homework. The rest of the day stretched out enticingly.

This afternoon they were going to visit old friends of her mother's in Waldenstein, and Donna had been invited to accompany them. While their elders talked, she and Donna would revert to childhood for a few hours. Old Mr. Conrad would throw hay down from the loft for them to jump and hide in. Then they would lie back, enveloped in its sweet smell, watching the dust float lazily in the sunbeams shining through the small window high in the peak of the roof. Mrs. Conrad would ask them to stay for supper—fried venison followed by fresh-picked strawberries and cream and three different kinds of cake.

Suddenly Eleanor was seized by an overwhelming and irrational joy. Everything was perfect; life itself was perfect. The face in the mirror received and held the intensity of the moment.

Off to one side, high in a corner of the mirror, something flickered—a gull's wing over a ship's mast, a shadow. A faint unease stirred the face in the mirror. "No, there's something else. Something not perfect. I can't remember." A vague fear trembled. Then it came to her. "Oh yes. Of course. That's it. I'm going to die."

❧

Emma stood by the kitchen washing machine as the agitator went back and forth, round and round, singing its own little song of despair.

"Keep it up, keep it up, wash again, wash again." Sometimes when Eleanor was little she made up funny verses that the washing machine sang, and they would repeat them together as the machine flip-flopped the clothes. "Eleanor, Eleanor, watch me sing, watch me sing," all on a two-note rhythm, a third apart. But today Emma was not in a mood for games with her machine. She hated it—the noise, the wringer that got the clothes all tangled up around it and, most of all, the self-satis-fied faces of their majesties George VI and his Queen who, set between crossed Union Jacks under a coat of arms, adorned the decal placed on the front of the tub of the "Coronation Model" machine.

Just as the clothes were in an intense tangle around the wringer, Eleanor arrived home from school for lunch.

"You here already?"

"Yes, I hurried because yesterday you said I must have dawdled, and how could you be expected to feed me and get me back to school on time if it took me half an hour to walk half a mile."

Emma bristled. "Okay. I'll have to let this be and get you something. Though goodness knows, when I was your age I didn't expect to be waited on hand and foot by my mother."

"When you were my age your mother had a whole pile of babies; all you've got is me."

"Don't talk back."

"Okay. Sorry."

A sullen Eleanor sat down to a cold and silent lunch, while Emma continued to struggle with the wringer of the washing machine. No sooner had she left than Nathan arrived from the barbershop. Another interruption, more food required. She served him silently. That was the way things often were now.

"How's your morning been?" she forced herself to ask.

"Pretty good. We had a dull spell around ten o'clock, but then it picked up again just when I was going to come and eat. That's why I'm late."

"Well, if it wasn't that, I guess it would be something else."

Emma could see Nathan hesitating, then he asked, "And how did your morning go?"

"As you can see, I haven't even finished washing yet, never mind got it out on the line, because this machine is so hopeless. And when I do get it out on the line, you can be sure they'll start spewing out dirt and dust next door, so that I'll have to bring it all in and wash it again."

Nathan was silent. Emma sat down and ate a few bites of bread and cheese. She remembered buying the cheese in the Dominion store on the main street last Friday. Apparently it wasn't the right kind of cheese. Louise Wamboldt, who wanted to make her an I.O.D.E. member years ago and dropped her once her true status became clear, was standing on the other side of the U-shaped counter. "Why are you buying that stuff that's all processed?"

Emma was stunned. Her cheese was wrong. "Mousetrap," Louise proclaimed.

For a second Emma almost took it back to the shelf. Then she pursed her lips defiantly and silently handed the money to the clerk.

Secretly, she wished she were like Louise—definite, sure of herself, her hair wrapped tightly in an elaborate roll at the back of her head so that no stray hairs ever escaped. In the local hierarchy Louise had a right to her pride. Not because she had once taught school and was a prominent Lutheran, but because her husband was captain of a fishing boat. In winter she could sport a dark brown mink coat with a fox collar.

Sometimes, in the evening when her husband was out at sea on the winter trip, she would make her way from the top of the hill she lived on down the snow-banked streets to drop in and visit Emma and Virtue. If it were snowing, she would stand in the hallway over the furnace grate, shaking herself like a cat, so that the droplets of water fell off the fur down into the furnace with a soft hiss. Both sisters would stand, one on either side of their living room doors, inviting her to enter. She always chose Virtue's room, not Emma's. Now, this lunchtime, Emma was eating cheese of which this arbiter of standards did not approve. She vigorously bit off a larger piece.

She could feel Nathan cautiously watching her, trying to placate her by his acquiescent silence. After the meal he moved from the table, took his dishes to the sink, and then sat down for a few minutes in the old wicker folding chair under one of the kitchen windows.

"If you're so busy, do you really have time to sit there?" Emma was already back struggling with the washing machine wringer. Nathan got up at once and looked at Emma sheepishly.

Emma stared at the chair, sitting there in innocent shabbiness. It symbolized everything that she hated about her life. "Take that chair out of here and burn it."

Nathan looked at her and started to say something, but stopped. After a few seconds he began to fold up the chair, but still Emma was not satisfied. "And when you've done that, burn the house down." She watched Nathan leave with the chair, but she smelled no bonfire. Neither did the house go up in a wild conflagration as she had requested.

Left alone, Emma managed to sort out the washing and pile it in a large basket. She was just beginning to pin the clothes on the line, when she became aware that she was not alone in the garden. A well-dressed man was standing behind her, and when she turned he doffed his hat.

"Mrs. Wentzell?"

"Yes." What now? Emma was in no mood for visitors. "Would you like to speak to my husband?" This seemed a reasonable presumption. Emma didn't have visitors—certainly not male ones.

"Actually, it was you I wished to speak with, if you have a few minutes. I'm Mr. MacIntyre, the new School Inspector."

Part of Emma wanted to tell him that nuisance visitors were all she needed to make her day complete, but her curiosity was piqued. "Come inside then. I'm sorry things are in a bit of a mess, but it's washing day."

She took him into the living room. At one glance she took in the worn edges on the plush sofa, the shabby floor covering, the tired curtains. She was sure Mr. MacIntyre saw them as well. She was dressed in her everyday doing-housework dress. She bade the stranger sit.

He began at once. "We have a bit of a problem with our school in First South. The teacher who took over there at the beginning of this term has had family difficulties and doesn't feel she can continue, and we wondered whether you could help us out."

Joy and fear sprang up simultaneously. "But I haven't taught for twenty years—since I got married. Everything must have changed."

"Some things have changed, of course, but the basics of good teaching haven't. Your sister is an excellent teacher, and I'm sure you are in no way inferior."

In no way inferior to Virtue. Well, she certainly had never considered herself so! "Thank you for your confidence in me. What is the school like?"

"It's really very much like the schools you were teaching in twenty years ago, I'm afraid. All of the grades up to eight, and all in one room. We're building a new school that will take in children from a wider area, so that we can then have a teacher for every grade, but that's still at least two years away."

"Would this be a permanent job?"

"Well, at least until the new school opens and this one is closed down. And even then, we certainly plan to rehire all the present successful teachers for the new school if they wish to be employed there."

All the despair of the morning fell away as Emma contemplated going back to teaching. Standing in front of all those faces every morning, talking to them about literature, history, music—all those things from which she was so sadly cut off. As a bonus, there might actually be some money. She could help Nathan save for the house. In the shabby living room, Emma saw the new house rising above the linoleum, glorious as the New Jerusalem.

"I'll have to think about it," she said. "I'll have to ask my husband."

"Yes, of course, I understand."

"How quickly do you need to know?"

"As soon as possible. I'd say, within a week at most."

"I'm definitely interested. I'll let you know as soon as I can." Emma stood up. Mr. MacIntyre also rose, and made a slight bow. Emma tried to steer him to the front door to leave, but he was already half way down the hallway and left through the back door, contesting the billowing sheets on the clothesline.

Twelve years ago—it had been twelve years—she sat in the garden in a chair—the same chair she just told Nathan to burn—and then, too, a school inspector came into the garden and asked her to teach. Seeing that this was impossible, he went inside and hired her sister. Now, at last, her time had come.

She went back into the kitchen, forgave the horrible old Coronation machine, and washed it out carefully. She cleaned up the lunch dishes, and began to think about making something special for dinner. She looked at the empty space where the old wicker chair had stood; yes, she really was glad she was rid of that, but equally she was glad Nathan hadn't burnt the house down as instructed.

Only after Eleanor went to bed did Emma broach the subject to Nathan. "Well now, that might be a good idea if you was well, but you know...every winter..."

"I think I could manage. If you could drive me at first...I'm sure I could learn to drive myself in a short time, and then I'd hardly be out in the cold at all. I could park right outside the school."

"But you've just had them polyps removed. Suppose they come back again."

"You can suppose anything, but right now I feel well enough to do it."

"Well, we'll see. We shouldn't rush into it."

"That's all very well, but they need to know in a week. I don't have much time."

"Well..."

She knew he didn't want her to do it, and she also knew it wasn't just because of her health. There was something ignominious about having a wife who worked. Obadiah could just about get away with it and hold his head up, because he and Virtue had no children. But Emma was a mother. Mothers didn't go out to work unless their husbands couldn't support them. Nathan could support Emma and Eleanor except, of course, for the desire for a new house. Every year they saved a little, but so little. Eleanor would be grown up before the house was ready. Emma knew Nathan was convinced that she would be ill; she was ill every winter with bronchitis that aggravated the asthma. She couldn't breathe without her puffer even when she stayed inside the house. How could she manage a classroom of rowdy children every day?

She watched helplessly as Nathan tried to find an ally in Eleanor.

At breakfast he said to her, "Your mother wants to go out teaching again." To Emma's surprise, if he thought that Eleanor would want her mother at home, he was mistaken. Eleanor was all excitement.

"Oh that would be wonderful. So is there a job for you, Mommy?"

"Yes. In First South. Mr. MacIntyre came to see me yesterday afternoon."

"And you'll take it, of course."

"I don't know. Your father doesn't seem to want me to."

"But why? Why Daddy?" Eleanor appealed to him directly.

Nathan retreated. "Well...the way I see it, your mother isn't strong enough to take on a big responsibility like that."

"But you'd be fine, Mommy, wouldn't you?"

"I'm sure I would."

"Then it's settled. Phone Mr. MacIntyre today and tell him you'll take the job."

"We'll see," Emma replied.

The next evening Emma tried to broach the subject again. Nathan was wandering peacefully about the kitchen, first tidying, then making his peculiar nightcap—a third of a glass of milk, a small scoop of vanilla ice cream, and a third of a glass of Sussex golden ginger ale. The spoon chinked rhythmically against the glass as he stirred and sat down to drink it. Apart from that everything was quiet.

Emma moved to sit at the corner of the table next to him, her finger-nails gripping the oilcloth. She must be casual, make it sound like nothing important. "Do you want to talk now, or are you too tired? It can wait until tomorrow I guess, though not too much longer."

"Wait? What can wait?" Had he genuinely forgotten, or did he deliberately refuse to remember?

"The teaching. I mentioned it yesterday, but we didn't really discuss it properly then."

"Oh that. Well, I thought we'd settled it. You don't really want to go out to work, do you?"

"I guess...I guess I just thought it was a good opportunity. For both of us. And I suppose I might like it, yes."

"Oh." Nathan looked up as if imploring the dark, blank window itself to witness the improbability of it all. "Well, that's quite something you wanting to teach again." He put down his glass and gazed even more fixedly at the darkness outside. "You'll only get sick again, Emma. You know you will. Look at what happened when you did that Sunday School play. It nearly killed you, going out in the winter in the cold and snow and blizzards." He brought out the last word as if it had the power of a spell to conjure away all notions of teaching. "You couldn't be serious, could you now? Not really."

"Of course I won't do it if you refuse to let me." An edge had crept into her voice now—the sharp pang of defeat.

"Well, refuse...I ain't refused, exactly. But you wouldn't like it after a bit. You'd be sorry you ever started."

Eleanor burst into the kitchen, nightgown flying, and confronted her father. "I heard you, I heard you! How can you be so selfish? You go out to work, I go to school. Why should Mommy have to sit here and just look after us? Why can't she have something for herself too?"

Nathan dumped the spoon with a clatter into the now-empty glass and retreated to dogged defiance. "Why I'm thinking of nothing but her. I go out to work because I got to. But she don't have to, and I don't want her slaving and getting sick when it's not necessary. Can't you see some sense?"

"I see that you want to keep her here just to do things for you, never to do what she wants."

"Stop this at once, Eleanor." Emma burst in. "This is for me and your father to sort out, not you. Now go back to bed and say your prayers and particularly ask God to forgive you for being rude to your father."

Emma knew that, in the end, it was impossible to win against Nathan. He was not subject to outrageous anger or fits of temper like herself, but he would get his way in the end. He just kept at it, dropping his arguments over and over like water on a stone until, at last, the stone was worn into the shape he desired. He had carved wood as a boy, Emma remembered, carved it beautifully, shaping and polishing it to perfection. She had never envisaged becoming his piece of wood, yet two days later she phoned Mr. MacIntyre to say that, regretfully, she had to decline his kind offer of the teaching position. She gave no reason, nor did he press for one.

Some days later, Eleanor came home from school fuming. "You turned down that teaching job, didn't you? How do I know? Because Jennifer told me today that her mother was going to teach in First South. She was boasting about it—'My mother's teaching school now.' And it could have been you. They asked you first."

"That may be true, but you are not to tell anyone—particularly Jennifer."

"I already have." Emma knew that the fact that it was Jennifer's mother was particularly galling to Eleanor, because Jennifer was now her chief academic rival. Mark and his hoped-for train set had long since disappeared down into the middle of the class order, and Jennifer, who lived in an impeccable white mock-Georgian house in the new part of town, was snapping at Eleanor's heels.

"Well, that's a pity." Emma refused to say more.

✌

Nathan was convinced that he had Emma's best interests at heart. He also knew that she didn't exactly see it that way. But he didn't want her to go back to teaching. The reasons were too complex for him to figure out. Still, he wanted to make her happy. He had a duty to make her happy because he was her husband and also because he had just taken from her something he knew she wanted. What else did she want? A house, of course.

In a lull in business he sat in the barber chair and read the local paper. There was a picture of another barber, an old man in Riverport. He was retiring. Kind of sad, Nathan thought. He told Emma he only went out to work because he had to, but that wasn't really true. He and Obadiah fell into barbering almost by accident, after his illness made it impossible to go on working in the woods, but he had no regrets. He loved cutting hair, the tidy snip-snip of it, the conversation and male companionship. He loved the smell of the soap and the after shave; he loved the smooth gliding of the razor over skin, cleaning roads through the white lather; he loved the slap of the razor on the leather strap that sharpened it; he loved the steady buzz of the electric clippers and the more subtle click of the hand clipper, and the rhythm of the scissors cutting through the hair held up by the comb. Most of all, he loved the constant flow of people, the talking and joking, and the trustful way they offered up their necks to his razor.

Sometimes they confided in him, even asked advice. One man whose wife had left him came in to pour out a story of grief and despair. Nathan listened attentively, but feeling that this man's problems were too much for his humble wisdom, suggested he go and talk to his minister. The man thought for a moment, and then replied, "I think I'll go and buy a bottle of rum!" Nathan was at once appalled and amused. He could hold both perspectives on the man's situation as easily as he could hold a scissors in one hand and a comb in the other.

But Mr. Creaser, the barber in Riverport, seemed not to mind giving up barbering too much. He told the reporter it was just too hard now that he was eighty, standing on his feet all day. Besides, there wasn't really enough work to keep a man busy all the time.

Suddenly, Nathan had an idea. Why couldn't he take on this man's work on a part-time basis? He was free Monday and Friday evenings, and Wednesday both afternoon and evening. If he drove the ten miles to Riverport, he could earn a decent bit of extra money in that time— money he wouldn't have to share with Obadiah. Emma's house would be just that much closer to reality. Then she couldn't complain about not teaching, because the money would be coming in anyway.

That evening, he told Emma about his plan. "So you're going to take away the little time we have together," she said. "I scarcely see you now. Go out there, and I'll hardly know who you are after a few months!"

Nathan was taken aback. He had not expected this outrage. "But if I can save everything I make there in addition to what we're putting away now, surely we'll be able to move so much sooner."

"You know perfectly well that we'll never be able to move. You can't sell the house without Obadiah, and he'll never agree."

"Why not? Surely him and Virtue want a new house as much as we do."

"I don't think so. Not unless it was a new house we lived in together with them, and that's not happening!"

"What makes you think that?"

"Because Virtue wants Eleanor. If we each built a house, she would no longer live with Eleanor. She praises this dump of a place every chance she gets. Mind you, she doesn't live on the side facing the galvanizing fan, and she's not here to listen to Willy Frank broadcast church services."

Nathan sat down and tried to reason. "It's worth the chance. And we'll still have Sundays. And it'll only be for a few years. When we've got the house built and paid for, I'll stop."

Emma turned to him now, her face lit unflatteringly by the single large ceiling light in the kitchen, and he saw the small lines forming around her eyes and mouth. She was still beautiful, he thought, but she was forty-seven. He had failed her; he had not provided her with the home she wanted. But in those far-off days, how could he and Obadiah know what their wives would come to want? In the back of his mind there lurked dimly the suspicion that, so extravagant were her needs now, that perhaps no one, no one could give her what she really desired. Still, he would do his best; he would go to barber in Riverport, even though she didn't want him to.

❧

It was evening, and Virtue looked up from the kitchen table where she sat marking papers. Obadiah was working on a painting for his art class. There was a new woman in town offering evening lessons for adults who just might enjoy painting as a hobby, and Virtue had encouraged Obadiah to join. She was away so much of the time, and even when she was there she had lessons to prepare, work to correct, and so on. Now he was sketching out some faces, and she made little approving noises when he raised the canvas towards her.

How lucky she was! Her sister was a spoiled brat. Moody, fractious with her own beautiful child and her husband who—well, wasn't a patch on Obadiah, of course—but still was an honest hard-working man. She heard the arguments in the evening; how could she help it? She and Obadiah never argued. In the evenings he helped with the dishes because, after all, she was working as hard as he was. Sunday afternoons they sat after lunch in their living room holding hands, her head on his shoulder, like young lovers, until one of them said, "Shall we go out for a spin?" and then the other would instantly agree, and off they would go in the car for a ride and end up in some small restaurant for an evening meal, happy simply with one another. Or so she told herself.

On the other side of the house, she observed, there was always a feeling of tension—Eleanor writing an essay for Monday's class, Emma shushing Nathan because when Eleanor was doing her schoolwork she must be given peace and quiet so she could concentrate, Emma wondering aloud what on earth she could make for supper. Why did they never go out to eat? Because they were saving for an imaginary house. It was an affront to her and Obadiah to want to move; couldn't she see that? She was certain Eleanor didn't want to move; Eleanor enjoyed having two families.

Emma had always wanted more, even as a child. Look at that ridiculous flirtation with that minister. She never said much, but Virtue knew Emma was setting her cap for him. And all that Latin he taught her. What use was that to any normal person? Anyway, she was the teacher now, not Emma. She knew there had been a possibility—such was the public nature of anything said in the house—but Nathan put a stop to that, and quite right too. A woman with a child out working! "You can't have it all," their mother used to say. "You can't have it all." She was living proof of that. So was Joan, though Joan now seemed to have gotten over the death of the child. It had taken a few years, but she kept on working, and now Douglas was buying a piece of land to build on so they could stop renting.

Virtue cocked her ears. Everything was quiet now on the opposite side of the hallway. Eleanor would be doing her homework, and Emma would be doing...who knew what? Reading some rubbish, probably. Nathan, of course, was out working in Riverport. Emma would kill him if she wasn't careful, driving him to work at two jobs for her own selfish ends. What rubbish. Then she heard Emma scolding Eleanor.

"Do stop using endless Kleenex to wipe your pen nib. Kleenex cost money, you know."

Virtue's hackles rose. Emma was always at the child, but this problem she thought she could solve. She got up, took her sewing box out of the cupboard together with some pink and blue flannel that was left over from she couldn't remember what. Carefully she cut the cloth with her pinking shears, folded four circular pieces of fabric, two pink, two blue, into quarters. Then she put the four quarters together into a circle, attached them by their central corners, and secured the whole with a pretty glass button. Voilà, a pen wiper!

Across the hall she went, into the kitchen, and quietly put the pen wiper down in front of Eleanor.

"What's this?"

"It's for you. A pen wiper. So you won't have to use Kleenex."

"Thank you."

There was silence. Neither Eleanor nor Emma raised her eyes to Virtue. Still, she was convinced she had done the best she could for the child. God would reward her. But she never saw Eleanor use the pen wiper.

❧

A ring at the doorbell at seven o'clock one cold December evening, and Eleanor ran to answer it. Guests, oh please, guests! There stood Louise, furred and booted, her tiny dark eyes piercing through Eleanor to the inadequacies of the crowded house. "Do come in. Mommy, Mrs. Wamboldt is here."

Eleanor longed for visitors, especially at Christmas. While it seemed everyone else was busy visiting and "seeing the trees" of their neighbours, very few people found their house. Certainly, none of the "important" people in town—the wives of the doctors and lawyers and captains of the fishing boats—ever did. Louise was the one exception, and she only came very occasionally, perhaps because she too was a Lutheran, Eleanor thought, and it was her Christian duty.

Emma came out to greet her. So did Virtue. Louise stood on the furnace grate, her skirt billowed out by the puffing hot air, while the customary, subtle tug-of-war took place. "Do come in." Emma said it first, and switched on the light in her living room.

Virtue joined in, "How nice of you to visit on such a cold night. You must be frozen. It's warmer in here." She offered to take Louise's coat, switching on the light in her living room. Louise hesitated. Eleanor was sure Louise ought to come to their side of the house, because she had been the one to answer the door, but slowly Louise, as always, inched towards Virtue's living room.

"I've come to see you both, so I hope you'll both join me wherever I sit." Louise said.

Eleanor was always baffled. Why did she choose Virtue's room? It was dark with a huge fern on a stand in front of the window that blocked all the light by day and seemed to eat up even the electric light by night. Also, it smelled funny, probably because it was shut up during the week and only opened on Sundays. But choose it Louise had, and so Emma and Eleanor followed her and Virtue in. Louise settled herself on the sofa with its maroon blanket covering (Virtue had not been quick enough to remove this protection) and began to knit as always, her tongue clicking away quite as rapidly as the needles.

First it was education. "Now they're building this new school out in Centre, all the little schools will be closing down. I guess you'll be out of a job, Virtue, unless they take you on at the new school." Eleanor watched as Virtue opened her mouth, but Louise did not wait for a reply. "It may have some advantages, but what about the time the poor kids spend on the bus getting there? And who's going to keep order on the bus? Not the driver. He's busy looking where he's going. And not the older children, they'll be worse behaved than the little ones. Thank goodness I gave up teaching myself before everything got turned upside down."

Then it was the church. "Pastor Schwarz preaches a good sermon, but he does offend people. And he has his favourites, the people he goes to see all the time and the people he never visits. I bet he never came to see you, Emma, when you were so ill. No? I knew it! And I tell you there's a direct correlation between whom he visits and what they put in the collection plate."

Eleanor sat lapping it all up avidly. This was real grown-up conversation, with Louise using words like "correlation," and daring to say what she really thought—daring even to criticize the minister! Then it became even more interesting—at least for Eleanor, as Louise moved into real storytelling.

"Do you remember the Wichts out in Dayspring? No? They went to the church in East LaHave because they fell out with the minister in Dayspring. Well, Mr. Wicht died when their only daughter, Karen, was nineteen, and after that, her mother—what was her name?—Edna, I think—she wouldn't let the girl out of her sight. Now Karen had a boyfriend, Gary, and they were planning to get married in the spring, but as soon as her husband died, Edna put a stop to that. Karen cried and pleaded, but old Edna threatened to kill herself if she left home, and Gary made it clear he had no intention of moving into that madhouse to live. So, after a while, he just drifted away. And then Karen found out he'd gone to the States, and that was the end of that fine romance.

"The two women, mother and daughter, lived together and tormented one another for a good twenty-five years. At long last Edna died, and Karen should have been glad, but there she was, totally alone in the house, getting on for fifty years old, and nothing to show for her life except a dead mother. And then, the most amazing thing happened. Gary, who had been married in the States, lost his wife in an accident, and back home he came. And there, waiting for him just as loyal as when he left, was Karen. They got married within a week! Some people were scandalized, said she should have waited till her mother had been dead a year, but I said, 'Why?' She's waited twenty-five years, surely that's enough. Of course, they can't have a family now, and Gary may have children in the States, for all I know, though they'd be grown-up in any case. So it's a kind of happy ending, I guess. Certainly it's a surprising one."

Eleanor listened avidly. She lay in bed that night thinking about Karen and Edna, and what it would be like to have your mother thwart the very thing you most wanted to do. Then she thought, "I could write about this. I could write a play." She wasn't quite sure how one wrote a play. It had to have acts. Some plays had five, but that seemed a bit ambitious for a first attempt. Others, she knew, had only three, and three would fit the subject nicely—one when mother and daughter were in conflict about the proposed marriage, one after the mother had died and the lover came back, and one in the middle, a "waiting" scene, when the daughter's life was desolate. Except—she could change the story just a little, and not kill the mother off, but have the daughter defy the still-living mother when Gary came back after twenty-five years. Karen would then find the strength to do what she had not been able to do when she was twenty.

Eleanor began to write. Christmas vacation gave her the time, so when she went back to school in January it was complete. Should she show it to Emma? It was about a conflict between mother and daughter; how would this go down with her own mother? But she could say, rightly, that it was all based on Louise's story, and had nothing to do with them. Deep down, Eleanor was not so sure that was true. Sometimes she felt that she was simply—what?—only what her mother wanted her to be. Otherwise her mother would be even more miserable and cross than she was anyway.

When Emma did read it though, it seemed her pride in Eleanor's accomplishment outstripped her vague sense that just possibly it might have something to do with the two of them.

"I like the way you handle the second scene, with Karen's friends, who all had children of their own to talk about, coming to have tea with Karen, who lives in a completely different world and feels very alone and left out," Emma said.

"Yes, I had to make something happen to show what her life was like during those years, but really, for her, they were years of emptiness, so it was hard to think about how to make a story about those years when really they were just nothing for her."

Now what she needed was a cast to put the play on—and a place to stage it. Surprisingly, everyone wanted to be in the play. She gave the chief part of Karen to Jennifer because, although they were rivals, she knew that Jennifer would do it best. Alicia, a tall thin girl with fine features that could be aged beautifully, would be the mother. Donna would be one of the friends, and Katie, because having boys in the play would be unthinkable, would be Gary. Two other girls, Margaret and Rose, completed the cast as additional friends of Karen. They would put the play on in the basement of the Sunday school. The curtain would be made of bed sheets held up on rope supported by four forked poles. Flashlights and candles would provide spotlights and atmosphere. Costumes and props were salvaged from attics. Eleanor had never been so happy or felt so completely accepted by friends.

It all ended one day a week before they were supposed to perform. They were rehearsing in Eleanor's living room, when things began to go wrong. Jennifer began to speak in a southern drawl: "Why Mamma darlin' I don' know what you got against mah lil man. He's naace an sweet as your apple pie."

"But mah darlin, ah jus can't bear the thought of yo'all livin so fah from your mother. Why don yo'all jus move in here?" drawled Alicia.

Everyone except Donna took part in the charade. At first Eleanor remonstrated, "Oh do stop being silly. We need to work hard to get it as good as possible. We've only got another week."

Then, as it went on and on, she realized that it had all been planned and orchestrated well in advance. She became furious.

"Get out! Get out! You aren't fit to take part in my play. You think you can do better than I did? Then write your own play." She physically pushed them towards the door.

After they had gone, she noticed some sheets of paper left on the sofa. She picked them up, and there was the revised script in Jennifer's handwriting. She sat down on the sofa in tears until Emma came in to see what was going on.

"They were making fun of my play. They hate me. I'm never going to have anything to do with them again!"

The next day Jennifer sidled up to her and said, "Hey, I'm sorry. It was just a joke. Can't you take a joke?"

"Not about my play, I can't."

"And can't we still do the play properly?"

"No." Eleanor walked away.

Eleanor lay in a small bunk in a tiny wooden cabin waiting to throw up. It was the middle of the night. All around her other girls, some friends, some enemies, mostly Lutheran, were watching from their bunks in anticipation and horror. A kindly young clergyman and his wife sat on wooden chairs near her bed, a basin at the ready.

Why had she allowed herself to be persuaded into coming to this horrible camp? Did she want to ingratiate herself with the friends she had so summarily rejected over her play? It was one whole week in July out of her summer vacation, and she was hating it. Every morning they got up at seven, raised the flag, and then ran around the field three times. Next they bathed and brushed their teeth in the lake, which was full of bloodsuckers. The study theme for the week was "God's Beautiful Wilderness."

She had known it was going to be awful from the moment she unpacked her suitcase on the lower bunk she had been assigned, stacking up around her such reminders of her crumbling identity as she had been able to transport. There were well-worn copies of books by L.M. Montgomery, the script of a new play she was writing, and her comforting winter pajamas. ("It'll be cold at night, I've no doubt," her mother said). Among these old friends, her new sleeping bag, the dark brown towels and face cloth Virtue bought her as suitable for life in the bush, and the navy blue shorts with the Eaton's price tag still on them, jostled strangely. She arranged things meticulously against pending disintegration.

But it was not L.M. Montgomery who provided entertainment after lights out. Jennifer, wise in the ways of dormitory life, had brought several copies of *True* magazine, which she was busily reading by flashlight to Linda, the camp counselor, who was sleeping with them. "Florabelle, in her panic, dropped the pale muslin shawl, exposing her white bosom to Malcolm's passionate gaze. As she bent to retrieve it he forestalled her, holding her forcefully in his powerful arms." And Linda was encouraging her. Linda was enjoying these stories of love and lust. Eleanor was both outraged and terrified. Linda was supposed to look after them, but she had no intention of doing any such thing.

The voices went on and on. Eleanor could not get to sleep. Also, for one used to being described as "so much beyond her years," she suddenly felt childish and out of it. After a while she went outside the cabin to pee. Strange birds swooped overhead. Bats? Noises wafted through the semi-translucent darkness—scurryings, rustlings. Eleanor did not like "God's beautiful wilderness" at all.

Her fear of everything must have been visible earlier that afternoon as she stood hesitating by the side of the lake in her new blue swimsuit. Reverend Schwarz, wallowing in the lake himself, called out to her, "Sissypants," as she stood there shivering, watching his huge upper body flounder and dimple in the dark grey water.

Now, on her third night at camp, she twisted her head on the thin pillow as a wave of nausea overtook her. She tried to concentrate on the brown towels. "So right for a camping expedition," Aunt Virtue proclaimed. She thought initially they were rather nice teddy bear colours, but now she decided she hated the towels as well as everything else—they reminded her of some horrible soup of bilious mush like the one served at lunch the previous day.

Only Donna cared at all, but even Donna listened to the scandalous stories at night. It was Donna she woke when her plight became obvious to her, Donna who went to the camp director and his wife (thank heavens it was not Reverend Schwarz), and who now hovered protectively around her bunk. But even Donna could not halt the sheer physical determinism of what was happening to her.

Finally, it came to an end. The young clergyman and his wife left with the incriminating basin. The lights in the camp dorm were turned off again. Everyone turned over, heaved a sigh of relief, and went back to sleep. Except Eleanor. She alone stayed awake through the night, although she was no longer sick. She felt a mixture of shame and underlying satisfaction. Her play might never have made it to the stage, but whatever else, tonight had been quite a performance—suspense, climax, catharsis even—and a wholly captive audience.

CHAPTER 9
Autumn 1955

"I believe that God has created me and all that exists. That He has given and still preserves to me my body and soul, my limbs and senses, my reason and all the faculties of my mind."

Eleanor sat at the end of the large table facing the black eminence whose words rolled out, certain, sonorous, echoing in the wood-paneled room of the church hall, shaking even the dust motes floating in the morning sunshine into submission. Around the rest of the table sat her Lutheran contemporaries—Jennifer, Katie, Ezra, Janet, Paul, Eric, and eight others—fourteen in all. For two years they would sit here every Saturday morning—studying, memorizing, examining every facet of the faith. Then, when they were perfect in all this, they would be confirmed and ready to take the sacrament, holy and dangerous. After that, they were ready to die.

Eleanor contemplated God; she contemplated her mind. The mind and the soul were those parts that chiefly interested God, that were most God-like. That was what "made in the image of God" meant. The body was casing, discardable shell. Nevertheless, what she saw around her were bodies—adolescent bodies, too thin or too fat, pimply, graceless. They were supposed to be aspiring to a state of grace, but this was grace in another sense. It had nothing to do with the body.

A world opened up—a world of symbols, of fish and roses and interlocked letters, imbuing everything with significance. Even the alphabet, the ordinary alphabet that they used every day, was a set of symbols, Reverend Schwarz asserted. Of course it was, Eleanor could see, in one sense a wholly arbitrary convention, but hallowed by use over thousands of years, so that "a" was "a" and could be nothing else. The whole world was charged with meaning that floated over everything, while below normal life continued on its mundane path. Except that, in the ideal life, Eleanor could see, the symbols would not be separate but would irradiate everything that one did or thought.

"'The world is charged with the grandeur of God./It will flame out, like shining from shook foil,'" Reverend Schwarz intoned. He told them this was from a poem by a man called Hopkins, who was a very great poet even if he had been a Roman Catholic. ("Never marry a Roman Catholic; the Pope is the Anti-Christ and will lead you into all manner of error.")

Reverend Schwarz, it seemed, was nothing other than the voice of God, his authority reinforced by the stained glass figure impressed on Eleanor from childhood—another large man, whom she now knew was Luther, holding his Bible and gesturing to his accusers, "*Hier stehe ich, ich kann nicht anders.*" ("Here I stand, I can do no other.")

The Bible, then, was the ultimate authority. Eleanor thought she knew the Bible quite well—at least better than most of her contemporaries. Every Sunday evening her parents read some of the New Testament aloud, and once the Revised Standard Version existed they would read the passage from both translations and discuss which was better. One Saturday she asked Reverend Schwarz what he thought. "There is no question," he pontificated, "that the new translation is clearer and more accurate than the King James' translation."

"But the King James' sounds nicer," Eleanor persisted.

"That's not the point," he said.

Eleanor sat back in her chair, unconvinced. Couldn't the sound of words subtly change their meaning? Or at least the feel of their meaning? This was a question she felt she was not going to get answered in confirmation class.

Gradually, as the weeks progressed, there were other questions, huge questions, frightening questions. They seemed to come to her alone, while the others skirted on the trivial edges of the literal. Jennifer listened obediently, worked diligently, and asked nice intellectual but orthodox questions like which of the Gospel accounts of the crucifixion came first and in what respect the other accounts differed from it. Janet, tiny and fluffy-haired, asked questions that were manifestly silly. "Can you run into a spirit with an airplane, Reverend Schwarz?"

Reverend Schwarz sighed. "No Janet, you cannot run into a spirit with an airplane, because a spirit is an immaterial substance, and even the air through which the plane moves, though it seems insubstantial, is in fact material."

"Material? You mean like clothes?"

"I mean it is physical, something you can touch and measure. At any given time, it is in a particular place. A spirit has no such properties."

One Saturday Eleanor finally said, "How do we know, how can we be sure?"

"Of what, Eleanor?"

"Of...of all of it. The angels, the shepherds, the Resurrection, everything."

"Because it is written in the Bible. Look at the Old Testament prophecies, 'But thou, Bethlehem...though thou be little among the thousands of Judah...' and all the psalms we have studied foretelling the Passion. You remember all those, Eleanor, I am sure you do."

"Yes, I remember them, of course, but suppose...suppose when they were written, they didn't really mean what the writers of the New Testament wanted them to mean?"

Wanted them to mean. Not even thought they meant. How had she said that? The devil must have tempted her to say that. Behold, your adversary, the devil, as a roaring lion, walketh about, seeking whom he may devour. Rather curiously, Eleanor was more certain she believed in the devil than in God.

For a moment she thought Reverend Schwarz was about to become a roaring lion and devour her. Then he said, with finality, "The Bible is the inspired and unerring record of what God has revealed to man concerning Himself and the Way of Salvation." That was Luther again. It was also the end of the argument. Then, almost as a concession, he added, "If you wish to discuss these things, Eleanor, which are of limited interest to the rest of the class, you can stay afterwards to talk with me about them."

She stared back at him. It was true that, with the possible exception of Jennifer, the rest of the class were in various poses of indifference, slouching in their seats, doodling with pencils, or staring vacantly into space, but that was just how they were all the time, here and in school as well. It wasn't because she had raised something particularly boring. In fact, it wasn't boring at all. Reverend Schwarz just didn't want to answer that particular question. Why? She had wanted him to refute her suggestion, but he didn't. He just refused to discuss it. He didn't like her anyway. He had called her "sissypants."

She sat sullenly in her chair at the end of the table when the others left. Reverend Schwarz also sat motionless at the other end, twenty feet away. Thin sunlight curled through the ornamental glass onto the oak table.

"So, Eleanor, you want to know how we can know these things. You are, of course, a clever girl, Eleanor, but you must remember you are not as clever as God. You cannot hope to understand God or His ways. It is very wrong of you to imagine you can and try to do so. The mind can be a snare, and a proud and haughty mind can lead to great evil."

"But God created the mind. He created my mind."

"God created your mind so that it might work to His greater glory, not to set yourself in defiance against Him. This is a great danger that you, above all, must be aware of."

Suddenly she wanted to cry. What he asked was impossible; she could not stop thinking! But sitting there before him—cold, impassive, dressed in clerical black, huge at his end of the immense table—she held back her tears. She simply said, "I see. Thank you," and left. He remained perfectly still as she walked out the door.

～

Emma was making apple pies when Eleanor came back from confirmation class. The scents of apple, sweet cinnamon and nutmeg wafted about on the oven-warmed air. Pure comfort.

"Can I have a piece now, while they're hot?"

"Oh, I suppose, if you must. The filling will run, but go ahead."

Eleanor settled into the pie. Emma looked at her daughter, concentrating on eating the pie, her face closed, impenetrable.

"Good class? What are you studying now?"

"We're on to the Creed. First article. We memorized Luther's explanation."

"Splendid." Emma began to recite the whole thing.

Eleanor said, "You know, I'm not sure I believe any of this stuff."

Emma was genuinely shocked. "You mean you're not sure you believe in God?"

"Well, sort of. At least—not as He is in the Bible."

Never, even in her most rebellious thoughts as a child, even while she was running around Waldenstein looking at the scratches on rocks and deciding that yes, there had been an ice age, had Emma gone this far.

"I want to believe it, of course. It would be impossible to be in a world without God."

"What do you mean, impossible?"

"I mean, there just wouldn't be any point. Get up in the morning, brush your teeth, eat breakfast, go to school to learn stuff, but for what?"

"What would you do if there were no God?"

"I would kill myself." The tone Emma heard was not of threat or defiance but of simple logic.

"Why?"

"Because there would be no point to anything."

Emma reflected that one could believe in God and still not see the point of anything and yet, against all logic, go on living, but at thirteen, perhaps living was not such an ingrained habit as it was at forty-eight.

Eleanor got up and rinsed her plate. "I'm going out to the barbershop."

"Okay, but don't be a nuisance."

"I won't. I'll just read."

❧

Eleanor loved the barbershop with its smell of soap and the coloured bottles of aftershave lotions, its camaraderie and jokes. When little, before she went to school, she sometimes entertained the customers by using the shop as a small theatre and reciting to the customers anything her magpie mind picked up—nursery rhymes, "'Twas the Night before Christmas," anything. Later she listened to the adult conversation there as she did with Emma and Virtue's friends.

Now the secret draw of the barbershop was *Life* magazine. There it was, brand-new today, and no one else was reading it. On the front cover Buddha sat, gold and shining, while the caption proclaimed, "The

World's Great Religions," and in smaller letters, "Third in the Series."

Eleanor picked it up fearfully, as if it were a tome of necromancy, and began to read. The spirit of the Buddha smiled down on her, impassive. The person who wrote the article not only knew about the Buddha; he seemed to find him plausible. "The heathen in his blindness bows down to wood and stone," she had been taught, but there was logic and coherence to the account that belied such a simple put-down. "In Buddhism there is no enduring personality as there is in Christianity, but many entries into life in various forms ending, for the fortunate, in absorption into a greater reality." Eleanor saw herself changing and dissolving, as if she were under water. First the distortion of refraction—because to Eleanor any change in the self would, necessarily, be distortion—then the decay and disintegration, the melting away into solution.

Scraps of conversation floated around her.

"Listen if dey makes too many of dem draggers, dey'res goin' to be nothin' left for de inshore fishermen. You mark my words."

"And what de draggers don't take, de Newfie's will. We never should of let 'em into Confederation, I say."

"Dis year, why dere's hardly any capelin for bait even. First dey predge in, and den dey predge out, and den dey're gone and de who knows where dey're gone to."

"The last stage of perfection," Eleanor read, "is to be absorbed into the Godhead." There was no agony, no dying God, no necessary pain. She read on, as she had read the two previous articles, with total terror, total absorption.

It was the wholly objective nature, the dispassionate stance of the articles that was so disturbing. In the first, on Christianity, the flood was treated as one of many such accounts in contemporary history. *The* flood became *a* flood. The dating and historicity of much of the New Testament was questioned. Christ was "a teacher and prophet." Again, the indefinite article stung Eleanor's mind with a sharp fear. She knew she should not be reading these articles. She knew this as surely as if they had been full of naked men with dangling penises.

She also knew, because her father would never read them or understand them if he did, that she would never be found out. When little, she had feared her mother's geography book with its picture of an erupting Vesuvius. Now this magazine was as explosive as Vesuvius but also enticing, and she could not tear herself away. She knew that the snake held Eve captive by staring into her eyes so that she could not look away, though that was legend, not fact. Now she herself was Eve, and *Life* magazine the unlikely serpent. "Oh God, help me not to think these things, remove these doubting thoughts from me." Eleanor repeated the formulaic prayer with one part of her mind while devouring the printed page with another. The comforting apple pie churned in her stomach. She continued to read.

At the end of an oak table God sat, stern and implacable. "The mind is a great danger, Eleanor," he said.

"You made the mind," said Eleanor.

"Not for this," said God.

Somewhere, out there in New York or another place as remote and improbable, a writer sat at his desk, thinking not of God, nor of Eleanor, but only of the most logical structure, the clearest description, the most appropriate word. For a moment, to calm her mounting panic, Eleanor thought of this writer—damned of course, you could not write these things and not be damned—but unknowing, indifferent in his damnation. Eleanor envied him.

❦

Always there was death. That was the point of life, the church taught—to prove yourself, to get ready to die. Eleanor looked at her mother and father and thought how very old they were. For her there might still be time, but they, surely, must be preparing for their end. Virtue too and Obadiah seemed to Eleanor suspended half between this world and the next already. How could they think of anything else, when at any moment the noose might close, the trap door open, for the final, inevitable drop?

On New Year's Eve they went to church. Others, some of her classmate's parents, were going to parties. Even Jennifer's parents, regular Sunday-morning churchgoers, did not extend their piety to this macabre festival but gave a party for their friends to which Jennifer was allowed to ask a few boys and girls from her class. This year, perhaps because of lingering guilt about the aftermath of the play, she asked Eleanor. It was a singular honour, and the thought of merging with that group of dancing, giggling girls and boys, of being able to allude to it later at school in coded signs and language—because those not invited must not be made to feel too bad—was almost irresistible. Emma did not insist she accompany them to church. "Go if you want to. You're only young once, I suppose," said with a sigh, either for the inevitability of the falling away from the true path or, more probably, for the even more inevitable passing of youth.

In the end Eleanor declined. What was more, she scored a major coup in persuading Donna, also invited by Jennifer, to come to church with her. Loyalty had been invoked: "Would you really sooner see in the New Year with Jennifer than with me?" And insufferable snobbery: "Look, anyone can go to a stupid party. Jennifer's invited a dozen people. But you're the only person in my class I'd want to share this with me." Also a dash of contemptus mundi: "It's important to do these things properly. Parties are not suitable for thinking seriously about what is to come. When you're dead it's too late!"

❧

Donna sat with Eleanor waiting for the service to begin. This didn't feel like the United Church she went to, where people whispered and chatted before the service and nudged and smiled at one another. The serious, austere faces of Nathan and Emma, Virtue and Obadiah were not reassuring. As for Eleanor, as soon as they entered the church she seemed to have moved into a strange and secret room and shut the door.

After a hymn and a few prayers, the sermon began. Donna knew she was expected to pay attention.

"The texts this evening are both from the psalms, those wonderful poems of David that reach down to the depths of self-examination as readily as to the heights of praise: 'Lord, let me know mine end,' and 'So teach us to number our days, that we may apply our hearts unto wisdom.'"

Two texts. This was going to be a very long sermon.

"The end of man is to know God—to know God in His immeasurable fullness and perfection. This is the task of a lifetime, always imperfectly realized, never completed. The applying of the heart to wisdom is the prerequisite for this task.

"But the psalmist here is using the word 'end' in another sense as well. To know God is the end of man in the sense of his purpose, and the final knowledge of God will only come with man's end in that other sense—death itself. That final end, that death, will come whether or not we have recognized and worked towards our 'end' in the first sense. And what a terror it will be then, for those who are unprepared!"

Why was he talking about death, Donna thought. Surely New Year's Eve was a time of celebration, or at least it always had been for her. You were supposed to be happy, expecting all the good things that were going to happen in the new year. That's why people had parties, wasn't it? Now he was finally getting to the new year part of the sermon, so maybe things would cheer up. But no. What was he saying?

"Suppose this new year is indeed to be for you the last. How would you spend it? Because as time ticks on, with its ever shorter supply of hours and minutes, things shift in their importance. The evening spent on the dance floor, the hour of idle gossip outside the post office, the minutes scanning the magazine rack in the drug store, all are subtractions from that small, precious, ever-diminishing total."

So the new year wasn't supposed to be a time of happiness at all, it seemed, but a year in which you just had to get ready to die. That did not sound like a lot of fun. She glanced at Eleanor, who was sitting transfixed. Eleanor was enjoying thinking about these things.

Outside, Donna heard a rogue rocket shoot into the sky, exploding with a pop. She had given up going to a party for this.

"So, my brethren, we must apply our hearts to wisdom. And what is this wisdom? It is foolishness to the Greeks—that is the world—we are told that. The world will always want its new cars and houses, its gossip and distraction, mistaking possessions for riches, activity for purpose. In wisdom we learn to see these things for what they are—a sham, an illusion. The wisdom we seek is found in the service of God, the service to others, the perfecting of the soul for its final journey."

At this point Donna deliberately stopped listening until finally she cued on the phrase "so give us grace that it may not find us unprepared," and knew that it was over.

At the end of the service, Eleanor turned to Donna and said, with in a tone of ceremonial joy and dignity, "A happy and blessed New Year, Donna."

Donna was too stunned to know how to reply. She turned to pick up her handbag and muttered, "Likewise."

CHAPTER 10
September 1956

"I shall learn Latin." Emma sat at the kitchen table looking at the pile of shiny new books Eleanor brought home from the first day of school. There, topmost, was the Latin grammar.

"But I thought you knew Latin, Mommy. That funny priest, who went back to Germany and then killed himself, at least that's what Aunt Virtue said he did, he taught you Latin, didn't he?"

"First of all, he wasn't funny, and secondly, he only taught me once a week for a year and a bit. And I've forgotten it all anyway. Now we'll learn it together."

She could tell Eleanor wasn't entirely happy about this. Was she afraid of competition? Did she feel that because her mother had done it before, she would have a head start? But there it was; Emma was determined to learn Latin, and Eleanor could hardly stop her.

The next day, Emma got her old Latin books from the attic and dusted them off. It had been so long. She could scarcely remember that girl—the same age as Eleanor now—who, all enthusiasm, had sat in a pew facing Reverend Selig and conjugated Latin verbs. That enthusiastic, confident girl was certain she knew so much and was capable of learning anything she didn't yet know. Now she was a middle-aged housewife, in poor health and conscious of how little she did know. Eleanor's life was burgeoning, while hers was shrinking. She tried to tell herself that it was wrong to feel this. Her beloved daughter—what could be better than watching her success? But deep inside she knew that one thing could be better—having just a bit of success herself. And she had just been prevented, cruelly prevented, she felt, from doing the one thing that might have given her that and made life more tolerable.

Yet, if she complained, others would insist she had nothing to be miserable about, nothing at all. She had a good husband who provided for her—worked himself to the bone providing for her. He didn't drink, smoke, gamble, or womanize. A husband who was free of all those vices was something that ought to rejoice any woman's heart. In addition to all those blessings, she lived in the bosom of a tight-knit family—oh yes, indeed, how tightly knit—with a sister and brother-in-law, both ready to help in time of need and, last and best of all, an exemplary daughter who was not "boy-crazy," who never gave her a moment's worry and got top grades in all her school subjects.

Emma could see their point. She could list all her "blessings," recite them every day on rising, but they didn't make her feel blessed. There was a hunger, a longing, but for what? Even she didn't know. It was the sense that there must be something more, something she couldn't find in life with Nathan, something she couldn't even find in her relationship with Eleanor. Anyway, Eleanor was growing away from her. "Well, that's what you think," she had replied when Emma suggested that a new hair style, copied from some magazine she picked up in the drugstore, might not be entirely flattering. She spent more and more time on Virtue's side of the house, talking about school and teaching because, of course, Eleanor was going to be a teacher "like Aunt Virtue," not like her mother, who obviously wasn't a teacher any more.

She opened the Latin reader to Caesar's invasion of Britain: *Exigua iam pars aestatis reliqua erat.* "By now little of the warm season remained." The words had a melancholy ring. Caesar had left it until almost too late in the season and now she, too, had left it until almost too late. But for what? What had she really hoped for? A child? Well, she had one. Knowledge? There was a library, and she certainly had time to read now that Eleanor was in school. What then? Meaning? Ah yes, that must be it.

Curiously, she felt the answer might lie in Europe, that exotic place suffused with music and literature and art. It hadn't saved Reverend Selig, of course. With the Latin book open before her, she allowed herself to daydream about ancient ruins and libraries that stretched for acres, and cathedrals where small choirboys piped glorious music from their tiny throats.

Emma stood over Eleanor, pushing her wet hair into shape. Every Saturday the ritual was the same. Eleanor washed her hair and then sat on a low kitchen chair while Emma "did it up." The fad of the time demanded wavy hair and metal wave holders, so Emma pushed and prodded the hair until the natural waves fell into place to be held by the metal clips. Then rollers went on the bottom of the strands. What it was to be fourteen! To feel life just beginning to open up in all its ripening possibility. Emma looked down on the beautiful hair, on the head bent studiously over a book, and wondered why Eleanor did not appreciate being young more. She herself had been—well, quite carefree. Life for Eleanor, she realized, was perhaps opening up in a different way. Now she was reading a history of English literature—a chapter on Thomas Hardy's poetry.

"Listen to this, Mommy."

> *Woman much missed, how you call to me, call to me*
> *Saying that now you are not as you were*
> *When you had changed from the one who was all to me,*
> *But as at the first, when our day was fair.*

"It's like a dance, isn't it? You can feel the rhythm in the line as you read it."

Indeed, Emma could hear the rhythmic ebb and flow of each line as Eleanor recited.

This was their special time together every week. Perhaps Eleanor really didn't love Virtue more than herself, Emma thought. They talked about everything—Emma's own girlhood, what life had been like in Waldenstein, literature, music, what had happened in school the previous week—everything except sex. At that barrier, real intimacy stopped.

"Jennifer has a boyfriend."

"Oh? What's his name?"

"Keith. He's in Grade Eleven. He's taking her to the next school dance."

"Isn't that a bit old for her? She's only fourteen, like you."

"Well, she doesn't think so. And Anna has ever so many boys that are crazy about her. They come up to her at recess and ask for a bite of her apple, just so they can be near her."

"And what does she do?"

"She laughs and teases them, and tells them they're silly, and pretends to run away so they can go after her and catch her. Then they hold her until Mr. MacDonald goes out to the playground and yells at all of them. But the next day the same thing happens."

Emma remembered her own mother's dark proverbial warning and passed it on. "'She'll go through the woods and pick up a broken stick at last.' Good men," she continued, "don't marry girls like that."

Still, Emma worried that Eleanor was missing out. Had she been so completely serious when she was a girl? She thought not. She and Virtue had got up to all sorts of pranks—harmless enough, but still mischievous. She thought of the verdict of Mrs. Black, the Grade One teacher, on Eleanor. She was "too serious." Perhaps it was her fault; perhaps it was because she hadn't given her any brothers and sisters to play with.

She had impressed on Eleanor, of course, that the one thing no girl or woman must ever do was to get pregnant and have a baby before she was married. "So," Eleanor asked Emma one Saturday evening, "how do you get pregnant and have a baby?" If this was the one thing to be avoided, surely one ought to have explicit instructions about how to prevent it.

"Well, it only happens if a man and a woman are very close together," stumbled Emma.

"You mean, like holding one another?"

"No, closer than that?"

"Well, how then? If you're swimming in the same place, could it happen through the water?"

"No!" Then she added lamely, "I think you're too young to know all these things. I'll tell you in a year or two."

"I'll bet Anna knows all about it now."

"Well, maybe she does, but that's nothing to be proud of."

❧

Eleanor was going to the Christmas school dance. This was not an unalloyed pleasure; dances were the one place she felt uncomfortable, unable to know what was expected of her. But Emma insisted she go, and made her a lovely dark blue velvet dress for the occasion. Of course it was a dress designed, like all her other clothes, to minimize the budding breasts and the narrowing waist under it. Still, it was a very pretty dress and Eleanor felt its soft luxury as she slipped it over her head. Then her mother carefully combed out her newly washed and set hair and told her she looked lovely. Did she? Eleanor was not sure what lovely was.

Donna came to pick her up; they were going together. She looked at Donna—the heart-shaped face with a dimple in the chin, the whole framed by dark clustering curls and large brown eyes; she couldn't possibly be as lovely as Donna, even though her dress was nicer.

As they walked up to the school through the darkness, they talked about forbidden subjects. "Would you like to have a boyfriend?" Eleanor probed.

"Well, I don't know. It would be kind of nice, but they seem to take up a lot of time. And they can be awful silly."

"Yes, look at Anna. She's nearly at the bottom of the class now, and she always used to be right in the middle."

"My mother says there's lots of time for that."

"So does mine. I think she's scared for me to have a boyfriend, but I don't know why. And she won't tell me anything!"

"What do you want to know?"

Eleanor paused because she wasn't sure she really wanted to know anything. At least, not until her mother was ready to tell her. There was a great mystery and a great fear. If she knew these secrets the universe might be unlocked, or it might explode. It might be enlightening or destroying.

"I guess I don't really need to know anything just now," she replied lamely. Then they were at the door of the school.

They climbed up to the assembly hall where everyone was milling about, still in disarray. Eleanor and Donna sat down demurely on the chairs arranged at the back of the hall. Eventually, the band got itself organized and the music began. Couples drifted out onto the floor, a spotlight following first one, then another.

Eleanor sat with her hands folded in her lap, trying to look nonchalant. As long as Donna was there beside her, she was fine. But soon a boy from Grade Nine came up to Donna, held out his hand and, wordlessly, Donna stood up and went with him. Now she was alone, and panic began to set in. What was wrong with her? Wasn't she pretty enough? Or was it something else? She remembered all the times she had snubbed the boys in her class, corrected their grammar, held their pronunciation up to ridicule. These scenes and others like them replayed themselves in front of her like a movie unrolling in the darkened dance hall. Why should these boys want to dance with her?

The walk home with Donna was cold and mildly scary. Why had she come to the dance at all? Finally, she reached her back door and flung herself into the warm hallway. Emma was there waiting. "I'm never going to a school dance again!" Eleanor said.

⁊

Even though nobody told her, Virtue knew Emma was studying Latin again. One evening when Eleanor was loitering in her kitchen she said, "You and your mother will soon be too clever for me, I guess. All this Latin you're both learning." Eleanor simply turned and left her kitchen.

Virtue stared blankly after her. Why should Eleanor behave like this? And to her, who had always protected her? She sat down for a moment and wiped her eyes, but there was no time to luxuriate in sorrow. Obadiah would be coming for his supper soon. Get out the steak, slice the onions, boil the potatoes, peel the carrots.

Just as Obadiah left to go back to the barbershop—Thursday evening, an eight o'clock closing—she heard Eleanor calling out goodbye to her mother. The back door slammed. The youth club tonight, of course. Virtue cleared the table, waited until she heard Emma running water to wash her dishes. Then she moved furtively across the hall. She stood in the doorway of Emma's kitchen, rubbing the small of her back nervously against the door casing, her arms folded in front of her. Emma, standing at the sink, seemed wholly absorbed in the washing up.

"I hear you're studying again."

Emma turned, as if surprised to find her there. "Not really. Not properly. I'm just brushing up on a bit of Latin from Eleanor's book. I'm sure I'll never use it."

"Oh, I see. You're doing it to help Eleanor."

"No, that's not what I said. Besides, Eleanor doesn't need help. She's perfectly self-sufficient. I'm really doing it just because I want to."

It came out before she could stop it. "Didn't help your preacher friend much in the long run."

"I hardly expect it to provide me with salvation. It just interests me, that's all."

Virtue gazed at her there, haloed by the bare kitchen light—a mother. Her childlessness shot a pang like a fresh arrow through her body, her useless body that had never borne or suckled a child. Yet, there was Emma, a mother who seemed to have nothing to do all day but what she fancied.

"Hmm, well there's a lot of things that might interest me too, but by the time I get home from a day of teaching thirty-five rambunctious children, and then do the cooking and the cleaning and the washing and ironing, there's not much time for interests." She pressed her folded arms more tightly together, still leaning against the door frame. Emma never asked her to come in and sit down any more. Though of course she would have refused if she had been asked. These interminable conversations held on the threshold allowed far more freedom of expression. Once she was seated in Emma's kitchen, she had the constrained feeling that maybe she was a guest and should behave as such.

Emma dried her hands and turned to face her. "You don't have to teach. I always thought you did it because you enjoyed it, just as I shall enjoy the Latin." Her words were controlled, but her lips were tense, her hands clasping the edge of a kitchen chair. Virtue pressed on.

"If it's so enjoyable, then why didn't you take that job when it was offered to you?"

"You know why. Because my husband didn't want to be dishonoured by having a wife who worked."

"Dishonoured. So that's how you see Obadiah, is it? Dishonoured!"

Emma briefly capitulated. "No, of course not. It's different for you and Obadiah because you don't have a child. There's no reason for you to stay at home all day."

That only stirred Virtue's anger. "Casting it up to me now. I don't have a child! So it's all my fault, I guess. Well just you wait. Eleanor cares a lot more about me than you. She even told me so one day. 'Mommy is so cross all the time, no matter how I try to please her. It's really nice and restful over here in your kitchen.'"

She watched her sister's face turn to a mask of stone. Emma turned back to the sink and picked up the dishpan, full of soapy water, and hurled it towards the kitchen door.

"What are you doing?" Virtue jumped to avoid the splashes, her panicked whine rising stratospherically on the final syllable as the soapy water flooded towards the doorsill.

"Get out! Get out of my kitchen!" Emma screamed. Virtue fled.

Emma had gone mad. She must have. She threw a pan of dishwater at her. She did it deliberately, not even caring about the mess it made. Virtue's mind flicked back through a mental file of the family to think where this dementia might have come from. There was no precedent that she could recall. She began to sob quietly, rocking herself on a kitchen chair and whispering softly, "Well, who would have thought it? All I said was..." After a bit she crept upstairs to get some aspirin.

⌁

Emma stood gazing in amazement at her kitchen floor. Tiny particles of food and dust floated out from under the Peacock stove and the refrigerator. A pencil rubber lay sodden by Eleanor's desk. Could she really have done this? Taking off her shoes and socks, she waded in. Part of her wanted to laugh. When she recognized this, she felt she really might be crazy, as Virtue now doubtless believed. Underneath it all, the resolve to leave this house strengthened.

CHAPTER II

January 1957

Eleanor loved skating. It was the one sport at which she could claim to have some modest ability. From November to March most of her class crowded the indoor skating rink on Friday evenings, but the trouble with the skating rink was that it was public and, worse, that you were expected to skate with someone. Lucky girls skated with boys. Still, skating arm-in-arm with your best friend, pretending to scorn the world of the opposite sex, was perfectly all right with Eleanor. She preferred skating alone, but with the others watching she felt odd, an object of pity or contempt. Best of all was skating outdoors, but for this the weather needed to cooperate.

There was little snow that January, still, as the sun moved every day slightly higher in the sky, it seemed, to Eleanor, paradoxically to fail in intensity. Its rays fell pale silver, solid and cold against her cheek. The back harbour, with no waves and little tide, froze quietly. Then the front harbor began to freeze—first just beyond the shore line, then up to the wharves and rocks, salt ice piling up in huge jagged cakes where the high tide pushed and broke it.

On the last Tuesday in January the school council announced that there would be a skating party on the back harbour the following Thursday evening. Now, after the announcement of the party, she stood at the third-floor classroom window and looked out at the frozen back harbour far below. It stretched like a wide translucent band from the town shore to another small peninsula on the far side. There one could skate alone in the dark, and it wouldn't matter. She would go to the skating party.

Nathan braved the icy January roads on Wednesday afternoons to drive to the barbershop in Riverport. He did not consider this a hardship, not compared to the difficulty of understanding his wife and daughter. Sometimes he blamed himself for having married Emma, since the life he had given her had obviously made her so unhappy.

Then he wondered if he should have let her teach school after all. But he was earning enough, surely! At least he was working hard enough. When he wasn't barbering in Lunenburg, he was in Riverport, day and night. The only day off was Sunday, and he would have worked then as well except for divine prohibition. And there would be a house, he was sure of it now. The savings were piling up, just not fast enough to satisfy Emma. The idea that she might have had other reasons for wanting to teach did not occur to him.

As for Eleanor, she was mostly a good girl, but now she wanted to go to this skating party on the back harbour tomorrow night. It was to be for the whole school from Grade Eight up, with a bonfire on the ice and hot chocolate and cookies at the school afterwards, she said. She was insistent that she must go, and Emma supported her. "She needs to get out and have fun with other young people."

Nathan was not convinced. Ice could be tricky. He knew all kinds of people who had fallen through up on the Nine Mile Lake when they were logging there. Look at Dilphin, his cousin! Dead in an instant! Once you fell through, you didn't have a chance. The cold, and the fact that you were under the ice sealed your fate. Just driving out to Riverport tonight, he had seen two single crows—bad luck twice over. What would he do if something happened to Eleanor? That time she had scarlet fever... But no one could have helped that. Skating on frozen salt water was just asking for trouble.

Nathan's mental landscape was populated with scenarios of disaster looming bleakly, implacably, on its frontiers. At any moment one might be swept in a logjam down a rushing river, burned in a lumber camp by a fire left alight all night by a careless cook, swallowed up in a smelt hole, choked in the frozen water under unstable ice. He had tried to talk Eleanor out of it.

"It don't sound very safe to me," he said.

"But of course it's safe. The ice is a foot thick. They've drilled through to test it."

"Well, that don't necessarily make it safe. What about smelt holes?"

"Smelt holes?"

"Sure, lots of them, all over the harbour. The fishermen go out, dig their holes, put up a little tent or cabin, fish for a few days from in there, then move the cabin and dig another hole. Then the old hole freezes over a bit, so you can't see it, but it's not solid. You skate over one of those and you're a goner."

Emma insisted that Eleanor be allowed to go. She told Nathan that he was simply wrong; Eleanor must go. Still grumbling and implying that Emma would be personally responsible if anything bad happened—she didn't understand the risks; she never understood risks; look what she had done to herself that Christmas ten years ago—he grudgingly consented.

⁊

The evening of the party was sharp and clear, with a small moon etched on the black sky. Bundled up at Emma and Nathan's insistence so that she was sure she would be too big to fall through a smelt hole should she encounter one, Eleanor sat on an icy rock at the edge of the harbour lacing up her Barbara Ann Scott figure skates. The skates were an extravagant present from Douglas. She was not sure if Joan knew. He still called her "Miss Mouse." She finished by twisting and tying the long laces several times around the top of the skates, then launched out onto the ice.

It felt quite different from skating on the ice in the rink. The artificial ice was soft and cheesy; it scraped away on the side of your skate blade. This ice was like polished rock, hard and impervious. She had never known before why skaters were said to fly over the ice.

About one hundred yards from the shore a huge fire sparkled high into the blackness. The wonder of it! Fire supported on a solid base of ice! Eleanor made a few experimental passes in front of it, then behind, then in ever larger circles, round and round.

As she gained confidence in the feel of the ice, the circles went wider and wider until, like a planet swinging out of orbit on its own secret trajectory, she moved straight off, away from the fire, out to the middle of the harbour. She was completely unafraid. Eventually she turned and looked back. There was the fire; there were the black silhouettes of her schoolmates flying to and fro against it, like manic performers. She was not excluded from them; they were playing it all for her, this exotic ballet of fire and ice. She felt strangely excited and began to skate again, this time sideways in a straight line, back and forth, so that she had the fire always in view.

Suddenly there was someone else, a black shadow in a rogue orbit like herself. James Rudolf, the doctor's son in her class, glided beside her, grasping her hand and waist. "A skate Mademoiselle?" She said nothing but let him take her where he would, with the fire always burning just on the edge of their line of vision. He was blond and tall for his age, but with a heavy jaw and broad nose. He looked at the breasts of primitive women in *National Geographic* magazines at school and, it was rumoured, at worse things in his father's medical books at home. Yet she let him take her with him in complete silence. Then, abruptly, he found her open lips between the layers of scarves and hood and pressed his tightly on them. A second later he was halfway back to the fire.

Eleanor stood still, astonished. When she moved again it was to swing out, out, and then, turning parallel to both shores, she flew off again in the direction of the narrow harbour mouth. The magical exaltation had returned, doubled in intensity. Music in her mind, structured, fugal, pushed her on. She was afraid of nothing, not even death. A Reverend Schwarz sermon transposed into a more urgent key. What would you do if you had one more minute to live? "I would skate," she cried aloud.

"Who's dat?" Immediately in front of her, so that she barely stopped in time to avoid running into it, was a tiny hut with a dim light seeping through the cracks. A miniature door opened, and a shadowy face back-lit by a kerosene lamp peered out. A smelt hut, with the smelter inside. So, they were real after all, the smelters. Her father hadn't made them up.

"I...I was skating. There's a school party."

"Well listen t'me, little girl. De party, from what I sees, is way back dere. Now ye're lucky t'be alive, d'you know dat? Because dis ice here is full o'holes just barely froze o'er. You goes down one o'dose, an it'll be a long day till you comes up again, my dear. Now you go straight in dere, near de shore, an' follow dat line back till you gets to de fire, an' you should be okay"

"I didn't know." A lie, kind of. She had known but hadn't believed. "Thanks. I'll do that." Eleanor sped towards the shore and back to the fire. At least he didn't seem to know who she was, thank goodness.

By the time Eleanor returned, people were taking off their skates and climbing the steep hill to the school. The library was warm and steamy with hot chocolate and plates of doughnuts set out on its tables. Eleanor glanced around for James, half hoping and half fearing he would come to her, but he was on the opposite side of the room, laughing with Jennifer. Apparently, he did not see her. She drank her chocolate, which was not as good as Emma's, and ate a doughnut, which was not as good as Virtue's. Then, not waiting for Donna, she walked home through the starlit night.

Pink-cheeked from the frost and exercise, she burst in upon Emma, who was sitting in the living room with the Latin book on her knees. "Did you have a good time?"

"Yes, it was wonderful, dark and shining, both at once. And the ice was so smooth and hard, much easier to skate on than the artificially frozen stuff in the rink. There was a huge fire as well out on the ice so we could warm up from time to time. Really splendid."

After a second, and superior, cup of hot chocolate urged upon her by Emma, she went upstairs to get ready for bed. The bedroom at night, with its curtains drawn against the ugly lumber yard outside, wrapped her in a warm, pink light. The walls were pale pink, there were two soft fluffy pink mats on the floor, and the bedside lamp was a little pink glass lady with an enormous skirt for a base and an even larger parasol for a shade. The bedspread, a luxury she had extorted from her parents only last year, was a deep rose satin. On top of the chest of drawers and the covered storage trunk in one corner sat numerous furry stuffed animals and dolls in stiffly starched dresses— reminders of past birthdays, Christmases, illnesses. The dressing table boasted a matching tray, mirror and brush set, precisely as dictated by *Seventeen* magazine. There was no make-up except for several small bottles of cheap and rather garish nail polish in a decorated cardboard box, given to her by some boy whom she had helped with math the year before. This desolate and shameful object was concealed in the upper drawer.

Emma came up to say goodnight, bearing a hot water bottle, covered in one of her many frustrated projects, a blue knit fabric of an exquisitely soft and silky quality that had begun life trying to be a baby dress for Eleanor and then, five years later, a sweater, and now, in its final metamorphosis, a completed hot water bottle cover. Emma pushed it under the bedcovers. "You'll want something to warm your feet after all that skating."

They said prayers together—silent private prayers, followed by the Lord's Prayer. Eleanor felt somewhat embarrassed now by this nightly ritual. Suppose her mother knew that her prayers consisted only of appeals to God, if He existed, to convince her of that fact? Impossible to tell her, impossible to have any idea what she might think. Her mother kissed her and turned out the light.

Eleanor could not fall asleep. She was skating by a fire, round and round, and whenever the darkness of sleep threatened to come up to engulf her it seemed she must either fend it off or fall into some inescapable hole, dark and flooded. After a while she turned on the light and tiptoed over to the bookshelf. In reaching for *David Copperfield*, she knocked down her old book of nursery rhymes that, to her dismay, landed with a crash on top of the trunk. She waited. Silence. Emma must not have heard. She was about to put it back, when she saw it had fallen open to one of Lear's rhymes:

Calico Pie.
The little Birds fly
Down to the calico tree.

Her mother used to read her that. There was an illustration of a bare tree festooned with what looked like patchwork quilts, with nondescript black birds fluttering down to nestle in them. Eleanor had thought it a jolly poem, full of good nonsense, but her mother had always seemed to see something terribly sad in it, as her voice lingered on the refrain:

They never came back!
They never came back!
They never came back to me!

Now Eleanor remembered the insistent sense of loss that her mother put into that silly nursery rhyme. She left the book where it lay and returned to bed. A luxuriant sense of melancholy filled her, and she slept.

Eleanor awoke from a deep sleep to a strange noise that seemed to be coming from her parents' bedroom. She lay warm under the covers, listening. It was a voice, almost trying to sound like words, but not quite succeeding. Then she heard other noises, the scuffling of feet, the bedroom door opening, a knocking on Virtue and Obadiah's door, quiet, urgent whispering, more sounds of feet scuffling along, some now going downstairs. Meanwhile the noises from her parents' bedroom became higher pitched and more urgent. "Noeful, noeful." It went on and on.

She jumped out of bed and ran to see what was going on. Her mother was sitting up in bed, distraught, one hand down on the covers, the other raised above her head in alarm or warning. "Noeful." The words played in Eleanor's mind, tricked themselves to "Woeful, woeful." Her father was trying to comfort Emma, but her mother seemed scarcely aware of him, or of anything outside herself and whatever it was her staring eyes were fixed on.

Virtue, draped in her long flannel nightgown covered with tiny pink roses, cowered against the wall near the door. Obadiah was nowhere in sight. It must have been his footsteps Eleanor heard going downstairs.

Now the crying changed: "Mona, monae."

Virtue raised her head. "It's the Latin. I always said it was too much for her."

"That's not Latin. I know Latin." Eleanor asserted herself, brought facts to bear on nightmare. There were things she was certain of in the midst of this chaos; she must cling to them. Her mother was mad. Suddenly she knew that this was something she had always feared, against all reason had expected—the breaking of all boundaries, the sheer terror of the meaningless cry.

As she stood shadowed in the doorway, Emma saw her and reached out her arms. "Mebus, maybus." Eleanor shrank back in fear. The gibberish changed into frenzied, hysterical cries and tears.

"Where's Obadiah?"

"Calling the doctor."

Eleanor stood on the threshold of the bedroom. She could not go in; it was too terrifying. What was in the bed was no longer her mother, but some inarticulate monster. Her mother could speak; her mother *was* speech. This object could only wail.

All at once, everyone was there—the doctor, Obadiah and Virtue, Joan and Douglas. It was Douglas who took her aside and put his arm around her. "I'm so sorry, Miss Mouse."

Eleanor shook herself free. "I'm not Miss Mouse. I shall never be Miss Mouse again."

When Dr. Willis came out of the bedroom he stopped to speak to Joan and Virtue. "A slight stroke, I think. We could take her to hospital, but it probably wouldn't make any difference to her recovery, provided she keeps quiet here. I've made certain that she will sleep for the time being."

He did not speak to Eleanor. As he went downstairs with Obadiah, she heard him mutter, "Unusual at her age."

All was quiet now in the bedroom. After a bit Nathan came out and held a whispered conference with Joan and Virtue. Only then did he come to Eleanor, standing quite still, leaning with her back against the railing of the stairwell. "Don't worry, dear. The doctor thinks it's just a slight stroke; she should be up in a few days. You go back to bed now. You don't have to go to school in the morning."

"But I want to go to school." Oh, how she longed to be enveloped by the familiar, boring routine of school. So that she might not be prevented, she went obediently back to her room. "Only a stroke." Why did he seem so relieved? Didn't her father know how serious a stroke was? Old Mrs. Acker who lived opposite the United Church had a stroke just before Christmas and died the next day.

All the rest of the night Eleanor lay rigid in her room, listening to the soft voices, unintelligible at this distance, murmuring constantly in Virtue's kitchen. Something momentous and awful had happened, but she had no idea, really, what it was or what kind of change it would make in her life.

At seven o'clock, she got up and locked herself in the bathroom. Everything seemed quiet now—at least in her parents' bedroom. The late-January light shone grey and bleak through the large bay window. It began to snow. The scrawny geraniums on the window seat were dropping a few sad yellow leaves and petals. She lifted the seat cover and sat on the toilet. There she stayed for what seemed a long time.

If only...if only she could talk to her mother about it, if she could just do that, just ask her what to do, what it all meant, it would be bearable. But her mother was now, and perhaps forever, out of reach, shrouded in some mysterious disease that prevented her from communicating with anyone. Maybe she could not even communicate with herself. Maybe—and here Eleanor was struck again with her original terror—maybe she was mad! All those times when she wanted her father to do strange things—like burn the house down—was that not a sign of impending madness? She could talk about this to no one. It must be her secret.

The living room clock struck eight. Gradually, she became aware of other voices and steps on the landing floor, but no one knocked on the bathroom door. The world outside the bathroom slowly penetrated her consciousness. If she wanted to get to school, she must hurry, and she did want to go to school. It would be the same as yesterday, or at least seemed likely to be. Nothing else was.

Quietly she opened the door and walked out. There was Aunt Virtue, wanting to embrace her. She didn't want to be touched by anyone, ever again. Especially Aunt Virtue, whom she knew her mother saw as a rival for her affection. She escaped downstairs and made herself some toast. There was milk in the refrigerator, so she poured some into a glass. She had no idea where her father was—perhaps still in the bedroom with her mother. She got her schoolbooks and went to the back of the hallway to put on her coat and boots.

"Where are you going, Eleanor?"

"To school."

"You don't have to go today, you know."

"I want to go, Aunt Virtue." She pulled open the door and was gone.

New fallen snow was the only thing that made Water Street beautiful. Even the piles of lumber and sawdust were covered up, and the electric saw was strangely silent as Eleanor walked by. Perhaps the men were late for work because of the storm, but Willy Frank must have made it to his shop. The loudspeaker was blaring, its vibrations jostling through the wind: "Praise my soul, the King of Heaven."

Eleanor walked on. She was early, but she decided not to wait at the corner where she usually met up with Donna. She did not want to see Donna. When she reached the school, she went straight into the classroom, sat at her desk, opened her English text, and began to make notes. No one would approach her now. She was safe.

The bell rang. First period, English. Mr. Ferguson, large, dark, and authoritative, strode into the room. Eleanor's desk was second from the front in the centre row. As always, he sat on the table of the empty desk in front of hers and put his feet up on the seat, his book resting in front of him on her own desk. From here he began to speak.

"Now today class we're going to start reading some of the poems of Keats. Keats, as you may know, died when he was very young. He never reached anything like my grand old age of forty. He also knew for quite a while that he was likely to die young."

Eleanor sat with her eyes down, staring at her desk. Dying. Was her mother dying? Mr. Ferguson was continuing, and she began to take notes.

"He loved the natural world, landscape, bird songs, flowers, people, and he also loved the world of art, whether it was poetry, painting, sculpture, or even archaeological pots that he came upon in a museum. And perhaps because he was so aware of his own coming death, he spent a lot of time thinking about the relationship between the things he loved that were alive, part of the world of nature, and the things that were dead, part of the world of art."

When you died everything disappeared—at least for you. Except maybe Heaven, if it existed. What did it mean that art was dead?

"He saw that things in the natural world were capable of giving and feeling joy and pain, but that they did not last. They changed and died; they were transient. Things in the world of art did not change; they were eternal. But the price they paid for that was that they could not experience joy or pain. They were eternal, but they were eternally the same. Now let's see what you can make of reading *Ode on a Grecian Urn* on page fifty-two."

So that was it; the art was dead only in the sense that it did not grow and change. It promised permanence, a world where no one shrieked in the night, where no one changed and died. Eleanor opened her book, hungry for the order of rhymes and stanzas on a white page. As she began to read her mind raced ahead, grasping the direction of the argument before it was fully articulated, observing the poem spread itself before her, quietly displaying its ideal design. This, then, was the world she would henceforth choose to inhabit, a world of artifacts, timeless in their perfection. A world without pain or joy.

❧

Emma's eyelids fluttered. Pale light pushed itself through tiny, fringed crevices, as she stirred. For several minutes she lay flat under the white sheeting, testing its weight. She tried to move, fell back. Her mouth felt funny. One side missing. She reached up with her right hand, traced the corners of her lips. All there, but odd. Gradually, memory. Something had happened in the night. Pure fear. She had screamed and screamed, but no one understood her. That was it. They refused to know her language. Malicious pretense.

Try talking now. Something familiar. "Our Father, who art..." What came after that? Give? Forgive? No. It would not come. She tried to say her name. "Em-ma...Emma." Good. She could manage that.

The bathroom. She needed to go to the bathroom. Slowly she sat up, pushing the iron weight of bedding aside. Her legs seemed to work. One, two, on the cold matting. Only her left arm wouldn't obey but hung limply by her side. She draped her dressing gown around her neck and shuffled towards the door. Before she could reach it, the door opened.

Virtue. Must have been waiting, listening for her. Virtue, at whom she had thrown a dishpan full of water not so long ago. Emma tried to smile a normal, nonchalant smile. The smile felt as if she had just been to the dentist. Even without a mirror she knew it was not right. Virtue took her arm. "How are you feeling now?" No reply expected, none given. Virtue guided her into the bathroom and proceeded to help her raise her nightgown and sit down. Then they went back to the bedroom. 'Do you want to go back to bed?'

"No... Dress."

Virtue took the flannel nightgown up over her head. Emma saw her body, shameful, breasts sagging, slack skin sliding off the bones. Virtue buckled it in. Bra, panties, slip, blouse, skirt, cardigan. Slowly they moved downstairs.

She sat in a chair and watched Virtue begin to make lunch. Virtue, she realized, was now in charge. She looked around her; nothing except the fact that it was Virtue cooking, not herself, was different. After such a catastrophe the kitchen itself should be transformed, ought to have gone out in sympathy, clanging its pots and pans, throwing its china from high shelves in a paroxysm of grief. But none of this had happened. The white curtains stood at starched attention; the linoleum floor gleamed from yesterday's scrubbing. Only she had changed, it seemed.

Virtue saw nothing ahead but self-sacrifice. She had managed to get a substitute teacher for this day. But for how many others would she need one? Of course, she must do what was best for Eleanor. It was hardly the child's fault. She looked at Emma sitting crooked-mouthed in the kitchen rocking chair. Emma had defied her, doubtless would like to defy her still. That, however, didn't look likely to happen right now. She thought of Emma as a small disaster area, subject to shocks and quakes that happier climes avoided. After each of these, someone, and it was usually herself, had to move in and mount a reconstruction operation. Then, just when you thought you'd succeeded, the whole edifice fell down again.

Part of her was furious with Emma for inflicting this on them all. But fault? No, not Emma's; she had just said so. Anyone's? Something worried her as she peeled the potatoes. She felt it tug at her. A tiny stab of guilt. No. Impossible. This time she had dreamed nothing, wished nothing bad. Her only crime was that she had wanted a child, and the only one around was Emma's. Was it so wrong to want a child? Didn't every normal woman?

Soon Eleanor would be home and she would take care of her. She found herself humming under her breath as the steak began to sizzle in the pan.

On the way home from school, Eleanor felt an undercurrent of terror, subterranean and swiftly flowing. As she approached her own back door she held herself resolutely still, poised just above the flow of the deadly current.

Walking into the kitchen, all was quiet. What had she expected? Cries, apocalyptic mourning? Her mother was sitting at the kitchen table eating a bowl of soup. Virtue presided solicitously over the soup and also over a huge plate of steak and vegetables that was, apparently, for her.

She felt embarrassment, horrible, inexplicable embarrassment. She met her mother's eyes briefly, then looked away. "Are you feeling better now?"

"Yes," Emma replied, after some hesitation. Eleanor, watching covertly, had seen her practise the word with her lips before speaking it. Emma's left hand remained folded in her lap. Her slice of bread was already buttered. Had Virtue done it?

Should she try to talk to her mother? What should she say? Was she really better now? Would she ever be better? If she looked deeply into herself, which she tried to avoid doing, along with the sense of devastation was a part of her that was just cross with her mother—a mother who apparently could no longer perform the simplest of tasks to keep the household and Eleanor's life running.

Virtue clanged around the kitchen confidently, keeping up a bright chatter. "Was it hard to get to school through the snow Eleanor? But you left early enough. It was smart of you to give yourself time. It's turning to rain now, so walking back should be easier."

Eleanor ate quickly, chewing down the steak without tasting it. Then she stood up. "I'm sorry I've got to go right back. I have this science project to write up with my new lab partner, Phyllis, and she lives so far out of town the only time we can get together is during school hours. She brings sandwiches, so she'll be there waiting for me now."

She half-turned to Emma. "Bye Mommy." She saw her mother's right hand reach out tentatively. She touched it and fled.

Days passed. Gradually Emma asserted her will. The second morning she refused to allow Virtue to dress her. It took an hour, but she emerged from her bedroom clothed and triumphant. After a week she could again do all the normal household things. The doctor was thrilled. "With your determination, this is nothing more than a little setback," he declared. Virtue, with a certain sense of chagrin, went back to teaching.

It was language that still evaded her. "Talk. Talk to me. Ask...questions," she demanded of Eleanor. So together they made a catechism of the daily routine. "What did you do?" "How was the weather?" "What groceries do we need for the week?" Slowly, ordinary vocabulary was restored, and the logic of syntax and grammar returned. The world rose up again as a structured whole, but wooden, static, without colour or feeling. Here and there gaps remained, shifting and treacherous—words that would not appear on cue to fill up the empty spaces, open pits and darkened craters that left their lunar scars on Emma's mind.

Eleanor hurried to shovel up the words as required, filling the frightening vacancies. Emma had always loved words. Now they were slippery enemies, hiding and taunting her.

As Eleanor helped the ordinary world to take shape again around her mother, it seemed simultaneously to be sliding out of her own grasp. There was so much she had wanted to ask, needed to know, things she had put off discussing—God—or had been sharply discouraged from discussing—sex. Would they ever get past grocery lists again?

When she ran out of excuses to keep Donna out of the house she steeled herself to tell her the truth. "My mother's had a slight stroke. She's okay, really. She just can't remember all the words she wants." Donna was matter-of-fact. "That's too bad," she replied.

Even Donna's visit could not restore any semblance of normality. Emma greeted Donna effusively—too effusively. "So glad to see you...gain. Long time..." Eleanor steered her quickly up to her room where they talked inconsequentially and ended up playing Monopoly. She could not talk about what really mattered, nor could she talk about anything else. The skating party had happened in another life.

*

Nathan was busy managing things. It was the practicalities that mattered. Once Emma could do the housework again, these were largely unchanged. The future? The future was the money he was saving to build a new house. That was what Emma wanted, wasn't it? He worked harder, longer hours. Work caged him round with a mesh of certainty. Thinking about things was only upsetting.

One evening in his brief supper hour he looked up at Emma, his mouth full of haddock, and said, "I guess it's a good thing you didn't take that teaching job. You'd've only had to give it up and make them find someone else in the end."

There was silence. A few minutes later he pecked Emma and Eleanor on the cheek and left for Riverport.

*

Virtue stood at her kitchen sink washing up the supper dishes. Her stomach hurt. Maybe she shouldn't have saved and reheated the sauerkraut and sausages. But no, it wasn't that. It was anxiety that was gnawing away in her entrails, shuddering against the bone. Why was she afraid? Emma was getting better now. She had a gift for drama, that was all. Of course, it could happen again; it could happen to her she supposed, but it probably wouldn't.

Anyway, Emma was not really the focus of her fear. It was Eleanor. How she had changed in a few short weeks. How she had changed towards her! But what had she done? Nothing except what she always did when Emma couldn't cope. She had cooked Eleanor's meals, washed and ironed her clothes, even secretly scrubbed the kitchen floor when Emma was in bed because she knew Emma would object. Her reward was to find Eleanor moving farther and farther away from her into some icy, impenetrable shell.

"Eleanor, come and have some nice hot gingerbread. It's just come out of the oven, and there's lots of whipped cream to go with it."

"No thanks, I've just had supper."

"But you could still have a little of this."

"Thanks, but I've really had all I want, Aunt Virtue."

Aunt Virtue! Virtue recoiled. This was new. It might have been a term of endearment, but now the tone was so formal and cold that she knew it was a placing of herself, a formal and respectful address devoid of affection. She watched covertly as Eleanor marched through the hallway into the living room bearing a stack of school texts, and arranged them round her on the sofa like a barricade. Did Eleanor in some way blame her for Emma's catastrophic illness? Or, more subtly, did she blame her for having survived unscathed longer than her mother?

A child, a child! She used to think, "A baby." Not anymore. It was as if the desire had grown inside her, maturing until what she now carried was a child, a Samuel, ready to be dressed in a red coat, and taken to the temple with thanksgiving. A child, bright and talkative. Virtue talked to him now as, in her imagination, she combed his curls. He was young enough to be trusting and loving. Eleanor was neither anymore.

CHAPTER 12
Spring, 1957

For three years now, Flora had worked for Mrs. Hirtle down in Vogler's Cove. The fifteen years before that she had been with Mrs. Marriott. When Mrs. Marriott died, her estate had passed to her niece, Mrs. Hirtle, two miles down the road, and Flora was moved with the rest of the goods and chattels. She could see that her brief outburst at Joan's wedding had done her no good, just a "tut, tut, there, there," from Emma and Virtue, nothing more. They were supposed to see that Harry treated her fairly, looked after her in "the manner to which she was accustomed," but Harry had no intention of doing anything of the sort, and Emma and Virtue either wouldn't or couldn't make him.

She worked for Mrs. Hirtle for almost nothing beyond her board, and being younger and more energetic, Mrs. Hirtle was also more demanding than her aunt. In winter Flora shoveled the snow from the driveway; in summer she mowed the lawn with a hopeless hand mower, and bottled and preserved endless quantities of fruit. All this she did in addition to the cooking and cleaning, washing and ironing. At least Mrs. Hirtle had no children, and her husband was dead.

Unlike Mrs. Marriott, Mrs. Hirtle stood on her position as the lady of the house, eating in the dining room while Flora ate in the kitchen. A Miller in the kitchen! What would her father have thought? They spoke little; Mrs. Hirtle seemed to think she was incapable of polite or substantive conversation, so Flora became practically dumb.

Once a year, Virtue and Emma would come to visit—not together, but separately. That meant there were two Sundays in the year when she got to wear her best dress, or at least the best she had, and Mrs. Hirtle allowed her to eat in the dining room with her and Emma or Virtue. She supposed each sister thought she ate there always, and she never told them otherwise.

"Now do make something nice for your sister, Flora," Mrs. Hirtle would urge. "I can spare a bit extra from the housekeeping money." So Emma and Virtue were treated to sumptuous fare such as was never seen by Flora otherwise.

Things might have gone on in this way forever—for Flora the eighteen years seemed like forever—but in the spring of 1957 someone else moved into the house—a young man, Mrs. Hirtle's nephew. Dan was an unpromising-looking sort, with long dark hair and what Flora knew Nathan called "bank robber sideburns." He didn't seem to have a job, but he was "family" and had to be looked after. Now she was cooking for three, not two, and cleaning and tidying as well. Still, she gradually became used to this sort of hardship; she expected nothing else. Sometimes she remembered that she had once had a home—a home where she had been loved; but mostly she put things like that out of her mind. They were too upsetting.

Usually Dan went out after supper to spend the long spring evenings hanging around with some fishermen when their day's work was done. But one May evening it was pouring with rain, so Dan stayed home taking long draughts of some mysterious dark liquid in a bottle. Flora was darning his socks, and when she finished, she went up to her small bedroom and sat for a long time at the window, watching the rain pelt down on the greening fields. Flora emptied her mind; she thought of nothing.

Eventually she heard Mrs. Hirtle climbing the stairs and going to bed. She sighed, got up, and prepared for bed as well. Six o'clock would come soon enough, and if she had not got the fire going and breakfast under way when Mrs. Hirtle came downstairs, there would be trouble. When she was under the covers she thought of pleasuring herself, as she had done in that brief spring so long ago, before Mama discovered what she was doing. But she remembered how strongly Mama had disapproved—and there was no one Flora adored as she had adored Mama—so she refrained and fell asleep.

In the middle of the night she felt something heavy on top of her, struggling with the covers as she instinctively grabbed onto them. The thing was holding her down and was grunting heavily. It smelled of strange sweet liquor that seemed to bubble out of its mouth as it covered hers. Flora couldn't move; she certainly couldn't scream. There was something hard at the end of the thing that was pushing and pushing, making a very big hurt in her insides. After a bit the thing slowly got up and went away.

Soon the early spring dawn began to lighten her room. Flora sat up and realized that her bed was bloody. She put her hands down to her nether parts, and they came back bloody also. What should she do? She knew she couldn't call to Mrs. Hirtle for help. It would end up being her fault somehow. Instinct told her to clean up the mess, but she didn't feel inclined to do this either. Then she noticed a button on the bed. It looked familiar. Indeed, it was a button like one she had sewn on Dan's jacket a few days earlier. Suddenly things became clear. She knew now what she must do; she must get out before anyone else woke up.

Flora gathered the few possessions she could stow in her broken suitcase, put on her wig and a decent dress and sweater, and crept out of the house. At least the rain had stopped. But where would she go? She could think of only one destination—Lunenburg, where those two sisters who were supposed to look after her lived in luxury. Now they would have to look after her or make certain that Harry did.

Out on the road she began to walk, one foot ahead of the other. Flora had no clear idea of where the road was taking her or how far it might be, though she had a vague memory from when she had travelled to Joan's wedding that there was a river—a river that needed to be crossed by ferry.

Flora had been walking for about two hours, and the suitcase was heavy, when a car drew up beside her. The man inside seemed shaken by her appearance—disheveled, down-turned lower lip, matted wig, crossed eyes, but having stopped, he couldn't just drive off. He asked Flora where she was going, and when she said, "Lunenburg, to my sisters," he replied that he could take her as far as the ferry. She then thought of a new problem. "But I don't have no money."

He reassured her, "You only need money if you have a car. Foot passengers go free."

The ferry, when they reached it, looked quite alarming to Flora. It was simply a large raft pushed by a Cape Island boat. But there could be no turning around now. She stood ramrod stiff against the railing, balancing precariously with the swell of the tidal river, until they reached the other side.

Which way should she go then? She asked the ferryman.

"Turn right when you get off here, then take the first left onto the Indian Path Road, then left again on the road in from Riverport, then right and that'll take you into Lunenburg. But it's about ten miles. You sure you're walking?"

"Yes, walking." replied Flora.

He shook his head and began to guide the cars onto the ferry for the return journey.

Flora picked up the suitcase and started walking again. This time no cars stopped; there were very few cars at all on this stretch of the road. It began to rain again. She could hear the rumble of thunder in the distance; it rained harder. The suitcase got heavier and heavier, until she decided she would hide it by the side of the road and come back later for it. The ditch she crossed to hide it in the trees was full of water, which she only noticed when her shoes were already squelching in it. Flora stashed the suitcase behind a large spruce tree, and put a small pile of brush in front so that she could find it again. Drenched through, she walked on.

The doorbell rang, and Virtue looked up from marking schoolwork. She guessed she'd better go. Emma had given up answering the door since her stroke—afraid she wouldn't be able to talk properly to whoever was there. Virtue scraped back the kitchen chair, made her characteristic little sniff, and went to the door. There stood Flora, dripping wet, making a mess of the floor she had cleaned only that day when she got home from school. First Emma's stroke, now this!

"What on earth's the matter? Why are you here?" Virtue had some vague notion that Mrs. Hirtle must have kicked her out.

"I left. I'm not going back."

"Well, come in. Emma, Flora's here."

Emma was already in the hallway. "Must get dry clothes. Virtue, you get?"

"Emma's had a stroke. It's affected her speech," Virtue explained to Flora. She couldn't tell whether Flora, in her deplorable state, took this in or not.

"I'm hurt too," she continued. "Hurt real bad."

"Where?"

"Down here."

"Oh, good Lord." Immediately, Virtue realized what Flora was talking about, and crimsoned.

So Flora was taken in and given a bath, and found some dry clothes.

Changing the sheets on the spare room bed, Virtue recognized that, whatever else, while she had been spared putting up Joan, she had to take on Flora—for the night, at least.

⁊

Virtue was on her way with Obadiah to see Harry. The situation at home was intolerable. In fact, a lot of things were intolerable, not least that she and not Emma was making this journey, because Emma could no longer argue with the wily and articulate Harry. As for Flora, she couldn't stay with them; she just couldn't.

Eventually Harry's house, one side painted, the other three weather-beaten, came into view. Virtue looked around at the unkempt farm, the general desolation; she was certainly glad she had escaped Waldenstein. The door of the barn was open; it must be milking time, so they parked the Oldsmobile near the house and walked down to it. There sat Harry beside one of two cows, his hands busy with her udders.

He glanced up in surprise. "And to what do I owe the honour?"

"Flora's come back," said Virtue. "She's staying with us."

"Where?"

"She's sitting in our kitchen this very moment."

"Well, send her back. What's wrong with her? Afraid of a little hard work?" He concentrated on keeping the milk pail steady; Virtue noted that after the first glance he refused to meet their gaze.

"She's been injured."

"So bad she can't work?"

"Not exactly. But she can't go back. It was the nephew of this Mrs. Hirtle that hurt her." Virtue thought this was the most tactful way she could express the situation.

Harry thought about this for a moment. "Well then, take her back and give this nephew a good talking to."

Now Obadiah cut in. "He…abused her."

"Abused. I bet she really enjoyed that. Most women do, eh?" He chuckled.

Virtue stood her ground. "You can't say that. Of course she can't go back. If we sent her back, she'd be his slave." Virtue suspected the status of Harry's wife wasn't that far removed from slavery, but it wouldn't be helpful to bring that up now.

"So, what you want me to do?"

"Well, you're the person responsible for her welfare, not Obadiah and me. You were supposed to build her somewhere to live years ago."

Harry gesticulated, his sweeping arm taking in the ruin of his entire farm. "And do I look like I've got the money to do that? Take a look around here. Does this look like a rich man's palace?"

"Well, you got all the money and all the land there was. And I'm thinking it was quite a lot. If you don't have any now, where did it go?"

Harry stood up, milk pail in hand, and moved to the other cow. "Times are hard for farming."

"I thought you were going to run the mill. 'Keep up a business in the Miller name.'" Obadiah, it seemed, couldn't resist rubbing it in a bit, and Virtue approved. She knew Harry despised Obadiah, his effeminate painting, his luxurious cars.

"Now you know that just ain't possible. A sawmill run with water power? How many of them do you see around here now?"

"Well, the farming must have been going pretty good, because you bought a big tractor and reaper just a few years ago."

"Oh that. Well, I got to tell you it never was much good. It's rusted something awful. And now it's sunk so far down in the field over there, I don't think I can move it."

"That's a pity." Obadiah just stood there. Harry kept milking.

To Virtue's disgust, Harry taunted him. "So, you going to help with the other barn chores or just stand there?"

Obadiah took a deep breath. "I'm not leaving until I hear what you're going to do about Flora."

"Okay, okay, I'll build her a shack if that's what she wants."

Here Virtue interrupted. "She does not want a shack. She wants a proper house, and Emma and I can make you provide it."

Then Harry produced his trump card. "So where does she want this proper house to be? You know I've sold off most of the land around here." He knew Flora would not want to live on the property anywhere near him.

"Well the more fool you. You just better work something out. I'm expecting a house finished before winter. If it isn't started within a month, I'm going to see lawyer Carter."

As they were walking back to the car Virtue looked back briefly. She thought she saw Harry spit on the barn floor.

⁂

Joan walked home from work at Knickle's Shipbuilding with Nancy, her friend and workmate. Nancy was a bit higher up the secretarial ladder than Joan. In addition to being a better typist, she took shorthand. When a letter needed to be dictated, she was called into the mahogany-paneled office of the company president. She had subtle ways of reminding Joan of this.

"When I was in the Master's office last Tuesday, he was holding up a newspaper report about a strike in Halifax. He said, 'Look at this, Nancy, just look at this. Picketing the offices of Nova Scotia Mining! It really does seem people just don't know how to keep their places as nicely as they ought anymore.' And I? Well, what could I say? I guess I'm just one of those people who still do know how to keep their places—or so he thinks."

Joan nodded acquiescence. Her place—what would that be? Somewhere below Nancy in the shipbuilding office, and definitely below her siblings in the family pecking order. But the latter was going to change, and all because of Douglas. She bubbled her excitement to Nancy.

"We're finally building a house. Douglas' business is going so well, he said, 'Why wait any longer? We need it now. So let's go for it. If we have to borrow a bit, we'll pay it off in no time.' I know it's not good to borrow—that pamphlet the minister gave us when we got married, it said, 'Wait for many things. Do not run in debt. Debt will fasten a chain about your neck that will compel you to look forever downward.'"

Nancy looked at her in amazement. "You've memorized that stupid pamphlet! I can't believe it."

Joan felt herself in the wrong somehow, naive. Why was it not good to take note of a pamphlet the minister had given you, all about how to live after you were married? She decided not to pursue this and returned to the house. "Douglas has got the plans all drawn up, and he can do all the finishing work himself, so…"

"So what? You deserve it after working and waiting nine years. That pamphlet was written by someone who was filthy rich I bet, and didn't know anything."

"Emma's been waiting a lot longer than that for her house. And now there's Flora…"

"Well, let them look after Flora. You certainly can't be expected to take her into your apartment. There's only one bedroom."

"That's true," Joan conceded. She didn't dare confess her real fear to Nancy; it seemed too mean. If they built the house, then there would be space for Flora and what was to prevent them from having to board her—for life.

❧

It was completely appalling, Eleanor told herself. First, she had to explain to everyone why her mother could no longer speak fluently, and now she had to explain why this strange creature, an aunt with no hair, crossed eyes, and a permanently pouting mouth lived in the house with her. Eleanor didn't fully understand the circumstances herself because naturally her parents thought she was much too young to be told or understand what had really happened to Flora. "Aunt Flora was hurt by the nephew of the woman she worked for," was as far as it went, so Eleanor imagined that Flora had been beaten up. But there were no visible bruises; she was simply left puzzled. Any further questions were met with a knowing silence.

Now Flora was always around. Supposedly, Aunt Virtue was "looking after" her, but in reality it was her mother who had to make her dinner because Virtue was away at school. In the evening as well, often Virtue was just so tired and had so much marking to do that Flora was in their kitchen. At least initially she stayed in the kitchen! So Eleanor retreated to the living room and did more homework and reading than ever before in her life.

"You might show...show a little s...sympathy for your Aunt Flora," Emma said on more than one occasion, but Eleanor did not feel any particular compassion. Why should she? She had seen this woman once a year, had never really talked to her even then, and as to the tragedy that had occurred forty-five years before—what did she know or care about that?

Flora was just an added complication in her life, a nuisance, really. Eleanor tried ignoring her, but Flora did not want to be ignored.

"How's your schoolwork going?" she would inquire, standing in the living room doorway.

"Fine."

"What you studying now?"

"Just now I'm studying about the history of the Reformation. Then I have some algebra questions to finish up before tomorrow morning."

"Algebra? What's that?"

"It's too complicated to explain."

"You just think I'm stupid same as everyone else thinks."

"No, I don't think you're stupid, but it really is too difficult to explain if you've never done any before. Now I need to get on with these things, please."

Eleanor would know she had been mean, and Flora would slink back to Emma in the kitchen and ask if there was any work she could do there.

The next night the same thing would happen. Finally, Eleanor persuaded her parents that she must have a small electric heater in her room, so that she could work there with the door shut.

"Damn him." Harry rarely swore, so his wife, Fay, knew enough to keep out of his way.

After a while, as he sat staring morosely at the supper she had prepared—baked beans with molasses and homemade brown bread—she ventured to ask what the matter was.

"Virtue," he snarled. "And Obadiah"

"Oh yes, I thought I saw a car in the yard last evening. Is his a two-tone cream and maroon?"

"Yes. Latest model. Nothin' less will do. Trades 'em ev'ry year. Virtue must make good money."

"So...what did they want?"

"Wants to ruin me, that's what he wants. Wants me to build a house—a whole house no less—for Flora."

"But I thought you always meant to do that, dear. I mean, didn't it say that in the agreement?"

Harry shoveled a huge forkful of beans into his mouth and yelled through them, "Don't you start, woman."

Fay cast her eyes down to her plate and said nothing more.

The next morning Harry went out to survey his much-reduced kingdom. There simply was no space for Flora on it that he could see. The old homestead had been sold, and apart from about one hundred acres of remote woodland that he still might have to sell if his finances didn't improve, there was nothing but twenty acres of pasture and farmland around his house. So what to do?

He got into his old truck and drove out the road. "Where you goin'?" Fay called after him, but he ignored her.

He followed the road in its wide circuitous route around the lake his old family home had stood on until he was at the far side where the Conrads lived. Ebenezer and his wife were old now, and all their children had moved away except for one daughter, Hilda, who had never married.

Ebenezer was planting some lettuce when he arrived. "Harry. What brings you here?"

"Oh, just a few little troubles that have come up lately."

"So...is there any way I can help?"

"It's Flora. She left where she was working and moved in with the lot down in Lunenburg, it seems. So Virtue and Obadiah came up to threaten me if I didn't get a house built for her."

Ebenezer moved from the lettuce patch and sat down. "Why'd she leave?"

Harry squirmed. "Don't know for sure. She took agin' a nephew that the woman had staying with her—or rather, the nephew didn't take sufficiently agin' her," Harry replied with a knowing grin.

Ebenezer did not smile. He shook his head and stared straight ahead. "Look, Harry, I'm not your man no more. My building days are done. I got arthritis so bad some days I can hardly pull myself out of bed."

Harry sat down as well and put his hand on Ebenezer's knee. "No, no, it's not that. I know you're too old for all that, but the problem is, you see, where can I put the house?"

"Why don't you build it in that little grove of trees just a hundred yards from your own front door. A pretty place, I'd say."

"You don't understand. Flora won't live that near to me. We..." He trailed off, unable to find the words—or maybe even the thought.

Ebenezer sighed. "So you're wantin' me to find a piece o'land on my place, here."

"Well, I'm thinkin' she might like a little place down near the lake— remind her of our old home. Of course, I couldn't pay much..." Now it was out, and Harry could relax. He knew Ebenezer would not refuse him. And Hilda, of course, could keep an eye on Flora as well. Things were working out fine for him.

By the following week, Harry got his oldest son, Peter, to come back from his job in Bridgewater, and the two of them began to build Flora a small house across the lake from where she had grown up. Harry felt very very virtuous; he was sure that so much labour should never have been required of him.

On a Saturday morning in early June, Eleanor sat at the large rectangular table in the church hall scribbling furiously. This was the final test; they would write this last exam, and then they could be confirmed. Eleanor did not look up once from her paper while writing out all Luther's explanations to the Ten Commandments, the Creed, and the Lord's Prayer. She was the first to finish, with Jennifer two minutes behind her. This was easy; the one thing she knew her mind could do was to remember words, the formation of words, their cadences, the way they rolled off the tongue. So the following week, when Reverend Schwarz gave back the papers, she was astonished to hear him say that there was only one perfect paper, and that was Jennifer's. "What did I get wrong?" The words were out of her mouth in an instant.

"Nothing much. You just left out one phrase in the explanation of the first article of the Creed. 'I believe that God has created me and all that exists; that He has given and still preserves to me my body and soul, with all my limbs and senses, my reason and all the faculties of my mind.' You left out 'with all my limbs and senses.'"

"Oh." How stupid, she thought. How intolerably stupid and careless.

"Very interesting that particular phrase should have escaped you, Eleanor," Reverend Schwartz said with a penetrating look. She winced.

Still, she had more important things to worry about today. Confirmation was happening in one week's time, and Eleanor was not sure she should go ahead with it. She had to sort this out with Reverend Schwarz, and she had to sort it out now. She stayed behind, shuffling her papers and books meaninglessly until all the others had left.

Reverend Schwarz seemed to be waiting for her, still and implacable at the other end of the long table.

"You wanted to talk to me, Eleanor?"

"Yes."

"What's the problem? Your little mistake? It doesn't really matter at all, you know. You must not think you always have to be first in everything. It's a bad way to go through life."

"No. It's not that. Not that at all."

"What then?"

This was hard to say. "It's just that I don't think I should be confirmed."

"And why is that?" He sat unmoving. He was the black-gowned Luther in the stained glass window; he was the black-gowned God in whom she no longer believed.

"Because...because I'm not sure I believe any of this. I think I know everything we're supposed to know, and I understand it, but I'm not convinced it's true."

Reverend Schwarz didn't seem as shocked as she had thought he might be. "Well, there will be time to discuss that later. But I don't think that's a reason for not being confirmed. We all have our doubts sometimes. If you're confirmed, then you will continue in the life of the church and I'm sure in the end your doubts will disappear."

Eleanor did not believe his reassurance, but she had been truthful, and if he still thought she should be confirmed, then she would be. After all, it was certainly easier that way. Her mother had made the white dress with a high collar and tiny loops and buttons down the back—the prefiguring of a wedding dress. And what would she tell her friends if she didn't get confirmed? The truth? That would be more shocking to them than any notions they might dream up. She would be a pariah. The girl who didn't dare get confirmed, because... Speculation would be rife. She sighed in relief, and left the church hall, closing the door softly behind her, to indicate that she was a good girl really and considerate and obedient in small things.

Yet she could not but wonder how, after two years of exhortation to honest and rigorous self-examination, she had now been encouraged to perform an act of dishonesty. What would the God (who might, after all, exist) who only by a special act of mercy refrained from striking dead errant Sunday School children who sat on the communion rail—what would He do to a girl who claimed to believe things she did not, who took the bread and wine "not discerning the body of Christ"?

When the day came and Eleanor stood and recited the Creed with the others, she no longer felt superior to them. They were blessed with the gift of faith; she was an outcast, a nonbeliever. Fearfully she opened her mouth and took the glutinous wafer on her tongue; she swallowed the wine and opened her eyes. She was still alive.

CHAPTER 13
1958

Nathan sat in his barber chair resting between customers. A slow Tuesday morning, which he quite relished. It had been three years now—three years of saving every penny he earned in Riverport without a single day off except Sunday, on which it would have been a sin to work anyway. Sometimes he looked at Obadiah, painting in his "spare time," whatever that was. Once, a long time ago, he had carved shapes—people, animals, a whole manger scene. He was good at it, so everyone said. But then life had intervened; Emma and a family had intervened.

He put the past out of his mind, and began to think about the house that now seemed a real possibility. There were still a few details to be sorted out.

"Obadiah," he began on this spring Tuesday morning, "Don't you think maybe it would be a good idea to move the shop?"

"What?" Obadiah looked up in surprise from his newspaper. "Whatever for?"

"Well, you know the liquor store is moving."

"Well yes. What's that got to do with us?" He swiveled his barber chair around to face Nathan.

"I've been thinking that it would be a better place for a shop than this—right on the corner there, where the men come up from the wharf, and a lot bigger. I've heard there's even a toilet in back, as well as lots of room for a little office to do the accounts and fold the neck towels." This was, perhaps, the first time in his life that Nathan had made a radical proposal—or a proposal of any sort—to his elder brother.

"But we own this place. We don't just want to throw money away renting somewhere else." Obadiah shook the paper, as if that settled it.

"We may own it now, but suppose we wanted to sell it, say the whole property with the house. I bet the plumbing business next door would buy it. It's the only way they can ever expand, and business is good, so they say. At least, we could find out."

"You mean move house as well? Aren't we happy as we are?"

Nathan did not reply, but he quietly set about discovering just what it would cost to rent the old liquor store. He also began to look around for a place to build a house. Most of the old town was full, and the lots, laid out in colonial times, were too small anyway. But out in "New Town," which had been all pasture when he and Obadiah arrived in town nearly thirty years before, all kinds of modest bungalows were sprouting up. At the very top of the hill with an excellent view of the harbour, he had seen a large lot with a prominent "for sale" sign on it. He told Emma, and the next Sunday afternoon they went out to look at it.

She appeared pleased but cautious. "It looks very nice, but I want to come back next week, when the moon will be full, to be certain."

Nathan was taken aback by this request, but in the context of the whole history of his turbulent life with Emma it seemed so minor that he acquiesced.

He was gratified that the moon did indeed fill out seemingly at Emma's request, and in one week's time on a warm spring evening they returned, bringing Eleanor to see the view. There it was! Straight ahead, beyond the gently sloping hill, the harbour glistened with reflected moonlight. To the left, pinpricks of light shone from the old town; to the right, a few houses lined the shore ending in a dark headland jutting out into the bay. Even further right, across the isthmus of the headland, another stretch of water was just beginning to shimmer. Behind them stood nothing but open fields stretching to the horizon.

"Ah yes, this must be it," Emma enthused. "We've waited so long, but it has all been worth it."

Eleanor chimed in ecstatically, "Oh yes, let's buy it, before anyone else does." Then, in the perfect silence of the night, Emma and Eleanor did a little pirouette on the land they were certain would soon be theirs, and Emma threw her arms around Nathan and kissed him.

✺

Virtue stood in Emma's kitchen weeping. It was eight o'clock in the morning; Nathan and Obadiah had just left for the barbershop, and Virtue finally knew a truth she could not bear. Of course, she'd had her suspicions—the odd word floating unguarded across the hallway, Obadiah's embarrassed reticence, Emma's unaccustomed buoyancy.

But now Virtue knew.

Between the corn flakes and the fried eggs that morning she had confronted Obadiah. "What's happening? What's going on? I have a right to be told."

Obadiah, staring hard at the yolk of his egg, broken, seeping into the white, said, "Nathan wants to sell the house and move."

Stunned silence for a second. Then logic. "Well, it's half ours. He can't sell without us. And what about the shop?"

"We're renting the old liquor store up on the corner. It'll be a better location—right up there where the men walk up from the boats. And the plumbers want to buy the house. We're getting a good price."

It struck her like a blow. It was already arranged. "You *are* renting. You *are* getting a good price. You mean it's all happening. You've done it without even telling me!" A smell of burning fat filled the kitchen. The empty egg pan smoked violently on the hot burner, but Virtue didn't move.

"Well, of course I was planning to tell you. There just didn't seem any point in getting you all upset until we knew for sure it was happening."

"And now it is. Happening."

"It looks like it. Nathan bought a house lot in New Town a few days ago, and Romkey Plumbing has made a firm offer for the house and shop."

"And where are we to live? I suppose that's all planned as well."

Obadiah swallowed the last of his egg and toast and looking at the clock got up to leave for work. "We'll talk about it later. It's nearly eight. I've got to be off now."

Virtue hurled the burning pan into the kitchen sink and raced across the hall. Betrayal! Obadiah and Emma both. And Nathan, of course. He had planned the whole thing. She never thought he had the wit.

Emma and Eleanor were eating breakfast as Virtue burst in and stood in the middle of the room, facing them. She had little idea of what she was going to say, but she knew she needed as much space for it to reverberate in as possible.

"You...why have you done this to me?" A cry of wounded outrage.

Emma looked up in astonishment. "Done? To you?"

"Yes, we've bought the lot for sale at the top of Harborview Street.

The view is fantastic." Eleanor said this briskly, almost matter-of-fact, but Virtue noticed that she immediately escaped to her room.

Virtue began to weep. "Surely this is our home, Emma. We've been a family. Why do you want to do this to me?"

"We're two families, Virtue. We have been for a long time."

"I've tried to get along. Maybe you don't believe that, but I've tried. We've never quarreled, have we?"

Virtue paused, suddenly remembering the night Emma had thrown a dishpan full of water at her. That wasn't really quarreling though, was it? It was just a fit of madness because Emma was getting ill. Maybe there had been some difficulties—particularly since Eleanor was born—but what was life without difficulties?

"Well, not really quarreled, perhaps," Emma replied. "But maybe just getting on isn't the best way to live."

"If there's things you'd like changed, we could talk about it." Tears glistened now on the bow of Virtue's navy and white striped blouse. "I just don't understand..."

Emma sat quietly at the table. "It isn't a matter of changing a few things. It's just not how other families live, two together, cramped and on top of one another."

Something broke within Virtue. So that was how Emma had seen all their years together, "cramped and on top of one another." Now Emma would queen it in the new part of town, looking down from the top of her hill. What she said next astonished even her.

"You're just doing this to take Eleanor away from me!"

For a moment the words hung suspended between them, dark and heavy in the moist kitchen air. Then Virtue turned and fled.

❧

The teacup in Emma's hand shook as she continued to sit at the table. Everything else was silent. The back door slammed as Virtue left for school.

What had happened? Was it irrevocable? Yes, it seemed to be. Had not she herself decided it was after the evening Virtue had taunted her, saying that Eleanor loved her best? She had thrown the dishpan of water at Virtue as if to wash her out of her life. All those years, the two of them together—sleeping on the same straw mattress, running through the snow to get help for Flora, sitting together at their school desk, getting married at the same time, marrying brothers, for heaven's sake. And then a child, a child they both wanted, but which, by some quirk of nature, had come to her. For just a moment she allowed herself to think of what it would have been like if Eleanor had never been born to her, if she had been childless like Virtue. A tiny shiver of sympathy trilled through her.

Gradually she became calmer. After half an hour, she reached up and took down a pile of house plans from the cupboard shelf and began going through them with complete absorption—rejecting, questioning, making notes, suggesting alterations to turn the merely possible into the ideal.

There was so much to consider. First the exterior. It would be a bungalow, of course; Nathan insisted on that.

"We're not getting any younger, you know," he said. "And remember when you were so ill? Wouldn't it have been better not to have had to go up and down a whole pile of stairs?"

The view, of course, was paramount. Nathan mightn't see this, but she did. The sea must be visible from every room except, maybe, the bedrooms. Those could look out on the fields, which were not unpleasant, but didn't compare with the sea view. The windows must frame the view as precisely as a camera lens. The parade of moonlight from harbour to inlet must move inside the completed house as uninterruptedly as it had on the vacant lot. She considered how this could be achieved.

She was feeling better than she had in a long time. Sometimes the words still refused to come, but with practice she continued to improve. Only someone who had known how superbly fluent she had been before would notice anything wrong. Even the asthma was only a problem in winter now. It was all finally coming right. Eleanor was becoming what she had always dreamed she might be. Sometimes Emma believed she had created Eleanor out of her own imagination. She had thought her, and so she had come to exist. Perhaps that was what the legend of Minerva springing from the head of Jove really meant. His mind had invented her.

Emma planned and dreamed. The poor builder drew plans, and she amended them. He drew some more, and still there were things to be changed. "Tweaking," Emma called it.

In the meantime, Obadiah and Virtue found a perfectly good lot only a few hundred yards down the street. Because it was lower, it didn't have a view of the harbour, but because it was on the other side of the street, it had a splendid sight-line to the Bridgewater road, and Obadiah, who liked cars, thought that was at least as good. Emma had sense enough not to comment.

<p>

The van arrived as Eleanor was leaving for school. At last it was all happening! This Monday in June, only one month after they had purchased the house lot, the barbershop was being moved to its new home up the street. The previous evening had been spent packing cardboard boxes with shaving mugs, hair tonic, shampoo, all individually wrapped lest they break. Now three burly men were lifting the barber chairs themselves off their stands, staggering slightly as they carried them, all chrome and black leather, out to the van and hoisting them inside.

She heard her mother mutter that she hoped it was "all for the best." It was clear Virtue did not think so. As Eleanor left for school, she heard Virtue loudly proclaiming to Obadiah, "I just hope people know where you've gone to, and that the landlord up there on the corner doesn't find another business that'll pay him more in a year's time and kick you out on the sidewalk."

Despite this, as Eleanor set out for one of the last school days of the year, she was ecstatic. No longer would she be the girl who "lived with her aunt and uncle—and her parents, of course—in that little house on the lower street." She imagined the new house, its shiny wood floors, its expansive windows, the smell of birch and hemlock and drying plaster. With Emma, she pored over plans and dreamed.

Two things she and her mother agreed were essential: lots of bookcases and a fireplace. Jennifer's house had two fireplaces, but Eleanor would be content with one. Nathan, however, had other ideas. The bookcases he conceded easily. He didn't see the need for books, but there were books, books scattered all over the place in unlikely corners, in the bay window of the bathroom, even under Eleanor's bed. He didn't seriously imagine they would disappear with the move. And he did see the need for tidiness. So there would be bookcases. But no fireplace.

"What in the name of land would you want a fireplace for?"

"It would be so cozy, so lovely to sit beside," said Eleanor.

Emma chimed in with a practical suggestion that was more likely to sway Nathan than romantic ideas of coziness. "It would give the living room a real focus and provide a bit of heat when we didn't need the furnace on."

Nathan was unmoved. "A dirty thing like that. And it'll add at least five hundred dollars to the cost of the house."

"Surely that isn't so much to get the house we really want, after all these years," Emma countered. Eleanor wondered if there was a small reproach here—after all these years?

"You wouldn't want it once you'd got it. And the chimney would have to be cleaned. Every year."

"Not every year. We wouldn't use it that much." Emma could argue every point.

"You don't clean it, you've got a fire on your hands. Burn the house down, it will. Dangerous as well as dirty. I tell you it'll make the house worse not better. Why spend a whole lot of money making something worse?" retorted Nathan with what struck Eleanor as unprecedented passion.

Eleanor could see that, within the parameters of her father's logic, this was unanswerable. But for herself, as much as for her mother, the house must have the shape of perfection; compromise could not exist. The next day she tackled Emma. "Why did you give in so easily? Daddy claims he's building this house for us. So why can't he build it the way we want it?"

"I gave up because there was no point in going on." Emma was standing in the kitchen by the sink, peeling potatoes for the evening meal. She was wearing a faded blue cotton dress, buttoned to the waist, gathered lumpily below. Over it hung a navy blue cardigan, washed shapeless. Eleanor looked at her with dismay. She seemed the very emblem of downtrodden domesticity. In some imprecise way she looked older since the stroke. There were no more lines, but things had subtly sagged.

Suddenly Eleanor saw, superimposed on this picture, another Emma, three years younger, before the stroke, standing in front of a full-length mirror in one of the best dress shops in Halifax. The suit she was trying on, like the housedress she was wearing now, was blue, but a distinctive, soft slate blue made out of the finest wool, with grey shell buttons. Tightly curved and darted, it fitted perfectly.

"It's gorgeous, Mommy, do buy it!" The salesgirl also babbled gushing approval.

Nathan was there as well, embarrassed, out of place, fidgeting. Emma, laughing, turned to him. "Wouldn't you fall in love with me all over again in an outfit like this?" She said it playfully, her body still facing the mirror, smiling back at him over her shoulder. Eleanor had waited for him to say yes, it was lovely, yes, she looked wonderful in it, of course she should have it. But Nathan only smiled rather foolishly, and after a minute Emma disappeared into the changing room to take it off.

"Why didn't you buy it?" Eleanor demanded.

"Oh, it was much too expensive. I really shouldn't have bothered to try it on."

Now here was her mother standing in a faded dress in front of the sink, refusing to fight for what she really wanted. "There's no point in persisting with your father when he's really set against something. He'll always win—not through argument, but just through wearing down. 'You don't really want... Surely you couldn't mean...' on and on. I tell you, there's no point."

Late that summer the house without a fireplace began to rise. First, the huge hole in the earth, then the concrete, defining the shape underground. By fall, a skeleton house was in place, with ribs of wood sticking upright above the concrete, and then a thick covering of paper and insulation before the boarding-in, and at last a roof over it all. Now they could continue to work over the winter, sheltered from the weather. Eleanor stood looking through the skeleton windows out at the sea, reveling in the fresh air, far from galvanizing or industrial smells of any sort. All around her the ribs of the house stood straight and expectant. Soon they would begin to breathe.

❧

As autumn progressed, it seemed to Joan that the whole world was a flurry of construction. It wasn't just her two sisters who were about to move; she and Douglas were building their own house as well. Douglas' business was flourishing along with the fishing industry. As long as the boats kept bringing in the cod for salting and drying, there was a need for boxes to put it in, and he was the sole supplier. There was money in boxes, it seemed. Now Joan wore clothes that were a cut above those of her sisters. She still worked but, when pressed, implied that this was only because she really enjoyed it. Perhaps after the house was finished she would think about quitting she said.

Everything had worked out for the best, she told herself—marrying Douglas, who was good and kind and earned a good living—what more could she want? Well, possibly a child, but that hadn't happened. Maybe God knew best when He took her child from her in the womb. Look at that spoiled, demanding girl Emma had raised. Virtue wanted Eleanor for herself, envied Emma! Joan wasn't that foolish. She knew when she was well off.

As for her past, she scarcely thought about it any longer. Why should she? That was all in another life. As she stood now in the kitchen of the apartment she was about to leave, peeling the vegetables for dinner, she actually found herself humming a little song her mother had taught her.

❧

When Eleanor went back to school in September there was a new girl, Molly, in her class. Molly's father had just moved to town as manager of the Bank of Montreal, and Molly, who had moved frequently during her schooling, came with an air of worldly experience that impressed everyone, even Jennifer. Eleanor, naturally, checked out her academic credentials, and when those didn't seem to be threatening, she made a friend of Molly. One day during recess, Molly happened to mention that she had been born in Bridgetown, but since her family had left when she was two, she couldn't remember much about it. "I've been back a few times, though, and it's quite pretty." Eleanor said she had an aunt who had lived there for a time about fourteen years ago.

"Oh, that must have been about the same time my dad was bank manager there. What's her name?"

"She's married now, but back then she would have been Joan Miller."

"Okay. I'll ask if my mom and dad ever knew her."

The next day it seemed that Molly was avoiding her until Eleanor confronted her at recess. "So, did your parents know my aunt at all?"

Molly hesitated. "Well, yes, they did, a bit. Not really well, but she worked in a bakery, didn't she?"

"I think so. She never really talked a lot about what she did, but I know she gave up teaching school because she hated it, and she's really good at decorating birthday cakes now. She always does mine." Joan's past had never been a subject of much family conversation. Decorating cakes was not what the Miller girls had been brought up to do, and Joan's failure as a teacher had always marked her out in the eyes of her sisters.

"Well, if that really was her..."

Now Eleanor was all interest. "Yes? So?"

"Well. I don't know if I should really tell you, if you don't know already."

"But of course you must tell me. She's my aunt."

"Well, my mother says that she got in trouble."

"Trouble? What kind of trouble?" Eleanor had a vision of Joan robbing Molly's father's bank; the vision was unconvincing.

"She had a boyfriend—kind of a boyfriend. And he got her into trouble."

Eleanor stared in incomprehension.

"Must I spell it out for you? He got her pregnant and she was going to have a baby. But then the baby came too soon and died and she went away. No one ever saw her again."

"Oh." Eleanor was shattered. Bank robbing sank into insignificance before the magnitude of this failing. After all, she might have really needed the money if she had robbed a bank, but how could she need to do whatever thing it was that made babies? She drifted slowly away from Molly, hardly knowing where she was going, moving through the crowds of smaller children playing hopscotch or marbles, back to her classroom. It all seemed unreal. It was impossible. She sat at her desk until the bell rang, thinking. It never occurred to her to question what Molly had told her. In her world, people told the truth. So— should she tell her mother? In fact, she had no choice, she decided. Your mother must be told everything you knew. Concealment was a sin, even if the concealment had nothing to do with yourself.

That afternoon after school, while Emma stood in front of her ironing board smoothing the white cotton sheets to perfection, Eleanor spoke.

"There's a new girl in school, Molly," she began tentatively.

"Oh yes, I think you mentioned her before. Nice?"

"Probably. Her family lived in Bridgetown when Joan was there."

Emma continued ironing. "Yes?"

"They found out something. Something about Joan. It's really bad."

"But what on earth could Joan have done?"

"She...she had a baby. But it came too soon and died. That's why she went first to the States and then came to us...so Molly says."

Emma let the iron sit on the sheet until the cotton began to smell, then grabbed it up in alarm.

"It can't be true. Your Aunt Joan would never..."

"That's what I said, but why would Molly lie?"

❧

Emma abandoned the ironing and sat down at the kitchen table beside the precariously balanced board, the sheet trailing helplessly on the floor. The question Eleanor had asked still nagged at her. Why indeed? Molly had no reason to malign Joan—unless she were one of those spiteful girls who enjoyed spreading malicious gossip. If the story were true, it would explain certain things. It would not only explain why Joan had left her job, but why she had fled first to Hannah in the States before contacting her by letter. In fact, it explained all the peculiar circumstances surrounding her appearance in Lunenburg fourteen years earlier.

It also, to Emma's mind, explained something else. It explained why Joan had lost her baby. This explanation had nothing to do with the medical fact that women who miscarried once were more likely to miscarry again; it was the hard and implacable fact that God punished sin, and a woman who had conceived a child out of wedlock would be unlikely to know the pure joy of a child within wedlock.

Now she faced the same dilemma as Eleanor. Should she tell Virtue? Keeping secrets was not the way things worked within a family, or at least within their family. On the other hand, showing her mother Reverend Selig's letter all those years ago hadn't worked out that well. Still, she couldn't bear the burden of this knowledge alone.

When she heard the back door opening, her heart beat faster. She had seen as little as possible of Virtue since their confrontation over the new house, but this she needed to talk about. She wouldn't go over right away; she would wait until Virtue had settled in her kitchen and begun to cook the evening meal. Half an hour passed. Emma put the ironing away and crossed the hallway. Virtue was not cooking supper at all, but sitting at the table reading the paper. Hearing Emma rustling in the doorway, she looked up.

"I'm sorry to bother you, but Eleanor has just told me something I think you should know." She told the tale briefly—Molly, the Bridgetown connection, Joan's "mistake."

"How could we not know?"

"Well, she didn't tell us, of course. How could she?" Emma said.

"And now Eleanor knows as well," Virtue responded.

"I'm afraid so." Emma sighed and went back to her side of the house.

≈

Something had changed, and Joan could not fail to notice. There was an awkwardness when Emma and Virtue were around Joan that had never existed before. It even seemed to her that they tried to avoid her.

"Do come out and see how well our house is getting on. I'm free on Saturday morning," said Joan one evening when she dropped by to show them some curtain samples.

"Sorry, I've got too much marking to do," was Virtue's excuse.

"And Eleanor needs some help with a school project on Australia," was Emma's.

"Oh...some other time?" Both Virtue and Emma rubbed their hands on their aprons and looked down at the floor.

"What's the matter? Have I done something wrong?" Joan decided to push the issue.

"Not recently," Emma said, finally.

Joan paled and steadied herself on the hall table.

"Oh," she said softly. "How did you find out?"

"Eleanor told us."

"Eleanor! How does she know?"

"There's a new girl in school whose parents lived in Bridgetown when you were there. And when Eleanor said she had an aunt who had worked there..." Emma's voice trailed away.

"Schoolgirl gossip. And you believed it! So that's the kind of loyal sisters I have."

"So it's not true?" Emma asked.

Joan crumpled. "No, it's true. But...not how you think. I had no choice."

"What do you mean, you had no choice." Now Virtue entered the conversation as inquisitor.

"I mean, he forced me. We went out for a bite to eat one evening, and then he offered to drive me home. He had a real nice Buick. But once I got into the car, he didn't go home at all. He drove down a little path to the river and...and...well, I couldn't get out and he pinned me down. I thought it would be all right, even then, but it wasn't..." Joan couldn't go on. She was leaning against the wall of the hallway now and sobbing.

"Okay. It's okay." Emma put her hand tentatively on Joan's shoulder. "We won't tell Douglas, I promise."

Joan sniffled and said, "Thanks, thanks so much."

It was growing dark when Joan walked up the lower street towards the apartment she and Douglas still rented. This was good, she thought, because it would make it less likely anyone she met would notice she had been crying. Sometimes she hated her sisters, her whole family. She had done nothing wrong, as far as she could see, except to choose a boyfriend who wasn't as nice as he should have been. Surely that was as much luck as anything else. And she had been punished, hadn't she? After all, she was childless. What was the point of building a new house with solid birch cupboards and a raised oven—the latest thing—in the kitchen if you had no family? For a moment she hated the house and everything that went with it. But then she composed herself and put on a good face for Douglas. He must suspect nothing.

❦

Before Christmas Flora was in her new house. Emma was pleased to see she had a freshly cut tree from what had been their father's forest, and with Virtue she helped Flora decorate it. Emma looked enviously at the wood-burning stove with its open front grate in the corner of the living room. Flora had managed to get, if not a proper fireplace, at least an open fire. There was a rocking chair that Harry had salvaged from "the old place," and a new sofa with a pull-out bed that Virtue and Emma had bought with her share of the money from the sale of timber that they had made sure Harry put into her bank account. Flora presided in the rocking chair and welcomed her sisters as guests.

"Will you come and pick berries with me in the summer, like we did the day of Papa's funeral?" Flora asked Emma.

"Yes, indeed." Emma replied.

❦

Eleanor decorated the large tree that stood on the floor in the living room. Intermittently she could hear tiny sounds of sniffling and nose blowing come from Virtue's living room as she decorated her small evergreen sitting on the table in a corner—the small tree another subtle indicator of her childless state. Only people with children needed large trees, it seemed. That was the way it went.

Both families in the house on Water Street knew there was something final about this Christmas. No one said, "This year is the last we shall spend here together." Yet the feeling was there even if unspoken.

Eleanor put the icicles on in the same meticulous rows that she had watched Joan agonize over ten years before. Obsession, she supposed. But a tradition, as well. This strange house was, after all, her home. All those who lived in it had nurtured her and, in their own peculiar ways, even loved her. For a moment she allowed herself the rare luxury of nostalgia. Then a particularly audible sniff from Virtue pulled her up short. Eleanor concentrated on nothing but the rows of icicles before her.

On Christmas Day they all ate together—Virtue and Obadiah, Joan and Douglas, Nathan and Emma, and Eleanor, the one person under forty at the table. Despite the superiority of Joan and Douglas' spacious new dining room, they all returned here to Emma's large kitchen, where the turkey, the cranberry sauce, and the many vegetables proceeded in order across the festive board. There were mince pies and, especially for Douglas, a coconut pie made from the milk and flesh of a real coconut. No one talked of the past; no one spoke of the future.

In the evening they walked together through the white landscape to the church for the Sunday School pageant, successor to that for which Emma had sacrificed herself years before. "I think they used to be better once, back when you were doing them," Virtue said graciously to Emma.

Eleanor held her breath waiting for the response, but Emma accepted the implied compliment with simple gratitude. "Maybe they were. It's nice of you to think so."

Later that night they came back along the quiet, deserted sidewalks down to the shabby lower street. As they turned the corner Eleanor saw the house isolated, vulnerable beneath its load of snow, in danger of being shouldered aside by its large, commercial neighbours. Would the plumbers knock it down once they owned it? For the first time she could recall, Eleanor actually felt affection for it. She went in first and turned on the Christmas tree lights. The glass birds with their white horsehair tails balancing on the ends of the branches sparkled red and green and blue. "Calico pie, the little birds fly..."

CHAPTER 14

1959

As late spring approached, Eleanor was due to write her first set of provincial exams—a set of uniform tests that, as their name implied, were set by the province. How would she stack up against all those others? It was one thing to be top of the class in Lunenburg Academy. But what a tiny fraction of the pupils in the province this class accounted for! Eleanor was sure there must be piles of brilliant students out there, effortlessly absorbing knowledge like little sponges. In the city they would have better labs, perhaps better teachers. Her mother could no longer help since her stroke.

English she was sure she would find easy. Words and the rhythm of words stuck in her mind, ineradicable. History also was easy, because she could always see the pattern, the cause and effect, the abstract design in the concrete events. But geometry—now that was different. Suppose there was a problem not in the text? Would she be able to solve it? Was she even clever at all, or simply a word-machine, absorbing and spewing out again?

The night before the exams began, she could not sleep. And she had to sleep. Without sleep, she knew, the mind couldn't function to its full potential. The clock on the mantel downstairs struck eleven.

Eventually, she called out. "I can't sleep."

Emma appeared. "Now you know there's nothing to worry about. You've worked hard, and I'm sure you'll do well." She kissed her and went back to bed again.

The clock struck twelve. "I'm still not asleep."

"Do you want some warm milk?"

"Maybe." Warm milk arrived, and, full of faith in its opiate powers, Eleanor drank it.

The clock struck one; the clock struck two. What should she do? It scarcely seemed worth going to sleep anymore. Maybe she should just stay awake and hope for the best. Then things became blurry. She was writing exams, endless exams, but not in school. They seemed to be taking place out in a field, and she had to run around the field twice before she was allowed to sit down and write. This was designed to favour the others, Eleanor could see. They knew she was hopeless at running; it would only tire her out unnecessarily and make her start later than the rest. She puffed around the course once, twice. Then she sat down at a desk that mysteriously appeared at the edge of the field under a tree. Suddenly she recognized the field and the woods behind it. It was at Lake Mush-a-Mush, the site of the camp where she had disgraced herself years before. Nothing good was going to happen here, she could feel it in her bones. She turned over the paper and read the questions. They were in some funny number code that she had to decipher: the numbers all stood for letters, and she had to figure this out before she could read the questions, never mind answer them. She put up her hand, "Yes, Eleanor."

"Do you know whether the answers have to be written in the number code as well?"

"Now Eleanor, just read the instructions at the top of the paper, and it should be clear," Mrs. Black was saying. Mrs. Black? She belonged back in Grade One.

"But it doesn't tell me in the instructions."

"Well, just use your common sense, child," Mrs. Black replied.

Eleanor looked for her pen, but it wasn't there. She looked around and saw that all the others had picked up tree sticks from the ground and sharpened them and were busy scratching on the paper with them. She scrambled around to find a stick, but then she realized she didn't have a penknife to sharpen it. "I don't have a penknife. Please may I borrow one?"

"That's against the rules," said Mrs. Black, and she began to leaf through a thick tome of paper.

Eleanor panicked. It was hopeless; they had designed this system just to make her fail. Then the clock was striking eight, and her mother was by her bed telling her to get up. She must have a good breakfast before setting off.

⁂

During the winter, work on the house had slowed. But now, at last, it was nearly finished. Emma insisted on sanding and varnishing much of the woodwork herself. After the carpenters had done a few doorframes and cupboard doors, Emma excused them from doing any more. They just didn't take the time to smooth it to perfection, to put on the multiple coats of shellac with the necessary painstaking care, making sure neither to leave any bare patches nor to allow any small drips to mar the surface. She sanded; she coughed; she sanded some more, dusted the surface and applied the shellac. Stood back. Was it perfect?

Sometimes, in the middle of it all, she stopped to question herself. Could she speak as well as a week ago? A month ago? It was hard to be certain. Did anyone else notice? She was afraid to ask. Every Sunday she sat in church and asked God to have mercy on her and restore her mind to what it had been before the stroke. But God didn't seem to be listening. Perhaps He had his reasons...

By July the house was finally finished. Now she was busy packing boxes of glass and china, cooking pots and pans, linen, everything. Her belongings, that appeared so meagre compared to the riches in the homes of her acquaintances, seemed to amount to an awful lot when packed into cases that were then transported by car to the new house one mile away. This went on for a week and a half. Finally, a small moving van came for the large items—the beds, the stove, the refrigerator, even the old Coronation washing machine. Into the new house they went, each to its appointed place. They looked displaced and odd against the plaster and shiny woodwork of their new surroundings. All Emma's efforts at perfection seemed chiefly to accentuate the shabbiness of the old furniture.

That night, as she and Eleanor set up the beds in the new house, Eleanor teased, "Won't you miss being woken up tomorrow morning by Willy Frank's music?"

"I shall steel myself to the...the..."

"Deprivation." Eleanor could fill in the missing words with a psychic rapidity. But it did spoil the intended irony.

❦

There was a week between the departure of Nathan and Emma and that of Virtue and Obadiah—a week for Virtue of packing up, a week of brooding reflection, a week of self-justification.

What did I do wrong? That's what she asked herself. It couldn't be her fault, surely. She had helped out as much as she could when Emma was ill; she had certainly loved and cared for Eleanor from the time she was a baby. Now she was being forced to leave the old home they had shared for all their married lives. What was wrong with sharing a house? There were still less people in it than there had been in most of the houses in Waldenstein.

She looked at the empty rooms that Emma and Nathan had vacated. The bare walls stared back reproachfully. "You have emptied us," they said.

"No, I didn't. I wanted you full of life and happiness."

"You only thought you did," came the inscrutable reply.

Why was she not looking forward to her own new house? Why had she insisted that it should be so modest, smaller than Emma's? "We can't afford anything bigger," she said. But that couldn't be true. She worked at a full-time job. With the exception of Nathan's Riverport earnings, Obadiah earned as much as he did. Deep down, did she not want to have a new house she could love?

A ring at the front door brought her back. When she opened it, there stood Rachel, her youngest sister, emaciated and weeping. Clinging to her was Violet, the smallest of her children, a girl of about ten, who was as thin and sad as her mother. "I've left Martin," Rachel said.

Virtue recoiled in horror. Why did they all come here? Joan, Flora, Rachel, the whole family seemed to regard this house on the lower street as a common shelter that was theirs by right. Well, it wouldn't exist much longer.

"Come in," she said weakly.

"Emma's gone already?" Rachel looked into the empty living room.

"Yes, they moved to the new house on Tuesday. We're going to leave at the beginning of next week. You can see..." She gestured towards the boxes that stood on the floor.

"Oh, I'm so sorry. But I just had to get out. He's really gone quite mad. He walks up and down beside my bed at night, telling me he wants me to die. And today he beat Violet so that I thought he was going to kill her." She pulled up Violet's flimsy dress and exposed her thin, bruised thighs. "On her back too. That's when I decided I had to leave. I'm not going back."

"Let's sit down and talk." It was the only response Virtue could think of.

"I'm not going back, I tell you. I'm not!" Rachel began to sob harder, with Violet now joining in.

"No, of course not. But we must think." So far, Virtue had not even offered Rachel a cup of tea. Now propriety asserted itself, and she went into the kitchen to put on the kettle. After a bit Virtue reappeared with the tea and some cookies that were not yet packed.

"Mommy, where are we going?" Violet whispered.

"I don't know." Rachel held her close. "I loved him so. That day he came to the schoolhouse and held me. He pushed my hair back and whispered he would care for me always. And now..."

"I know." Virtue paused, but in the end couldn't stop herself. "We did warn you that he was...well...not the best match."

Rachel sank back against the sofa. "What shall I do?"

The cry of the youngest, Virtue thought. Always expecting someone else to help her, tell her what to do.

"Will you go back to teaching?" Virtue was thinking of the practicalities.

"Oh yes, if there's a job for me." Rachel stopped crying for a moment.

"Of course I don't know for sure, but I think there may be a vacancy at the new school in Centre where I'm teaching now. Would you like me to get in touch with the Superintendent?"

"Yes. Yes, I suppose so."

Then Rachel just sat there on the sofa with her teacup as if she could never move again. Virtue wondered whether she might sit there forever, waiting for meals to be brought and fresh clothing. Possibly at night she would simply stretch out on the sofa to sleep.

Time was passing. Virtue was mentally counting the boxes she could have packed. "I'm afraid the spare room bed has already been taken apart," she said.

Rachel was silent.

"But Joan and Douglas have been in their new house for six months now, and I'm fairly certain they could give you a place to stay—at least until you get a teaching job."

Joan, Virtue knew, would be in no position to refuse. She had been taken in and looked after herself for years when she first came to the town. And she had a secret, a secret that Virtue knew.

Virtue phoned Joan, and when Obadiah came home from the barber-shop, Rachel and Violet were gently put in the cocoon of the Buick's cream leathered back seat and driven quietly to a place of refuge.

CHAPTER 15
Autumn 1959

Emma had her house, and she should have been deliriously happy. Every day the autumn light glowed on the polished wood floors. Every day she sat drinking her breakfast tea as the sun warmed the small dining area with its spectacular view of the harbour and the open ocean beyond. But something was wrong. Emma closed her right eye and looked down at the newspaper in front of her. The letters went dark and hazy. What was the problem? Could she be going blind in one eye? She looked up and tried to focus on the view but found the same thing. The whole landscape was shrouded in darkness, as if she were looking through smoked glass. When she tried the same thing with the other eye, the letters on the paper sprang into focus; the sea sparkled.

More than that, she couldn't seem to concentrate on what she was reading. Emma picked up a history book about Henry VIII, and tried to remember where she had stopped reading. She never used bookmarks, because she could remember the last sentence, the precise last words that she had read. But not now. With mounting panic, she scanned the pages. It was no good. She simply could not remember where she left off.

Had she had another stroke? She didn't think so. The stroke had been, like its name, a blow, sharp and swift. This was something more gradual and insidious. When had it begun? She thought back. Everything had been so busy—the endless sanding of the woodwork, then the packing of the boxes, the actual move, the unpacking. It left no time for introspection. Only now, when she was alone in the house, with Nathan at work and Eleanor back to school, did the awful truth dawn. Emma thought she was losing not only her sight, but her mind.

Now, ironically, she feared being left alone. When Virtue came home from school, Emma would tell her about it, and Virtue would assure her that no, it could not be true; it was all just her imagination. Things like this didn't happen. A few good nights' sleep would fix everything. Then she remembered. Virtue would not be coming home—or at least not to her home. Virtue would be coming back to that other brand-new house down the street. Nathan would be grabbing a hasty supper and then going off to Riverport. He had said he would give up the second job once the house was built, but there were still a few outstanding bills, so he was going to keep on until Christmas, at least.

That left Eleanor, but she could not tell Eleanor. It wasn't fair to burden a teenager with this sort of thing. Eleanor would not be consoling. She would panic, and insist that Emma go to the doctor—at once! Eleanor believed in doctors; Emma had given up on them a long time ago. She had no intention of going to the doctor.

Another thought struck her; it was all intended. She was being punished, punished for her whole life. Everything she had ever done had been wrong. Emma had been proud of her mind, oh so proud. She knew it could perform tricks that her sisters' minds could never accomplish. She had flaunted it over Virtue when she had got her Grade Ten with flying colours while Virtue struggled again and again to get her Grade Nine. She had been proud that Reverend Selig had chosen her and her alone to learn Latin.

Looking back, she could see that she had been punished for that as well. It was not mere girlish foolishness that had led her to pick up the page of the letter he had dropped and give it to her mother, but part of a divine plan to discredit her in his eyes and make her, who had admired him so greatly, the unwitting instrument of his departure from Waldenstein. Ah yes, it was all beginning to make sense. And it was not only pride of which she was guilty. She had a good husband, a caring sister, and even a child, and had this satisfied her? No, it had not. She had set her heart on a house of her own. And not just any house—a house with a fabulous view, with a modern kitchen, polished wooden floors, silk curtains at the windows. "Fool, this night shall thy soul be required of thee." The stroke had been a warning, but she had not heeded. She had gone on looking at house plans, forcing Nathan to do two jobs, determined to make her own dreams come true regardless of those of anyone else. Now, she was going to be punished.

After a bit Emma got up and washed the dishes. Then she went up to the attic and began to sort through some boxes that had not yet been unpacked. This at least she could still do. For now, she must confide in no one.

⟋❦⟍

"Isn't it funny how our minds work." Now that she lived in the new part of town, Eleanor walked home from school a large part of the way with Jennifer, and the conversation was never dull. So on this last Wednesday in September, as she and Jennifer started out on the steep gravel path through the cemetery, she casually threw this out.

"What exactly do you mean?" Jennifer replied.

"Oh, I mean so many things," Eleanor responded, stumbling a bit as she hiked down the hill. "Like how, just now, part of my mind was worrying about not falling, but I was also thinking that old Mrs. Morash, who crocheted a blanket for my doll's bed when I was little, is buried just off there to the right, and also that Mommy is making lasagna for supper, and how nice that will be."

"Yes, of course, I do that too—all the time. Sometimes it's the way one thing leads to another. I notice something as simple as, say my eraser in school, and I think about how Jerry borrowed it one morning to rub out his math answers, which were all wrong, and now he's out fishing and not in school anymore, and is he happier than we are or not?"

"And schoolwork, that gets all mixed up with other things as well. Like when you read about Gaul being divided into three parts, and you think 'three,' and then you suddenly see a triangle, and you're into geometric proofs, and after that...oh, I don't know, you might go anywhere."

There was a third girl with them as well, Caroline, who had never been a particularly close friend of Eleanor's, but who now was her closest neighbour and walked to and from school with her and Jennifer. "I don't know what you're talking about. I don't think my mind is like that at all," Caroline said.

This was even more interesting to Eleanor. A dissenting voice. "So, how does your mind work?" They had reached the sidewalk at the bottom of the hill path now, and Eleanor turned to concentrate fully on Caroline.

"Well, I don't know. It just works. You know, 'Incoming thoughts to the right; outgoing thoughts to the left. Please do not crowd at the exits.'" Caroline had a wry sense of humour. She continued, "I just don't get it. You people with such good grades—I'd like to have your brains just when I was writing an exam, but I don't think I'd want them all the time. It must be so mixed up in there, so much stuff running around helter-skelter." They all laughed.

Eleanor had never been happier. This last year of school began with such interesting things to read, new avenues of knowledge to explore. She particularly liked some of the set texts—*The Tempest* by Shakespeare, and *Mill on the Floss* by George Eliot, a woman who pretended to be a man when she wrote. Also, Mrs. Schmeisser had chosen her to play the part of Mabel from *Pirates of Penzance* in the Christmas Gilbert and Sullivan revue. She had the most wonderful song! Now she was walking home with friends who actually seemed to like her. Of course, there had always been and still was Donna, but being accepted by these girls was definitely flattering.

Eleanor was almost losing the fear that had beset her after her mother's stroke whenever she approached the door of her house. Now she called out cheerily, "Hi, I'm here."

"A good day?" Emma smiled. She had rehearsed the smile and the greeting so that it couldn't possibly go wrong.

"Yes. And we had the most interesting conversation coming home— all about our minds and how ideas get associated and mixed up." Eleanor half expected that Emma would take this up and continue the discussion, but she didn't.

"I've made your favourite lasagna for...for supper." Eleanor scarcely noticed the hesitations anymore, and now she plunked herself on the living room sofa and began to read. How nice to have all this space to oneself, to be able to glance up from one's reading and look out at the sea!

She could hear her mother fussing about in the kitchen, assembling the lasagna, no doubt. When she got to the song "Full Fathom Five" in *The Tempest*, it was so wonderful she had to share it. "Come here, Mommy, and listen to this!" Emma stood in the doorway between kitchen and living room, and Eleanor read it all. "Makes death rather lovely, doesn't it? Eyes changed to pearls, everything transformed into something rich and strange."

"Yes," said Emma.

This was not the kind of bland response Eleanor expected. She sat up on the sofa and turned around. "What's the matter?"

"Nothing, nothing really."

"Just come and look at this next bit with me."

Emma didn't move. Now Eleanor was becoming alarmed. "What's wrong?"

"I...I can't read."

"What do you mean, you can't read."

Now Emma came in and sat down opposite Eleanor. She hadn't meant to reveal this, not so soon at least. Somehow it had happened. "It seems...well, I think the talking, the...speech...is getting a bit worse, and this morning when I tried to read the paper it was really difficult. My one eye couldn't seem to focus properly."

Eleanor was relieved. "Oh, if it's only that, you should go to Doctor Baines, and he'll get you a new prescription for glasses."

Emma said nothing more.

The lasagna was perfect. Nathan expressed his appreciation, pecked Emma and Eleanor on the cheek and left for Riverport. Eleanor went to bed that night somewhat reassured.

⁊

Emma never went to the optometrist. She knew there was no point. Surprisingly, Eleanor did not bring the subject up again. But at the beginning of October, the pain began. Now she had no choice. She had to go to the doctor.

Nathan drove her to the doctor's office the following afternoon. After a fairly cursory examination punctuated by inarticulate puffs and grunts, Dr. Willis muttered that it could be another slight stroke that had temporarily affected the part of the brain that controlled reading. If so, she should recover gradually over some weeks or months as, indeed, she had before. He advised rest and caution. He gave Emma some pills for the pain, patted her on the shoulder and told her to take things easy.

The pills eased the pain, but they seemed to make everything else more confused. One night, on the radio, she heard a strange kind of music. "O Fortuna!" it cried. She could still muster enough Latin to understand that. Fortune! This was her fortune—to be dying alone in a small town on the edge of nowhere with no real friends, not even her sister Virtue, whom she had cast aside and who no longer loved her. Eleanor and Nathan could not compensate or even understand. The sea was empty, a void.

✦

Eleanor walked to and from school between Caroline and Jennifer, enclosed in a transparent cage. She could see through the cage; her voice could be heard, but nothing tangible or real could pass through it. She made the right gestures, asked the right questions, and revealed nothing of what was really going on within her life. It was all a performance, playing at being her usual self. Sometimes she thought of telling Donna, but she only saw Donna at school, and anyway, having distanced herself, Eleanor felt she had no right to burden Donna with confidences.

October came and went. The sea tossed fretfully against the grey sky. The trees were bare. Eleanor dragged home a huge volume of the complete plays of George Bernard Shaw. She had never read Shaw, and there was no particular reason why she should read him now, except that his plays appeared to be the largest volume in the school library.

After supper Eleanor retreated as usual to the small room that had been set up as her study. There was her old, functional desk, and the rocking chair that had stood by the window of the house on Water Street. But instead of sitting at the desk to do her homework, Eleanor huddled in the rocking chair and began to read *Saint Joan*. Suddenly, in the middle of the second act, her mother appeared. "What are you...read...reading?"

"*Saint Joan*. It's by Shaw. I've never read anything by him, and I thought this looked interesting when I saw it in the library today."

Eleanor was flooded with guilt; she knew that in some obscure way she had been found out.

"So you haven't been doing...doing your...schoolwork, then?"

"No, well, not exactly."

"What do...do you mean, not exactly? I left you alone all evening because...I thought you must have a great deal of...of...homework to do, but now I see you...you've just been reading a...a...play all evening. A play."

Eleanor blushed. "I thought it would be, well, generally helpful. To know about Shaw, I mean."

"Maybe. But that's not...not why you're reading it. You're reading it to...to get away from me!"

Eleanor was dumbfounded. The blunt accusation was hurled with such passion that she could think of no defence. Besides, deep within herself, she knew it was true. She had implicitly deceived her mother. Why else had she gone into the room where nothing but homework ever happened and shut the door? Why was that necessary? To escape, to escape.

Emma went out of the room abruptly, closing Eleanor in as she had been. Eleanor sat still for a long time. The house was very quiet. Nathan was in Riverport. When Eleanor finally ventured out to the bathroom to prepare for bed, the rest of *Saint Joan* was still unread.

$\sim$

Emma was afraid to grasp the enormity of what was happening to her. It was too complex and terrible. She needed to think—but she could not think, that was the root of the problem. The idea of death was easy to grasp if not to accept. For much of her life the idea of death had filled her thoughts. "Lord, let me know mine end." But suppose she had known this end? What then?

It was the disintegration of the self before death that was impossible to comprehend. She had thought of herself as a complete entity, mind and body and soul working together to produce this thing, this person, called Emma. Even when she had been so ill twelve years before, the self had stayed together. Now parts of the whole were rebelling, flying off in different directions, becoming nonexistent. She could not read. She was imprisoned in this small compass, this body, but a body that increasingly seemed divorced from everything she had been.

Daily life provided no distractions. The written word was closed to her, and the spoken came only in fits and starts through the fog of her meditation.

"How have you been today?" [Virtue]

"Don't you think you should go back to Dr. Willis?" [Nathan]

"I'm going in town for Virtue. Can I get you anything?" [Obadiah on the telephone.]

All of these were questions. People didn't talk to her anymore; they simply asked stupid questions, and the answer, whatever they asked, was always the same and impossible to articulate: "I am dying; none of these other things matter in the slightest. They no longer have anything to do with me."

Sometimes she feared she was going mad. In the past she had thought of madness as an escape, a cowardly exit. Now she knew it would be the final descent to uncontrolled terror, not escape from the past or the present but living with them, omnipresent, in the fractured form of unreason—feeling and image ceaselessly impinging without a logical narrative structure. It would be the end of the story of life, without the oblivion of death. Scraps of old poems still floated in and out of her consciousness: "My mind to me a kingdom is." That was rich! "O Lord have mercy on me and grant what I desire. For, as I think, my desire is not of earth." Where did that come from? Oh yes, a book Johannes had left with her. Augustine. *Confessions.* But Augustine had been holy; she was an outcast, punished for her pride, beyond redemption.

The soul—where was the soul? Body, mind, and soul, the ancient triad. Memory, a faculty of the soul. It had seemed so secure. Now it too might disappear, as reading had disappeared, as reason itself was disappearing, all tied to the fragile mind, which in turn was tied to a physical apparatus that worked or didn't. Memory was the very self, the past that was constantly present—"time present of time past." And what of expectation, the "time present of time future"? Of that she must not even think.

Emma busied herself with tasks she could still perform, cooking recipes she had memorized and cleaning. Week by week it became more difficult. The simplest things required intense concentration.

One Saturday she could no longer set Eleanor's hair. She tried and tried to part the hair and clamp the waves in the usual way, but her fingers would not behave. Eventually she was beaten. There was a dreadful scene. "Why can't you do it?" Eleanor shouted. Another unanswerable question, Emma thought. A hostile question. "What can you do anymore? You've always done this for me, always!"

"For me, for me!" Emma repeated. "Do you ever...ever...think of anyone but you...you? Now that I can't do...anything, since I'm...I'm useless, you don't want me. You'd like me to...to kill myself, wouldn't you?" Tears streamed now, furious tears. "Well let me tell you...tell you something. I'm not going to. Not just because you...you want me to. You'll...you'll just have to...to put up with me a...while...a while longer."

⌖

Eleanor stared at her mother and then ran to her room, her wet hair falling about her shoulders, raging and crying. The hair seemed the final betrayal of some unspoken contract. From earliest childhood her mother had always cared for her hair, "her beautiful hair." Behind that specific hurt—worse, much worse—was the terrible thing her mother had said. Why had she said that? Yet it was true; it was true and not true. The present was intolerable; life without her mother was intolerable, too. Had she wished her mother dead? Could she fleetingly, for a moment, have imagined that? Ah yes, she could have. Wicked, most wicked, and her mother had known. Her mother knew everything. Alive or dead, she would always know everything. There was no escape.

Slowly, clumsily Eleanor set her hair and dried it. She could hear that Emma was getting ready for bed. She knocked on the bedroom door and went in. Her mother stood in her old pale blue dressing gown looking out the window into the darkness. She did not turn around.

"I'm sorry. I shouldn't have said that. I know it's not your fault that you can't do everything like you used to."

Silence.

"I'm sorry. I'm truly sorry."

Emma picked her dress up from the bed, walked to the clothes closet and disappeared inside it. When she emerged, Eleanor was still standing there. Emma faced her. "You always say that. Go to bed."

CHAPTER 16

November 1959

What was happening was just unbelievable, impossible for Nathan to comprehend. He had been a good husband, never looked at another woman, tried to give Emma what she wanted. Indeed, he'd done better than that. He had given her what she wanted. There stood the house: living room, dining room, kitchen, utility room, two bedrooms, even a small den in which Eleanor could study or Emma could retreat to read. Except that now Emma couldn't read. Everything that he worked for was useless. He didn't want to admit it, but he now knew something was horribly wrong with Emma. She was going to die. He just couldn't quite say it yet. He certainly couldn't say it to Eleanor.

A lot of things had gone wrong in his life. He was forced to leave school; then he was compelled to go and work in the woods for a man his family despised; he had become very ill. Then suddenly he was grown up and barbering with Obadiah. He'd worked and worked to make Emma happy—always an uphill struggle. Now, just when everything should be so right, it was all wrong.

There was Eleanor, his brilliant daughter, but Eleanor had always belonged to Emma. All that book-learning. Could it really be so important? Still, it was nice to have people come into the barbershop and say how well they heard Eleanor had done in the last set of exams. But with every set of exams she moved further from him.

It was a struggle, but he finally got Emma to go back to the doctor. She was willing to go because the pills no longer controlled the pain. This time even Dr. Willis seemed concerned. He said she could take as many of the pills as she needed—as many as ten a day. "What about the long-term effects?" Emma asked. He just smiled his slow sad smile, and told her not to worry so much. "The important thing is that you shouldn't suffer now." He also said that he would get her into the hospital in Halifax as soon as possible. This should have been what Nathan wanted to hear, but now it only confirmed his worst fears.

Two weeks went by. Finally, on a Friday morning, Dr. Willis phoned and spoke to Nathan. "I've got a bed booked for Emma in four days' time. That's Tuesday, the first of December. If you could drive her up to Halifax, she can be admitted any time after ten in the morning. They'll do some tests, and we'll find out what's really wrong."

***

Of course it would only be for a short while, Emma reassured Eleanor. "But just in case you need to cook anything..." She sat down with Eleanor and all her recipes—some in proper books, some pasted in scrapbooks, some scrawled on bits of paper floating loose in the other books and falling out whenever any page was turned—and went through them haltingly and painstakingly.

"I always use a bit more baking..."

"Baking powder."

"Yes, baking powder, in this one. Don't forget to fry the meat before, before...you...put it..."

"Before you put it in the stew pot?"

"Yes. Yes, that's right. You'll be okay. Just follow..."

"The recipe?"

"Instructions." Triumph, her own word. "If forget...if you forget, ask Virtue."

The evening before she left for the hospital in Halifax, Nathan and Emma stood together in the front hallway. Eleanor was sitting there also by the telephone, about to call Jennifer for some math homework she had missed while at the operetta rehearsal. Nathan was on his way to Riverport. Emma could not bring herself to ask him to stay home even this one evening. Suppose he refused? In the hallway, within full sight of Eleanor, Emma embraced him, tears streaming down her face. As he clasped her, she looked at Eleanor and held out an arm, passionately gesturing her inclusion. Stony-faced, Eleanor sat still, apparently beyond the reach of love or tears.

A white mist of snow covered the ground the next morning as Nathan and Emma drove to Halifax. Fear blew through the gusts of cold antiseptic air in the hospital lobby, hovered around the chill efficiency of the admitting secretary: Emma was no longer in control. She gave all the answers on the form and braved the typist's icy frown when she stumbled. The ultimate humiliation, she could not sign her name. After trial and hesitation, she said, "I don't think...I can...write anymore." The last word had a sound of finality. Not "just now," or "while I am so ill," but "anymore."

She was given a private room. Nathan checked with the nurse. "Do I pay more for this?"

"No, not in your case, Mr. Wentzell. The specialist has decided this is what your wife requires."

"Oh, that's all right then."

He kissed Emma and turned to go. She was unpacking her night things with the nurse's help. "Wait. Wait," she called softly. Even more softly and moving towards him so that the nurse would not hear, she said, "Ask Eleanor...to get me a new..." The word would not come, and Nathan was no help. "A new...dressing gown." At last, she smiled with relief and exhaustion.

"Sure," said Nathan. "I'll do that. We'll be up to see you before the end of the week."

<hr>

The following Saturday Eleanor and Nathan drove to Halifax together. Eleanor knew where she would go for the dressing gown. She led Nathan firmly and accurately to the shop where Emma had tried on the perfect suit years before. She did not remind her father it was the same shop, though she did wonder if the depth of carpet and consequent hush inside might jog his memory. Apparently not. He stood, bewildered but acquiescent, while Eleanor selected the perfect gown— fine woven wool in a pale dusty rose, with satin piping around the shawl collar and the cuffs. A pair of satin slippers in the same shade completed the outfit. She did not ask permission; she said this was what she would have and told Nathan what they cost. He unrolled a wad of bills without comment.

"Is it a gift?" the salesgirl asked.

"Yes," said Eleanor, and the salesgirl carefully folded the gown in tissue paper, put it in a silver box, and tied it all up with a satin ribbon.

The hospital room shone white and narrow in the light of its single window as Eleanor and Nathan entered. Emma looked very small; her skin seemed to have yellowed. When she saw them she smiled but did not speak for fear of spoiling the moment.

Eleanor presented her with the silver box and helped her to open it. "Ah, too much, too much."

What did she mean, too much money, or too good for her? Perhaps it had been a mistake.

Emma managed another word. "Beautiful." The old faded blue gown was taken away, and the splendid new one put on in its place.

Gradually, with much hesitation and correction, she managed to tell them what had been happening to her. She spoke first of the many tests—blood tests, a brain X-ray, innumerable pills and needles. She stopped, but there was something more. With tears of shame filling her eyes she told of being taken into a lecture room. "So many young...men, all...all looking at me, and then they tried...they tried to get me...to do...to do things..."

"What kinds of things?" Eleanor asked.

"Raising my arm, touching my nose with my eyes shut. And the worst was...the worst, I couldn't do...do them all. I couldn't do these silly...silly things for...these silly...men...doctors, and then they asked me...things...questions, lots of questions, and I...I couldn't answer all of those. And once...once...I heard one of them laugh...he laughed."

It was the kind of humiliation Eleanor could imagine all too well, could taste like acid in her mouth. Trying to make a joke, she replied, "You should have stuck your tongue out at them."

Emma laughed bitterly as tears filled her eyes. "They tried...they tried to get me to stick it out...to see if I could...but I couldn't." The final, cruel absurdity.

On the way out a nurse collared Nathan and said the specialist wanted to see him. Eleanor stood a respectful distance apart while they conferred. Afterwards, Nathan was reticent. Eventually, on the drive home, he admitted that they were going to do a few more tests and then they might operate.

"On her brain?"

"I guess. They said it might be brain cancer."

"I know," said Eleanor.

⌘

The following Tuesday evening Eleanor sat in a chair in a corner of the small dining room, just off the kitchen. She was reading the newspaper there because it gave her the illusion that this activity was merely temporary. She ought to be doing something else—homework, or cleaning the house, or preparing next day's meal for Nathan and herself.

She had just returned from the final rehearsal for the Christmas operetta. The Gilbert and Sullivan revue was an ill-assorted mix of four of their operettas, strung loosely together by an absurd plot that belonged to none of them. But in her role as Mabel, Mrs. Schmeisser was letting her sing the original of "Poor Wandering One" rather than the shortened version in the revue copy. So Eleanor was reasonably content.

Despite her guilt about the multitude of tasks pressing to be done, Eleanor had no intention of getting out of the chair until she had finished reading the newspaper. Light from a new lamp pooled on the corner where she sat, wrapping her in an illusory glow of security. The news was somehow consoling. The cold war and the threat of universal annihilation put one's personal problems in perspective. At a more basic level, it simply filled up the mind. "I like reading like a drunkard likes drink," her mother had said. Now she could not read anymore.

At nine-thirty precisely a car pulled into the driveway. It sounded like her father's. When it drove into the basement garage beneath her, Eleanor knew it must be Nathan. Never before, even on nights when business had been almost nonexistent, had he closed early and come home before quarter past ten. She waited for the slam of the outer garage door. It did not come. Then there were footsteps coming up the basement steps into the kitchen, and he was opening the door at the top of the stairs. Without thinking, she stood up as if waiting to receive an announcement. The paper dropped to the floor at her feet. She did not move.

"They phoned me. They say we should come up to the hospital right away." He paused. Eleanor said nothing. She had known this message was coming; she had stood up in anticipation of it.

For a minute they both stood motionless, locked in a common, unarticulated fear. Then Nathan said. "I think I'll just phone Obadiah and Virtue. Maybe they'll want to go too."

Virtue and Obadiah not only went, they insisted they should do the driving on the two-hour journey. Eleanor was once more in the warm, leather-smelling womb of Obadiah's car, just as she had been during those long Sunday afternoons when she was four and Emma's asthma was at its worst. Then Eleanor had escaped the worry of Mommy being ill by driving with Virtue and Obadiah in their car, squeezed between the two of them in the front seat, consoled by the warm puffing air that embraced her. Now the whole night was a dark tunnel, soft and enveloping, with just a small funnel of light leading them on. She wanted to drive like this forever, never arriving, doubly enclosed by the protective sphere of the headlights and the surrounding blackness.

As they neared the hospital, Eleanor suddenly remembered her hair. Her hair! It was in ringlets! This had been Mrs. Schmeisser's idea of how Mabel should look and, with great effort, before she left for the hospital, Emma had found Eleanor's old curls, cut off at eight and carefully laid out in a chocolate box. She had cut a band of brown hairnet and sewn them on individually so that, when the band was attached, the old curls would hang down below Eleanor's present hair, which would likewise be set and combed into ringlets. It was utterly ridiculous that she should turn up at the hospital with her hair as it had been when she was five. It was preposterous! But what could she do? To tear the netting and pins out now in the dark would be to risk ruining the wig. Anyway, there was still the rest of her hair, set for the performances on the next day. There was nothing for it but to leave things as they were and hope the nurses would not think her demented or, worse, moronic.

Suddenly, Obadiah was parking the car, and such trivial concerns no longer gave relief against Eleanor's mounting panic. In the incandescently white lobby she tasted the flavour of fear, icy and bitter. Then the elevator, the long corridor, the nurse coming out to meet them. "She's rallied just a bit." What would they see?

The room was the same as it had been on Saturday, white and narrow, but illumined softly now at night. Emma lay in bed breathing noisily. Her eyes were open, but she was not moving. A large Scandinavian nurse sat in the corner chair reading a magazine. When they came in she looked up, then retreated behind a slow, impassive smile.

Virtue went first to the edge of the bed. "How are you Emma?" Tears fell down her sallow cheeks. Eleanor saw her mother nod her head slightly in acknowledgement.

As if he needed to explain their sudden appearance, Nathan said, "I was out at Riverport. They phoned. They said to come, so we came—right away." Again the slow, faint nod.

Chairs appeared, and they sat down. There was a huge emptiness in the room. They waited like third thumbs, unconsciously timing their breathing with Emma's. The night ticked by. Lacuna, Eleanor thought. Lacuna. She clung to the word. Her mother had never managed to learn Latin again.

Hours seemed to pass. Eventually another nurse rustled in. "I think perhaps you should go now. She needs to rest, and I'm sure you all do as well."

Virtue began to sob softly. Eleanor stood, rigid with terror. Now that they were leaving, something was required of her, something final. It had to be the right thing. So much in the past was wrong and irretrievable. "I'm sorry," she had said. "You always say that," her mother had replied. She moved towards the object of love and fear on the bed. She said, "I love you," and kissed her. As she bent over, Emma managed to touch her ringlets.

Then it was over, and Eleanor ran away, down the dim corridor, past the sleeping, the comatose, the dying, to Obadiah's car.

Driving home in the back seat, she began to drift into a light sleep. From nowhere, came the whistle of a train. There had been a train once, a long time ago. First there had been rocks and ants that crawled all over her, and then her mother had held her and sung to her while she cried and the train wailed inconsolably in the distance. Now as the train approached and passed, she noted first the crescendo and then the fading, falling tone and thought, "Doppler's effect." For the rest of the journey she sat bolt upright, not yielding to sleep.

Emma knew that they had come, and that there had been something final about it. Perhaps she would never see them again. They began to merge confusedly with all the other people she would never see again—her mother, her father, Reverend Selig.

"I would wait for you." There he was, standing looking at her across the back of the church pew. He seemed very sad and she reached out to him, but then he was gone, just like that. Some people thought you met everyone again after you were dead. The golden city—but what she saw in front of her drugged eyes was the underworld of the Romans—multitudes of whispering ghosts, flitting across darkened fields, unspeaking shadows.

Someone else was beside her bed. Was he real or phantasm? Black suited, he opened up a little vial of something. He was putting it on her forehead, her hands. What was it for? He was putting something to her mouth—ah yes, that was the bread and wine, and she tried, obediently to swallow. She still believed in the faith; she thought she did, and she surely would receive God's mercy because He had punished her so severely in this life. The sin of pride, the worst of all, had been hers, but all sins could be forgiven.

Then that person was gone, and there was only the fair-haired nurse in the corner, busy with her book. She could read. Emma wanted to say, "You are so lucky. You can read." But she knew that what came out was nonsense. The nurse put down her book and came towards her. "Water?" Emma tried to swallow a bit, but it wasn't water she wanted. She wanted to start again, to do everything differently. Still, there was Eleanor. Then a greater anguish: she would never know what became of her, her wonder child. Would she grow up to be someone amazing? Would she marry? Would she have children of her own? She would never know. She sank back onto the pillows and moved into a confused half-slumber certain of only one thing. Eleanor had been there. Not the troubled and troublesome Eleanor of later years, but the child with ringlets, the fairy girl she had adored.

The next morning Virtue sat alone in her new kitchen, spartan and immaculate, doing nothing. It was all unreal; it was impossible. Why was God doing this to her? Why was Emma doing this to her? First Emma had said, or as good as said, she didn't want to live with her anymore, that, in fact, she had never wanted to live with her. She went away to her own house; now she was going away again, finally and permanently.

Indignation gave way to doubt, just a fraction of doubt, edging its way around fortified barriers of certainty. Maybe it's your fault. The voice came from somewhere deep inside.

"But how? How could it be? I looked after Eleanor when Emma was sick."

And when she wasn't as well, the doubting voice said. You envied her the child. You would have taken Eleanor from her if you could. You know that's true. Now look.

"I will make amends. If Emma is spared—I'll make it up to her, somehow, please, somehow."

❧

That afternoon Eleanor turned up at school for the matinee performance of the operetta. Make-up was happening in the library. For a minute she stood in the doorway, uncertain where to go. Mrs. Schmeisser caught her eye and beckoned her towards her own chair. First she rubbed on the creamy base, then the rouge on the cheeks. Eleanor sat passively, for once enjoying the comfort of sheer physical sensation—the large, warm, gently efficient hands going over her cheeks, her neck, smoothing the shadow on her eyelids. "I'm sorry about your mother." How had she heard? Eleanor did not reply, and Mrs. Schmeisser continued smoothing the make-up until her art had achieved perfection.

Standing in the stage wings among a crowd of other soloists and chorus members, she found herself singled out by Mr. MacDonald, the principal, who had both terrorized and tried to comfort her in Grade One. Now fear had turned to respect, but Eleanor never felt at ease with him. "We missed you in math this morning. What happened to you?"

Unlike Mrs. Schmeisser, he didn't know. He moved towards her, his hand half raised. He was going to put the hand on her shoulder. "If he touches me, I shall cry," she thought. That must not happen. Eleanor looked at him, and he withdrew.

"Is something wrong?"

"No. I mean, not now. I'm on stage in a minute."

She went, singing her song of pity and consolation to Frederick—in real life a spotty eleventh-grader whom she studiously ignored.

"Take heart, no danger lowers," Eleanor sang.

"Take any heart—but ours," the chorus replied.

"Take heart, fair days will shine/Take any heart—take mine," came Eleanor's firm assurance, followed by a burst of joyous, athletic runs and trills, culminating in a top C, with the chorus joining in for the grand, climactic affirmation.

Three times in the next two days, while Nathan drove the winding roads to and from Halifax, Eleanor sang that song to applause and general astonishment. When she looked back on it, no one was more astonished at what she had done than herself.

The last performance came and went. Eleanor didn't go to the party afterwards; she was too tired, she said. By eleven that night, she was sound asleep in bed.

Eleanor woke to the sound of the phone ringing. She sat bolt upright in expectation. It was still very dark. What day was it? Friday? Or perhaps by now Saturday? Motionless, she listened to Nathan's slippers flopping along the hallway. The ringing stopped. His voice murmured into the receiver. She could make nothing out.

Her bedroom door opened. "Your mother has died." Her mother. Of course, her mother, but how odd that was how he had expressed it. Was that how he really thought of Emma? Or had he unconsciously adjusted her identity to fit the person he was addressing? She heard him continuing with vague, broken phrases about life holding some hard things, difficult to understand. Poised like statues—she, sitting rigid in bed and Nathan, leaning up against the bedroom door frame— they looked in silence at one another and wondered how to behave.

There were no tears. Nothing in their past life together had prepared either to be of any help to the other at this moment. After a while Nathan said, "Do you think you can go back to sleep?" Eleanor said yes, she thought so. And she did.

At nine o'clock the next morning she woke up. A gradual sensation that something awful had happened possessed her. There had been a phone call in the night. Ah yes, she remembered. Her mother was dead. She turned on her back and stared at the empty ceiling. What ought she to feel? Uncontrollable grief, she supposed. Then why did she have no desire to cry? Had she not loved her mother? Had she ever loved anyone? She felt nothing but a great weariness and a sense that it would be impossible to do anything ever again. She could not get out of bed because she could not decide what to wear, what to eat for breakfast, what to say to people, what to do next. They would expect her to cry, her aunts. "Have you no feelings?" they would say, wiping their eyes with embroidered handkerchiefs.

Gradually, she realised she was not alone in the house. Of course Nathan would not have gone to work, but the noises seemed to indicate her father was not the only person out there beyond her bedroom door. She could hear small voices, whisperings, the occasional blowing of a nose. They seemed to be coming from the other bedroom. Eleanor got out of bed.

There in her mother's bedroom—still her mother's bedroom—stood Joan and Virtue. The bed was covered with her mother's dresses.

Virtue turned, saw her, and immediately came to embrace and kiss her. Eleanor stood back, forbidding herself to be touched. "What are you doing?"

"We're just trying to decide which dress to take to the funeral parlour."

Oh yes, the funeral parlour. Endless details, things to be done, everyone full of business. But how dare they? How dare they take her mother's clothes out of the closet, spread them, casual and vulnerable on the bed, assess them for quality, style, suitability? Anyway, in these circumstances, what was suitable?

She stood in amazement as they chose the navy silk dress with the large lace collar. Not new, but "good quality," said Virtue. Eleanor thought, "Good enough to last for eternity?" and suddenly began to laugh. The aunts looked at her but said nothing. Maybe, Eleanor reflected, she could get away with anything now.

When they left she went into her mother's closet and nestled against the dresses they had rejected. One by one she went through them, remembering the occasions for which they were worn: the housedresses, the dresses for going uptown in the afternoon, the summer church dresses, the winter church dresses. And in the back, something she had never seen her mother wear. It rustled, stiff with red taffeta flounces. She pulled it out—a long evening dress with a scoop neckline and a fabric flower on the collar. It was the very same dress she was wearing in the photograph Eleanor had come upon when they were cleaning house years ago. "My red party dress I had at Normal College," her mother had said. So she had saved it, but never worn it, all these years. A secret identity, hidden, but not destroyed. Her mother would be buried in navy blue silk; the aunts felt it was fitting.

Nathan, grave and Sunday-suited, appeared and said they must go to pick out a coffin. To pick out a coffin! Just like that. Of course, it made perfect sense. People were buried in coffins. Presumably their "loved ones" picked out the coffin they liked. Eleanor felt she had strayed into a world of absolute logicality based on premises that were completely mad—those premises being that her mother was dead, her mother was to be buried, and she, Eleanor, was helping to arrange these necessary details.

The undertaker was familiar; he came to her father in secret by night to get his hair cut because he wore a toupée. Eleanor had read that Death was a gentleman, and Mr. Noble was clearly his appropriate emissary. A pale oval face with thin lips and a straight, narrow nose was surmounted by fine silver hair—some real, some not—divided with geometric precision down the centre. A widower, he lived alone but "had money," it was rumoured. His dead wife's? The suits he wore were of the finest English cloth and cut; the black gloves he donned to follow the coffin were softest kid. His shoes were supple as slippers.

Now he was standing at the door of the white funeral parlour, waiting for Nathan and Eleanor. He led them through the flower-laden hallway, up a long stairway into what at first appeared to be a furniture loft. Coffins! Wooden coffins, metal coffins designed to look like wood but more impervious to water (and other things), blonde coffins, dark coffins, coffins lined with purple for old people, tiny white coffins for babies. They did not seem sad; they did not have any emotional properties, these coffins lined up in neat rows. Eleanor felt she might have been choosing a living room sofa.

"You don't want a dark lining, of course," Mr. Noble explained, "because your mother was so young." Eleanor had not thought of her mother as young; it had not occurred to her. So they chose a coffin in a light shade of oak with a pale peach lining.

"Very suitable."

When they returned to the house, Reverend Schwarz was waiting. His formality was a deep relief to Eleanor. She had not really talked properly to him since her confirmation. Now he stuck to the prescribed prayers, took down the hymns they wanted for the funeral, and departed.

There was so much to do. The tasks were never-ending. Neighbours whom she hardly knew appeared at the door with casseroles. This was designed to save them work, but they all had to be invited in, their awkward expressions of sympathy acknowledged. Cards and letters arrived in huge bundles. Eleanor supposed they would all have to be answered sooner or later and that it would be she, not Nathan, who would do the answering.

Eleanor felt constantly observed, on show. "How is she taking it?" There was a tightrope to be walked between "brave" and "heartless," "coping marvelously" and "doesn't feel a thing." Why this preoccupation with what she ought to be feeling rather than what she actually was feeling? Because she didn't know what she was feeling.

Custom, which Eleanor decided was completely barbaric, dictated that the family—and this included not only Eleanor and Nathan, but also Virtue, Obadiah, Joan, Douglas, and Rachel—must sit in the funeral parlour the evening before the funeral while friends and more distant relatives came to "view the body." Eleanor could not understand why anyone would wish to do this. She was finished with the body, the frail, betraying body, for good and all. Still Eleanor sat there, trying to look solemn—not overcome, grief-stricken but "assured of the blessed hope of the resurrection," for three hours. She shook hands, stood up, sat down (depending on the age and sex of the person addressing her) and made what she hoped were suitable noises.

The same sense of performance and detachment persisted throughout the funeral. But here the immense sadness was contained as if in an ornate cup by the very words of the liturgy. The individual was subsumed in the universal—a whole world of loss and mourning—a condition inevitable, impersonal, eternal. "O God the Father in Heaven, have mercy upon us."

"We'll manage somehow, I guess," Nathan assured her.

"O God the Son, Redeemer of the world, have mercy upon us."

"Of course she is in Heaven," said Joan.

"O God, the Holy Ghost, the Comforter, have mercy upon us."

"You must take a handkerchief," said Virtue.

Virtue was using her own copiously and conspicuously. Eleanor felt annoyance. What right had she to mourn the sister whose life she had often made so unhappy? But gradually it occurred to her that perhaps Virtue's misery was real, a terrible blending of mourning and remorse, and above all grief for herself and her own youth, all wrapped together in this childhood bedfellow, this sister, gone forever, cut down "like a flower."

Reverend Schwarz was preaching now, a strong sermon, the kind of thing he did best. It was superfluous to eulogize the dead. God would do that at the Last Day. But for those who died assured of His grace (and here the full measure of human certainty could be extended to our dear departed sister in the faith), that Last Day would be a wonderful, not a fearful event. So let us all prepare ourselves, he exhorted, as she had done throughout her devout though short life.

Eleanor heard the tone and emotion, not the content. It moved her to feel not grief nor yet rejoicing for her mother, assured of grace and salvation in which, for the moment, she could almost believe, but to an exalted determination to do something herself, something more than just get top marks and memorize other people's ideas. In a peculiar way she felt released. She must not waste her freedom but seize it to live for herself and her mother as well.

As they went out, Virtue collected the cards from the flowers. Eleanor looked at them on the short journey to the cemetery and saw, to her surprise, that one was from her school class. Perhaps they had not hated her after all.

It was cold and windless as they walked to the grave. There was no snow; the dead frozen grass stuck out of the brittle ground like tiny porcupine quills. The back harbour at the bottom of the hill was beginning to freeze, and Eleanor remembered, incongruously, the skating party.

Then the committal itself, the well-known words, the end. Finally Eleanor did feel something for her mother. It was pity. She had never before felt pity for this woman, dynamic even in the face of disaster. But now her appalling assertiveness and all the fearsome passions she embodied were stilled, and she seemed strangely in need of protection.

Afterwards there was tea at the house, and aunts and uncles and cousins crowded indiscriminately into the living room. They had nothing to say, but they talked noisily and tearfully all the same. Gradually they began to drift away, and eventually only Virtue, Obadiah, Joan and Douglas remained. It was then that Nathan turned to Eleanor and said, "What shall we have for dinner tomorrow?"

Suddenly Eleanor thought she was going mad. The rituals of the past days were over; her role of bereaved daughter was brutally stripped away, and she was back in a world where people shopped, cooked, ate meals. It was a world impossible to enter; it was a world that would go on forever. It would go on forever, and her mother would not be in it, and she could not bear it. She simply could not bear it. But no one must know she was going mad. No one must suspect. So she said, "I don't know." That sounded sane enough, didn't it? She genuinely didn't know.

As the others apparently noticed nothing and Nathan began to recite a litany of beef and pork chops and hamburger, slowly sanity returned, and she could bear it. Tomorrow she would be cooking dinner.

❧

Emma was no more. And she, Virtue, was still alive. But what was she now that the sister against whom every waking hour had been measured did not exist? There had always been Emma—Emma trotting along with her on that night they walked through the snow to get help for Flora, Emma sitting beside her in school, Emma reading infuriatingly on her bed while she was called downstairs to do the chores, Emma living with her in the old house on the lower street—then Emma having a child. After that, things were never the same, of course, but they were still together, weren't they? She had never wanted to leave that house, never. It had been all Emma's doing. Now Emma, in the middle of this life-long argument that had strangely sustained them both, had left; she had slammed the door for good and gone away, leaving her—what? A figure without a mirror, an argument without a riposte. And Eleanor.

Naturally, she would look after Eleanor, but it wouldn't be easy. On the way home from the funeral, sitting in the back seat of the funeral car, Virtue had put her hand on Eleanor's shoulder and said, "Of course you'll be looked after, Eleanor. I'll always be here for you, you know that." Eleanor had flicked her hand away and stared out the window.

❧

Nathan felt bewilderment. It was all quite beyond him. He'd worked hard, tried to do the right thing, and it all came to nothing. For him, there had always been Emma, ever since the winter day he had plowed through the snow to visit her at home. There she had sat in a blue velvet dress on a little chair. Still, he had taken her and tried to give her what she wanted, but it had not been easy. Her wants were like mirages that disappeared when you got close to them, slipped away into some larger desert of wanting, that you could never fill up. The house: he had built the house. She claimed she liked it. But by then her brain was beyond liking, beyond happiness. She had lived in that house for only four and a half months. What purpose could God have had in doing this? But one mustn't think that way. There had to be an explanation. He just couldn't see it at the moment.

He looked around the new sterile house. There, hanging over the back of a kitchen chair, was Emma's wine-coloured cardigan sweater, sagging gently, elbows worn. It was waiting patiently for her to come home and put it on. He steeled himself, picked it up, and put it away in her closet.

On Christmas Day it snowed. Nathan and Eleanor waded silently through the drifts down the middle of the unplowed road to Virtue and Obadiah's house for dinner. Here they were joined by Joan and Douglas, Rachel and Violet. There were no presents, no Christmas tree; it would have been improper. Virtue served up the turkey almost apologetically, frowning to show she could not possibly enjoy it, and that the act of cooking it had been a penance, done only for others, who must have food to survive.

The long Christmas day blended into an interminable Christmas vacation. There was more snow. No one came or went. Nathan and Obadiah struggled to the barbershop, often on foot, and for a meagre return. Eleanor sat in the tiny study and read. Now she was reading *Maria Chapdelaine*, a story about a French family living in an isolated Quebec community in the era of her own grandparents. The girl Maria was her own age, and as she read she came upon the account of the death of this fictional girl's mother. Maria had prayed for her mother, saying her rosary over and over. All Catholic, of course, but still... Eleanor could see it so vividly, the fire burning down, the girl sitting by the window with her beads, the mother dying in the next room. Then fiction did what reality could not, and Eleanor wept.

At night there was music. A few weeks after Christmas, almost as if it were an apology for the lack of gifts on the day, Douglas brought Eleanor a small transistor radio. Now, late at night, after Nathan had gone to bed, she would lie in the darkness listening to distant stations that seemed, through some quirk in the atmosphere, to appear only after eleven—WQXR New York, and a CBC station from Montreal.

Alone in the quiet bedroom her interior life expanded to the sounds of things she had not known existed—symphonies, bits of opera, organ music unlike any played in church. "Music for a while, shall all your cares beguile," sang a high male voice with a peculiar cutting edge. "Till Alecto free the dead..." Who was Alecto? It occurred to Eleanor that perhaps teenagers growing up in those far distant, magical cities—Montreal, Toronto, Boston, New York—knew about these things from early childhood. But would that necessarily be better? Could any gradual, early exposure compensate for the joy of this sudden discovery?

One Sunday night late in March, just two weeks before Easter, when Eleanor tuned in to the Montreal station, she was overwhelmed by a sound that threatened to swamp the tiny black transistor with wave after wave of unearthly music. Choir and orchestra swept up together in a solemn momentum of vast proportions and complexity. It swirled out so that the bedroom itself seemed to be the centre of a transcendent universe.

Still, emotion alone was not enough; Eleanor wanted understanding. She strained to hear the words, then realized they were not English at all; they were German. She knew only a little German—the residue that had been passed down casually from her ancestors—but for this it was enough. "*Kommt ihr Töchter, helft mir klagen*": "Come you daughters, help my mourning."

It must be an appeal for aid, the classic appeal at the beginning of an epic, as Mr. Ferguson had taught them. Perhaps this unknown work then was a kind of epic, an epic of mourning. Yet the rising phrases implied an indomitableness as well, triumphantly struggling against the dark minor chords and the chromatic progressions.

Never had she heard music like this. Then, just as she thought she was beginning to comprehend some meaning hidden in the elaborate texture, there came on top, high and clear, the piercing voices of boys singing one of the very hymns she had sung in church that morning: "O Lamb of God most Holy / Who on the cross didst suffer." Simple strength and innocence superimposed itself on the intricate, confusing harmonies underneath. What on earth was this? Wonderful beyond anything she had imagined, it came unsought like an answer to a question unasked.

⟆

Virtue sat in her new living room looking out the large picture window. The picture, so-called, was not inspiring. There were other squat little bungalows up and down the street as far as the eye could see. She had a new house—just what every woman wanted—what Emma had wanted, at least. The street was empty. On this unseasonably cold Saturday a week before Easter everyone was staying cozy inside. But Virtue did not feel cozy; whatever temperature the new thermostat proclaimed, the newness of the place was cold, clinical—new paint, new dusty-rose carpet on the floor, new stiff and flowered sofa where she perched uneasily lest she soil it.

It was all gone now. She had lost her sister who, despite the tensions of recent years, was still a part of her. She had slept in the same bed as Emma for sixteen years. They had done everything together—except have a child. That Emma had experienced on her own, and then she, Virtue, was the one who was alone, it seemed, until Eleanor became hers as well. But Eleanor had pushed her away. In the car after the funeral, when she had put her hand on Eleanor's shoulder, she had deliberately, cruelly, pushed it away. Eleanor was lost to her, and that was the most hurtful thing of all. Perhaps Eleanor had not meant it. Perhaps…it was at the funeral, after all. People did crazy things at funerals. Perhaps she would try again. She got up and went to look for her coat and boots.

⟆

Eleanor glanced up from the book she was reading and saw Virtue making her way up the snowy road. She was wearing her best fur coat—"mouton." Eleanor knew that was French for "sheep"; whether Virtue knew this or not was unclear.

All winter the food parcels from Virtue had kept arriving, and Eleanor consulted her, as her mother had advised, when she was cooking something about which she was uncertain. There were phone

235

calls almost every day. But Eleanor kept the conversation to practicalities—how her schoolwork was going, what she was making for supper. Now, as Virtue took off her coat and gave it a little shake before hanging it up it the outer closet, Eleanor felt afraid. Virtue had come for a purpose, and whatever that purpose was, Eleanor didn't want to know.

Virtue began by complimenting Eleanor on what a good housekeeper she was. Everything was so neat and tidy. Eleanor didn't tell her that it was, in fact, Nathan who did all the cleaning. Then they moved on to the safe topics—cooking and school work. Eleanor felt both bored and fearful—bored with the present topic, fearful of what might come next.

Meanwhile, Eleanor saw that Virtue's right foot kept up a small staccato tapping on the wood floor, a quick motion scarcely audible. It accelerated as all other topics of conversation were exhausted, and Virtue said, "I've been thinking that maybe I could do more to help out. I don't know…it just seems…" The foot-tapping increased to a frenzy as the voice trailed away. Then she said it: "It just seems wrong for you to be living here all on your own and us down the street all on our own. Wouldn't it make more sense if you moved down to stay with us? We have a nice spare room, and I'd see that you had a good quiet corner to do your schoolwork. Then you wouldn't have to worry about meals or anything."

"But what about Daddy?"

"Well, I thought he'd be happy staying here and not having to worry about looking after you as well as the house and shopping, and everything else. And," she added, "of course he'd come and eat a lot of dinners with us—as often as he wanted."

Eleanor just wanted to say "no" and walk away, but given that Virtue was in her house, that was not an option.

"I couldn't do that," she said.

"But why? Surely it would be the best thing. Your father wouldn't mind. He's always wanted what's best for you."

"No, it's not just that."

"What is it then?"

It came to Eleanor that if she left this house now she would be deserting the last vestige of her mother—her mother had wanted this house, pored over the plans, revised them, sanded the cupboard doors, obsessed over every detail of construction. She still lingered in the very woodwork, in the window frames holding the views of the sea. But she couldn't say that to Virtue.

Meanwhile, Virtue continued, "You know how much I've always cared for you, Eleanor. I've thought of you as my own. You spent as much of your childhood in my kitchen as in your mother's."

"And that's just the problem," Eleanor wanted to say, but didn't.

At last, after a long pause, she found some words, some formula that might serve. "It's really kind of you, Aunt Virtue. But I can't do it. I can't even say why. It just wouldn't be right. It wouldn't feel right. But"—and here she got up and gave Virtue a hug—"I do care for you, of course I do. It's just that..." Everything trailed off in tears for both of them.

"You know I'll always be here for you, Eleanor," said Virtue.

"I know," Eleanor replied. And she gave her aunt a kiss.

⁊

Surprisingly quickly, Eleanor and Nathan's lives settled into a routine. Nathan did the cleaning and laundry; Eleanor did most of the cooking. They moved in separate envelopes of dumb grief. They spoke of practicalities and kept busy.

With some astonishment, Eleanor realized that her time at school was coming to an end. Already it was May, and the dismal mud and melting snow were giving way to what generally passes for spring in saner climates—buds, new leaves, a few flowers.

For Eleanor these things scarcely existed. It was the season of examinations and scholarship results. She reviewed assiduously. Her walks to and from school with Jennifer and Caroline became extended study sessions as they quizzed one another on history dates, French and Latin vocabulary, geometric theorems—all with a fierce undercurrent of rivalry, at least as far as Eleanor and Jennifer were concerned.

Caroline, with her orderly mind, affected to stand aloof from the competition. "What's the point of getting really high grades? I know I'm going to pass, and pass well enough to get into university."

"But don't you want to get a scholarship?" Eleanor was incredulous that anyone should be satisfied with just doing "well enough."

"I don't need a scholarship. My father can afford to pay for me to go to college."

Even Eleanor's academic prowess showed only that she was poor.

Once the exams were over they began to plan for the graduation dance. Graduation itself posed no worries for Eleanor. She was certain she had maintained her place at the head of the class and would carry off the bulk of the local scholarships. But the prospect of the dance opened up an abyss of fear and embarrassment. She must go to the dance; everyone did. James had already asked Jennifer to be his partner. Caroline was dithering between two boys in the year above them in school, now in university, both of whom were dying to go with her; they phoned her, pestering, every night. No one had asked Eleanor. Terrible memories of earlier high school dances that her mother had pushed her into attending surfaced. The tension of sitting with a row of other undesirable girls, of seeing a young man approach (could he be coming to you?) and then the blank despair of hearing him say to the girl next to you (always the girl next to you): "May I have this dance?"—it was too much, too humiliating, the knowledge that in the end these other undesirable girls were still more desirable than her.

When the phone finally rang one evening and it was the tentative voice of Johnny Heckman wondering if, by any chance, she might be willing to accompany him to the graduation dance—that is, if she were not already going with someone else and if, really, she wouldn't mind, if she would be happy to, in that case he would, he would be very pleased—uh, delighted, if...Eleanor eventually cut short his torment and said yes, she would love to go with him. He was not handsome; he was not particularly clever or interesting. He was simply male and had the courage to ask her. That would have to do. She got the pale peach dress that she had worn as bridesmaid at a cousin's wedding from the closet and sent it to the cleaners.

Though the beginning of May was scarcely spring, by the last week in June it was already hot summer. At four o'clock on the Friday after-noon of the dance, Eleanor sat in a cooling bath thinking about her mother. "Woman much missed, how you call to me, call to me." She missed her mother, certainly, but—and here an uncomfortable reali-zation hit Eleanor—she did not want her to come back. Suppose now, she thought as she sat in the bath, there came the familiar quick tap of steps down the hallway. The bathroom door opened and her mother's face smiled in at her. No! No! The smile would be fearful, the voice sepulchral. The figure would be clad in wrinkled nightclothes, clinging loosely to the body, shaking with the fearful, laboured beating of her heart. Her mother had crossed a final barrier of pain and silence; there could be no return.

The telephone rang. Should she answer it? It was probably only Virtue or Joan fussing about tonight. On the other hand, it might be Johnny getting cold feet and backing out. She had better go.

Wrapped loosely in a towel, and leaving a trail of drips and wet footprints, she made her way to the insistent ringing.

"Hello?"

"Is that Miss Wentzell?" It was a faraway male voice announcing that he was the Registrar of Acadia University. If they offered her a scholarship of five hundred dollars a year, would she accept it? Eleanor knew it was their top award.

"Yes, I would…but does this mean that you are offering it?"

"Yes, of course. We ask first because we want to make sure we don't offer an award to someone who might later turn it down in favour of something from another university."

"Oh, I see." Actually, she was just beginning to see. It had not previ-ously occurred to her, preoccupied as she was with the possibility of being rejected herself, that a rejection might be feared by the university as well.

"Congratulations then! I'll send you the official letter, and one to your school principal as well, and we'll look forward to seeing you in September."

"Yes, yes, that will be splendid." Words of thanks began to stumble over one another until, by the time she put down the receiver, she was certain they would be convinced they had made a mistake and would offer it to someone else after all.

The future opened, incandescent, before her. It blocked out most of the actual dance that evening, which was probably just as well, because Johnny, while stolidly conscientious about buying her the right colour corsage, opening doors, and generally doing the proper, gentlemanly thing, could not be said to be an inspiration. Her one indelible memory of that evening was of dancing close to the band on the stage, haloed for the moment by a blue spotlight, while he leaned towards her and whispered, as if imparting the most delicious secret: "There's a new soft drink on the market. Sprite. They say it has a touch of lemon."

As she took off the peach dress late that night, the satin bow flashed in the bedroom light—a coffin lining for the dead.

᠅

Eleanor was class valedictorian. She accepted this honour complacently as her due. Gratitude did not seem relevant. One had something to say; one was given the chance to say it. This stance might be seen as arrogance, but was really an isolation beyond arrogance. She was not courting applause; she simply wished to speak. She wished to speak for the sake of the words and ideas themselves of which she was the custodian. If they could move and persuade, so much the better. But in the end they had their own existence, beyond moving and persuasion.

She stood in her white graduation dress, her valedictory notes in her hand. Out there somewhere in the dark auditorium were Nathan, Virtue, Obadiah, Joan, Douglas, half the town. They were all proud of her, so they said, but she felt that they no longer quite knew what it was they were proud of, what she had become. For if she were connected to others—and sometimes it seemed she was not, not at all—it was through that tradition of words and ideas and music that were first passed on to her and now were evolving far beyond the original gift. "This passing on of knowledge is the passing on of life," she was about to assert in her address, believing it with a faith as passionate as it was touchingly naive.

Now she stepped forward to the front of the auditorium stage, holding this conviction like a chalice. It was not a lot, this fragile continuity of ideas and minds—she had seen the mind destroyed—only a few rhythmical words, a few scraps of music, a dead language. But it was what was left; it would have to do.

The audience disappeared as she moved into the bright whiteness of the stage lights. She embraced that amplitude of whiteness. She opened her mouth and began to speak.